Unlovable

Tamara Chavalle

A catalogue record for this book is available from the National Library of Australia

Publisher:

Australian Self Publishing Group, Pty. Ltd / Inspiring Publishers
PO Box 159, Calwell, ACT 2905, Australia.
Phone: 61-(0) 2 6291-2904
http://australianselfpublishinggroup.com

National Library of Australia Prepublication Data Service

Author: Tamara Chavalle

Title: **Unlovable**

ISBN: 978-1-923250-89-5 (print)
ISBN: 978-1-923250-90-1 (ePub2)

Dedication:

For mum, my beautiful babies and nieces. I am blessed to have you all.

Alex. Thank you for pushing me. When this book became too hard you convinced me to keep going. I'm so glad you did!

And Maddi. Your story made me brave enough to tell mine. Xx

Content Warning

Unlovable includes content that might not be suitable for some readers. I've included a list of these elements at the end of the book. If you have concerns, please check it out so you can decide whether to continue reading.

Please be aware that these warnings may contain spoilers!

Unlovable, while presented as a work of fiction, is based on true events in my life.

Chapter One

I was nearly twenty-three the first time I met Sam. He was gorgeous. He was a little over six foot tall and had muscles for days. Dark skin, short, black hair and the kindest face. With a smile that reached all the way to his big, hazel-coloured eyes. I hadn't seen anyone quite like him before.

I never had the guts to talk to him when he came into the bar where I worked, until the day I found myself face-to-face with him. It was a Friday afternoon in late September. He was there with a group of other guys. I'd seen most of them before too but had never paid them much mind.

When he and one of his mates walked up to the bar and ordered a couple of beers, I wasn't surprised to hear that his voice was as lovely as I had imagined it to be. He sounded sweet and kind. I just hoped that I wasn't shaking from nerves as I grabbed the schooner glasses from behind the bar.

My friends at work would always tell me to just go over and talk to him. I knew that I wasn't some dog myself but he was so attractive, there was no way I had the courage to approach him. I didn't have very high self-esteem. Guys had always treated me very badly in the past and I really didn't think that someone like him would give me the time of day. He seemed so perfect.

So, imagine my surprise when he said hi. He told me, as I began pouring the first beer, that he had seen me a few times but never had a chance to talk to me. Somehow, I managed to place the first beer up on the bar without spilling it everywhere. I was so nervous. I started pouring the second beer as he continued to speak but a moment later the strangest thing happened. The glass I was holding suddenly broke. The whole bottom half fell right off. It took me a few seconds to realise what had happened and let go of the beer tap.

I looked up to see the two guys in front of me laughing. I couldn't help but join in. The sheer ridiculousness of what had just happened was too much. I realised at that moment that he was just a regular guy, not the mysterious unicorn that I had built him up to be in my mind.

When his mate came back to the bar a short time later with a piece of paper I was confused. But my confusion turned to flattery when he spoke. As it turned out, his mate, the cute unicorn guy, had apparently liked me from afar for weeks but never had the opportunity to talk to the pretty blonde barmaid—me. I flushed at the compliment, I couldn't imagine anyone feeling that way about me but he went on to explain that the incident with the glass, the icebreaker as it turned out, had made his friend realise that I was just a normal person. How ironic, I thought. The guy handed me the piece of paper with a name and phone number on it and urged me to call him.

Sam and Magnolia. It had a good ring to it. I blushed as I started to imagine what it would be like, going on a date with him.

A moment later, I looked over to see the group of guys getting ready to leave. Just as I was about to look away, I locked eyes with him. Sam gave me the biggest, sweetest smile I'd ever seen in my life. I smiled back as he headed for the door, and then I looked down at the piece of paper. The smile didn't leave my face for the rest of my shift.

As soon as I finished work a couple of hours later, the first thing I did was call my cousin Bec. I had been harping on about the guy for weeks and I knew that she'd be proud of me. Well, maybe not proud since I hadn't built up the courage to approach him first. But I still knew that she'd be thrilled for me. And she was.

After a few minutes, our conversation turned to our plans for the following evening. We had a friend's twenty-first dress-up party to go to and we needed to finalise our costumes. Bec was twenty-two as well and just a few months younger than me. Then there was Hayley who was twenty-six. They were my cousins and my best friends. They were the daughters of my mum's sisters. We grew up in the same street where our mums had grown up as kids, in a suburb called Lane Cove. A quiet, leafy suburb about ten minutes north of Sydney.

Our grandparents still lived in the very same home where our mums had shared a room as young children. That is until our pop won the lottery. He had been playing the same numbers religiously for years. He never missed a draw, despite never winning more than a few dollars here and there.

When his numbers finally dropped, he was the sole winner of almost $350k, Aussie dollars that is. Back then, in 1958, that amount of money was enough to construct the second story of their house and put in the pool that we grew up swimming in together. My pop also purchased three separate properties in the street as they came onto the market over the next couple of years. He rented them out and then eventually gave one to each of our mums once they'd graduated from university.

We often joked that my cousins were basically sisters. Hayley and Bec's mums were identical twins and so were their dads. We already had a strong chance of twins in our family as it was and so no one was surprised when Hayley's pregnancy at twenty-two had resulted in the birth of twins as well.

Oh, and then there was my younger brother. I was only three minutes older because, surprise, surprise, he's my twin. I looked older too, until he had a massive growth spurt when we were seventeen. James shooting up to 6ft3" almost overnight meant that people usually assumed he was older, much to my amusement and his annoyance.

We may not have looked like twins but we have the same blue eyes, blonde hair and fair complexion as Hayley and Bec. When the four of us went out together people always assumed that we were all siblings. My brother decided to follow in our dad's footsteps and become a doctor. You didn't need two guesses to figure out who the brainiac of the family was. I had no trouble admitting that it wasn't me.

My mum, a quiet achiever by the name of Bonnie, had always planned to do medicine but then in her last year of school she had a change of heart and decided to study veterinary science instead. She met a guy in her final year of university. He was studying finance and swept her off her feet. By the time she graduated university they were engaged. Thankfully my grandfather didn't trust him. The guy was too slick. Pop said he was just like a snake. There was no way my grandad was having his daughter lose her inheritance the minute she got it and so he kept the house in his name and charged the guy rent. That snake guy proved pop right a year after graduation.

That was when my mum found out that she was pregnant. At first the guy seemed like he was going to do the right thing and look after his fiancée and baby. But then they found out that they were having twins and it was all too much. Just like that, he was gone. On 10th November 1976, at the age of twenty-five, mum found herself a single mother of twins. It wasn't the way she imagined having a family but she was so in love with us that she didn't care. She knew that she'd figure it out with her family's help.

And she did. By the time James and I were born, with her parents' help, she had bought into a successful veterinary clinic right down the road from our house. Nan and pop looked after us at either our house or theirs when she went back to work after her maternity leave was over. That man may have walked out on us before he even bothered to meet us but we were surrounded by so much love that his absence wasn't noticed.

Mum met the love of her life two years later through mutual friends. She wasn't ready to date but when she found herself seated next to an attractive guy named Cameron at a dinner party, she couldn't help but be intrigued. And she couldn't say no when he asked for her number as she made her excuses, desperate to get home to her babies. He wasn't at all phased when, after their fourth date, she told him about James and I. They were married two years later, to our whole family's delight. Especially mine and my brother's. We may not share his DNA but he's the best dad anyone could ask for.

I love animals just as much as my mum does. I grew up wanting to be a vet just like her but a year of bartending in the US, after dropping out of school, turned into two-and-a-half years of living in California and the beginning of a completely different career.

I'd originally planned to spend a year working my way from California to Vegas, down through Texas and then across Nashville, Louisiana and Florida, before working my way up to New York and then coming home. I was planning to work in restaurants and bars, depending on what the minimum age to serve liquor was in each state, since I was only eighteen. But instead, I fell in love. Anthony worked for a tech company in Silicon Valley, so when my visa was getting close to expiring, he managed to get me sponsored by his company as a marketing assistant. We rented a two-bedroom apartment together and embarked on the adventure of a lifetime. It was my first real relationship and it was an amazing and fun experience. Until it wasn't.

The love of a lifetime broke my heart and so I ran home with my tail between my legs. I had started a marketing degree while I was in the US and so, luckily, I was able to have that credited towards a similar degree once I got home to Sydney. My parents were excited to have me home finally. My parents, brother, cousins and a couple of friends had been out to visit me at different times while I was living in Palo Alto, a suburb in the Bay Area of San Francisco but it wasn't the same.

I had missed my family terribly. Especially when things started to unravel in my relationship and so I was happy to be back at home. I was thankful that my parents were willing to help me financially so that I could continue my studies. The only condition was that I needed to get a part time job to fund my twenty-two-year-old lifestyle outside of uni. That's how I found myself working in that pub on the Friday afternoon that Sam walked into my life.

Chapter Two

It took me a few days to build up the courage to actually call him. I went to grab the piece of paper out of the pocket of my black work pants, only to realise that the pants were no longer hung over the back of my desk chair where I'd left them. I'd been back home for over a year but somehow my mum still didn't understand the difference between clothes that were on the floor, and clothes that were not.

I raced back into my room but it was nowhere to be found. And then I remembered the jar. My mum had always had a system for things she found in pockets. It was actually an old biscuit tin and not an actual jar. It was older than I was and she'd used it to store things she found in our pockets whilst she was doing our washing as kids. I smiled to myself as I remembered the wonderful trinkets that mum would find and return to me from the tin as a young child.

It took me a few tries to pry the lid off but when I did the piece of paper was sitting there, right on top of the random assortment of trinkets and coins. I took it out carefully, replaced the lid and then raced back to my room. I grabbed my pink Sony-Ericsson flip phone from the charger and dialled the number in front of me. With each ring I could feel my bravery slipping until finally the phone clicked over to voicemail.

I was so mesmerised by the sound of his voice on the recording that I almost forgot to leave a message.

"Hi, this is Magnolia from the pub. Your mate gave me your number, so I thought I'd just call and say hi." With that I left him my number and said goodbye.

As soon as I hung up, I wondered if I could somehow delete a voicemail that I'd left—but of course I couldn't. The only other thing I could think of, to take my mind off whether my message sounded okay, was to dial Bec's number. My youngest cousin was unlucky in love just like me so I knew that she would understand why I was second guessing myself.

Bec answered on the second ring. She nearly deafened me as she screamed excitedly down the phone.

"Have you called him yet?" she asked. "When are you going out? And where? We need to figure out what you're going to wear!"

"I left him a message." I laughed, still feeling self-conscious about how I must surely have sounded on the phone. "I guess I'll just wait to see if he bothers to call back. Maybe he didn't know his mate was giving me his number." I said, feeling a little silly as that familiar feeling of self-doubt washed over me.

"Of course he'll call you, my girl. He'd be mad not to." I could always count on Bec to know when I needed reassurance. "You deserve a good guy, he sounds lovely." she added happily.

"We'll see, I guess." I said, appreciating my cousin for her kindness but not agreeing. Her words made me feel uncomfortable. I had never been good at taking compliments, not since my early teens, so I decided to change the subject.

We needed to figure out the plan for later in the evening. It was the fourth day of spring, and the weather didn't seem to have gotten the memo because it was freezing. In the warmer weather we often walked down to Lane Cove Plaza to get an ice cream and then we would walk home as we ate it. It was a good half an hour round trip on foot and so it was the perfect number of steps to burn off two scoops of our favourite, love potion. Well, nearly.

The first part of the plan that night was to have an early dinner. Bec and I were going to go and pick up pasta and pizzas from our favourite little Italian place in North Ryde. We often sat in my car down by the ferry wharf, nearby Woolwich, to eat it while we shot the breeze but that night, we were picking up a few catering containers of food for the whole family to share because it was our Nan's birthday. We agreed to meet at my house twenty minutes later before ending the call.

A couple of hours later we were getting out of the car, ready to walk up to our grandparents' place with dinner when my phone rang. I didn't recognise the number at first but then it clicked. Bec realised before me. I stared dumbly at my phone for a moment before realising that my cousin had taken the phone out of my hand and answered it.

"Hello, this is Magnolia's phone." I knew that my cheeks were already bright red. I was nervous just thinking about talking to him. My cheeks always gave me away, it was a hazard of having such fair skin. A moment later the phone was thrust back into my hands. Somehow, he sounded even hotter over the phone. He apologised for missing my call earlier, explaining that he had been at football practice. Well, that certainly explained the muscles, I thought to myself with a smile.

I found myself chatting with him easily, ignoring Bec as best as I could as she danced around blowing kisses at me. It was only a minute's walk from my car to nan and pop's front gate. As we walked up the driveway, I excused myself. The front door was open, and I could hear our rowdy family talking inside. I handed Bec the bags of food I was carrying and told her I'd be in soon. She tried to protest just as James walked out, asking what had taken us so long. She ordered him to carry the pasta before racing him inside.

Sam had heard the conversation, despite me covering my phone with my hand. Insisting that I should get inside to my family, he asked if I was free the following Saturday night. For the first time since I met my Californian Dream—turned nightmare—I actually had a good feeling about a guy. We agreed to meet at 7 pm at a nearby pub before saying goodbye.

Saturday night rolled around finally. I was pleasantly surprised when Sam arrived ten minutes early. I was sitting in my car when I saw him walking in the front doors. I had planned to wait another five minutes before heading inside but seeing him walk in, in his jeans and dress shirt, gave me the confidence I needed. I grabbed my bag, smoothed my long denim skirt down and headed towards the pub.

We hit it off straight away. Sam was a mechanic by trade. He lived fifteen minutes away in a suburb called Ryde with his parents and his older brother Brian. Sam told me that he played football on the weekends, which I already knew. When he admitted that he was seeing someone my heart dropped. My first thought was to make an excuse and leave but he must have seen the look on my face.

He told me that the previous weekend, actually the Friday night after I had sheepishly accepted his number from his mate, he had planned to have a big night with his mates and so he'd left his mobile phone at home. The following morning his parents had scolded him about his phone waking them up through the night. The woman he was seeing had tried calling him more than forty times. He had already decided that he was probably going to end things with her the moment he spoke to me but then the phone calls had made up his mind. He hadn't had a chance to tell her yet, because he'd been avoiding seeing her face to face.

Our original plan was to just go for a drink but we were both enjoying ourselves so much. We ended up sitting in my car outside of his house for a couple of hours chatting. He hadn't driven and only lived five minutes away from the pub, so I was happy to drive him on my way home.

It seemed like the most natural thing in the world when he finally leaned over to kiss me goodbye. We sat there in my little car, in his pitch-black street, kissing for about an hour. It was almost midnight when we came up for air and saw the time. He apologised for keeping me out so late and we both laughed. Some of my friends didn't even go out until 10 pm and I often worked until at least 2 am on the weekend. I told him as much and we laughed again.

And then he asked if I wanted to go out for dinner one night through the week. I wanted to but I remembered that he hadn't broken things off with the other woman. I'd forgotten about her when I let him kiss me but he promised to call her the next morning. He'd only been seeing her for a few weeks, and they were both in agreement that it was just a casual thing. I cautiously agreed, remembering what it felt like to be cheated on. I decided I would give him one chance to prove that he wasn't one of those guys.

I finally pulled up outside my house shortly before 1 am I snuck inside to see my parents watching a movie. Well, my dad was watching while mum slept soundly next to him. I hadn't spent much time at home since I was at school. Of course, I was overseas for a couple of years but ever since I got back, I was always either working, at university, at some party or at one of my cousin's places.

I always found it so sweet that even after all these years, my parents were still so in love. I smiled as I kissed my dad on the cheek and headed towards my bedroom. I wondered if I had finally found my Prince Charming too.

Chapter Three

S am stopped seeing the other woman and we quickly became an item. That first spring and summer that we spent together was like something out of a movie. My family loved him, and I felt like his parents and brother liked me, even though he never told me as much. The first time my cousins met him was at Bec's parents' house. Hayley's twins were spending the night up the street at her parents' place and so we were planning on having a big night.

I was nervous and excited. It was so important that my girls liked him but I also wanted him to like them. They were my best friends and I needed them to like each other. We had originally planned to have a BBQ but we realised, as we wandered up and down the aisles of the supermarket that afternoon, none of us really knew how to cook a steak. And so instead we ended up buying the ingredients for beef stroganoff.

I was so nervous about the evening ahead that I decided it would be a good idea to do shots, just a couple, to calm my nerves. I had always been a bit of a lightweight when it came to alcohol though and so by the time Sam arrived a little before 7 pm, with flowers for me and wine for everyone, I was quite tipsy but he wasn't fazed. Not even when Hayley and I jokingly demanded to know whether pasta bows or shells should be served with the stroganoff. I was having such a great time watching how well everyone got on that I didn't even hold it against him when, much to my cousin's delight, he chose shells instead of bow ties. I had such a good feeling about the type of man he was, funny, smart and gentle. I wondered again, as I watched him interact with my family, could he be the man I'd been waiting for? The one who was going to put my broken pieces back together?

We were almost inseparable from then on. We spent our days at the beach or some pub or club with his friends or mine and the nights with our limbs entwined and not a care in the world. Everything about him was lovely. I never imagined that my heart would ever heal from the misadventure of that guy in America but for a while, Sam just about made me see it for what it was, a once in a lifetime adventure on the other side of the world.

The more I told Sam about my time in the US, the more I realised that the friends I had made there and the places I'd been were all worth the drama and heartbreak that I had endured at the end. I had been to places like San Francisco, Los Angeles, New Orleans, Dallas, Detroit and even Hawaii; I had made lifelong friends. As the weather turned cold, I started to wish that I could introduce him to my friends back in America. He was keen to go on an adventure together so we agreed that when I started working full time again after graduation, we would save up to go see them.

At the end of the year 2000, at twenty-four years of age I graduated from university. I had stayed in touch with my wonderful American boss, Lisa, who was based over in Florida, and so when the Australian head of marketing at my old company, who was based here in Sydney resigned, just two weeks after I graduated, the interview process was really just a formality. I had learned most of what I knew about marketing in the context of their technology and how it benefited their customers and so now that I had the required formal qualification, the job was mine.

When I started my new job in the new year, the first task I was given was to continue working on a big customer event that was being held in San Jose, California in April. I was excited to learn that I would need to attend the four-day event in person, meaning that my flights and accommodation would be paid for. Sam and I decided that we would take the opportunity, rather than waiting until I'd saved enough money to pay for my flights myself.

April came quickly enough. We arrived at LAX on a Friday. By the time we arrived in San Jose, it was almost 6 pm. I'd done enough travelling to know that our weekend would consist mostly of sleeping and wandering around the shops and bars close to the hotel. I took great pleasure in seeing Sam's excitement when we hopped off the Caltrain in San Francisco on the Sunday. We'd made the decision after a big sleep-in to head up and check out the city I'd called home for those couple of years. It was the first time Sam had ever been further than Brisbane, which was just an hour's flight north of Sydney and from that first train trip he was in love.

For the four days that I was working. Sam happily spent his time going to different sporting events. A friend had managed to get tickets to watch the A's baseball team play at home in Oakland so a group of us went on the one evening that didn't require my team's attendance. It wasn't really my thing, but I enjoyed watching Sam's excitement as he talked baseball with my colleagues. I wasn't even upset when he got annoyed at me for asking so many questions about the game.

I didn't blame him really. We had been together for eighteen months and I knew better than to try talking to him when he was watching a game. I'd learned pretty quickly during the previous NRL season how seriously he took his sport. At the time I assumed it was just rugby league since he himself had played at a professional level for a while but that day I learned that it was baseball too.

Sam was a good guy, kind and considerate and so instead of getting offended and ruining our day I simply excused myself, and went off in search of the toilets and something to eat. When I arrived back to our seats twenty minutes later with a huge box of hot chips and a bucket of fried chicken, I was relieved to see that he was in a much better mood. Especially when he realised that I had bought the spicy chicken he liked, despite my hatred of anything containing pepper or chilli.

Once the work part of the trip was finished, we spent the next ten days travelling to spend time with Lisa back in Saint Petersburg, Florida, and then to see my friends Brandon and Veronica in Austin Texas. It was so wonderful to be back in

America. I had run home so fast that I'd never realised just how much I missed that part of my life until I was back. Sharing the experience with Sam was fun too. Apart from Sam getting annoyed with me that day at the baseball and a couple of evenings where he wiped himself out from drinking too much, we had a wonderful holiday. As we boarded the flight home, we promised each other that we would come back the following year—if not sooner.

A day trip up to my company's headquarters while we were in the US reminded me of a hobby that I had enjoyed when I lived there, especially when Anthony and I were living together. Baking and decorating cakes. My company's headquarters often hosted cultural days and baking contests. I had only been working there for a few weeks when an email was sent to everyone about a cancer fundraiser being held the following week. I spent most of that weekend making a caramel mud cake and then decorating it to look like a crocodile

I was so proud when my cake won an award but even more than that, I was thrilled by the amount of praise that I received from everyone. People I'd never even met started approaching me in the office kitchen and in the hallways to tell me how delicious my cake was. Having complete strangers praising me so openly was something I had never experienced before. It was such a lovely feeling. I soon started making all sorts of cakes and desserts for my teammates and friends, I was even paid to make a couple of wedding cakes. When I arrived back home in my heartbroken state, one of the things that healed my heart was how much Bec enjoyed sharing my new hobby with me.

We would spend hours making huge novelty cakes for family birthdays and baby showers. Once I started studying and working, I found myself with less time to bake but once that first US work trip was done, and with Sam spending a few nights a week at football training, I found myself with more time to start baking again. Bec was single at the time and so, we found plenty of time to indulge ourselves. Sam got a kick out of being our taste tester and we were thrilled when he asked us to make a cake for his footy team's mid-season party.

Bec and I had a blast making the huge cake with the angry looking Rabbit hand piped across the top. We both marvelled at how good the cake looked and by the end of the night we had lost count of the number of people who asked us to make a cake for their upcoming special occasions. As we drove home afterwards, having left a very drunk Sam to continue partying with his friends, Bec and I made plans to start our own baking empire.

We agreed that we would build a portfolio by doing discounted cakes for all the people who'd asked after our services that night. We came up with the name 'Magnolia & Bec's Cake Creations'. It wasn't the most creative business name but we felt it was personal and just right for our little side hustle. In the first few months we averaged a cake every three weeks. Each time we delivered one of our creations, from bullseye to Miss Piggy and even a huge superhero frog, we were bombarded with enquiries from people who'd been impressed by how tasty our cakes were.

By Christmas of 2001 we were refusing order requests. There were two reasons. The first was simply because we didn't have the time. I had taken on a more senior, regional role at work which required me to attend video meetings at all hours of the evening, as well as travelling for events every few weeks. And Bec had met Damian. They had been together for a few months and were still in that wonderful early relationship Bubble where they couldn't stand to be apart.

Bec's new relationship and my work commitments had allowed me to ignore the bigger problem for a while—Sam. At first my boyfriend was really supportive of my little hobby-turned-business. He had seen how excited and animated I became when people praised me. His friends fussing over me seemed to make him proud too. But then his attitude changed. He started questioning me about the amount of money Bec and I were charging for our cakes.

A couple of weeks earlier Sam and I were at his mate's thirtieth birthday party. I was standing at the cake table cutting slices to hand out during the speeches when Sam approached me. I knew that he'd been drinking heavily all night which was nothing new but what I wasn't expecting was his bad mood.

"What the hell, babe?" he slurred angrily, pointing at what was left of the cherry ripe mud cake.

"What's wrong, Sam?" I asked, confused by his outburst.

"Derek just told me you charged him $150 for the cake!" he said so loudly that a group of people nearby stopped talking and were staring at us.

"Don't scream at me." I whispered before grabbing his arm and leading him outside. "Why are you going mad on me?" I asked, feeling flustered by his outburst.

"Because I told you to stop ripping my mates off with your stupid cakes!" he screamed back at me.

"That cake is huge. It cost us almost $140 to make. It took us twelve hours!" I exclaimed, frustrated by his attitude.

"That's bullshit. You're just making money off my friends." he spat back angrily. "How many times do I have to tell you?"

"Fine." I mumbled before storming off. I didn't want him to see that I was crying. In the two years and three months that we had been together he had never screamed at me like that before. I had always hated how much he drank but I'd always just tolerated it because he treated me well most of the time. I knew that Sam was no angel but he was nicer than Anthony, so at least that was something. I was used to leaving parties and functions alone so that he could stay back and get shitfaced and I'd long since learned not to talk during sports matches so I didn't annoy him but that night, for the first time in our relationship, I walked away from him feeling not just embarrassed but scared.

I hadn't felt so low in such a long time. By the time I reached my car, after sneaking back inside to grab my bag, I was shaking. I sat there for almost twenty minutes, hoping Sam would come and apologise but eventually I admitted defeat and started my car. It wasn't until I was almost home that I realised I'd forgotten to collect the money for the stupid cake.

Chapter Four

When I walked through the door at home an hour after storming out of that party the last thing I wanted to do was talk to anyone. I wanted to go and hide away in my room with some chocolate and a book but seeing Mum, happily tidying up my baking cupboard, just reminded me of Sam's outburst. I saw the look on Mum's face when she realised I was crying.

"What's wrong, sweetheart?" she asked.

"Sam got cranky at me about ripping off his friends with the cakes again." I told her, sniffing into a serviette I'd found in my bag.

"Did you tell him how much work you girls put into those cakes?" she asked, looking annoyed. "And how expensive they are to make?"

"I've tried but he just gets annoyed. I'm starting to hate making them." I hadn't even admitted that to myself but I realised as I said it, that it was true.

"But you and Bec are so good and you have so much fun together making them. It would be a shame to stop doing it."

Mum said as she pulled me into a hug. "Maybe you just need to stop making them for Sam and his friends?"

"Thanks, Mum. I'll talk to Bec tomorrow." I realised that she was right. Sam's constant complaints about the cakes had been making things uncomfortable for months, yet it had never occurred to me to cut him and his friends off.

"Anyway, I'm tired, good night."

"Good night, darling." Mum said, still looking concerned. "Love you."

"Love you too, chook." I replied, using her childhood nickname for me before heading to my room.

Bec, Damian and I went for breakfast the next morning. I had messaged Sam to invite him but I wasn't surprised when he didn't respond. I knew that he would have been passed out after his big night of drinking. When I told Bec what had happened the night before she was annoyed. We had spent every night the previous week decorating that huge stack of expensive mud cakes to make it look like a tiger in a football jersey. Being berated and accused of ripping off his mates was not only unnecessary, Bec and Damian both agreed that it was downright offensive. I kept the part about feeling scared by Sam's outburst to myself, because it seemed silly in the light of that new day.

We made the decision that morning to take my mum's advice and stop taking orders from Sam's friends. I felt conflicted about it because I knew how much all of the guys loved our cakes but Sam had been complaining for months and I didn't blame Bec for being angry about it. I certainly had been the night before too.

"You guys worked your arses off on that cake." Damian said. "Bec told me you ended up wrecking your back from bending over to decorate it?"

"Yeah." I said sheepishly. "That always happens. It's an old injury that plays up in my old age." I laughed, trying to lighten the mood.

"You don't need to put up with him screaming at you either by the way." Bec said sternly.

"He's never done that before. It was just a misunderstanding." I assured her. "I'll talk to him when he surfaces later." I ignored the look of concern on their faces and changed the subject, I didn't want to talk about me anymore and I didn't want to think about what kind of mood Sam might be in later.

"Anyway. Enough about me. What are you guys up to over the holidays?" Seeing my cousin with such an adoring boyfriend really filled me with joy. It gave me hope that my own relationship could still be like that again too.

It was just after 4 pm when my phone finally lit up with half a dozen messages from Sam. I had been hoping to spend the day with him, but I didn't want to interrupt his sleep. I had never forgotten the story of the woman Sam was dating before me and her forty-plus phone calls in one night. I was always conscious not to call him unexpectedly and so after the single text that morning about breakfast, I left him alone and instead spent the day cleaning and packing for a conference in Melbourne that I was attending for work that week.

I wasn't surprised to read the messages.

SAM 💜
hi babe
Everyone missed you last night
I missed you
Why did you leave without saying goodbye? Elena said she saw you grab your bag and storm off. Did someone do something to upset you?

I had never drunk so much that I forgot what I was doing. Sam, on the other hand regularly got so wasted that he would supposedly lose whole days. I had never even been around anyone who drank the way Sam and his mates did. It was not at all unusual for him to spend $500 in one weekend. Enough back then, in the 1990s, to stay in a swanky hotel for the weekend, or buy an old bomb of a car.

Early in our relationship, Sam used to get his mates to drop him at my place on their way home from the city. At first, I was flattered that he wanted to see me so desperately but then early one morning I watched on in confusion as he walked to the end of my futon and proceeded to wee on the floor. My confusion turned to disgust when he hopped back into my bed and went back to sleep, leaving me to clean up his mess.

I thought about Sam's drunken toilet antics as I read his messages again. When he woke up after that first incident, he was confused about why I was in a strange mood, but I was too embarrassed to tell him what he had done. I assumed it was a one-off but then it happened again, and again. I began to dread his late night and early morning texts, announcing his impending arrival at my door but I didn't want to rock the boat by telling him that his behaviour upset me. I was so sure that he would break up with me if I made a fuss. I put up with his behaviour because I was so sure that he was too good for me.

That's why I simply started to make excuses about why Sam couldn't come to my house after his big drunken nights out. And it's why I swallowed back the feelings of hurt and disappointment when his messages mentioned nothing about his nastiness from the night before. I wasn't stupid enough to believe that he didn't remember anything about screaming at me, I had been drunk a number of times in my teens and still remembered everything I did on those crazy nights. I should have called him out on his behaviour and demanded an apology, but I didn't. I decided it was easier to just let it go. I gulped down my disappointment and messaged back with a simple:

Magnolia
Hey, I was just tired.
How's your head?

His response immediately cheered me up.

SAM ♥
can I come and see you?
We can go and get Italian and have
a picnic at the wharf?

Sam knew that sitting down at Woolwich pier, watching the boats glide towards the Sydney Harbour Bridge off in the distance while eating salmon agnolotti was my favourite thing to do.

Magnolia
Sounds good. Do you want to come
here and then we'll take my car?

SAM ♥
can I stay at your place afterwards?
I won't see you until the weekend
otherwise.

Sam may not have remembered the previous night but he clearly remembered that I had to go away for work.

Magnolia
Sure. I have to go and have a shower.
I'll see you soon?

SAM ♥
ok babe, I'll see you in about an hour.

I threw my phone on the bed and headed for the shower. Forty minutes later I bounced happily down the stairs and into the kitchen to find Mum pouring ingredients into the slow cooker.

'You look happier,' Mum said, looking up from her dinner prep.

'Sam's coming over. We're going to have dinner down at the wharf,' I announced happily.

'Oh, good so he apologised?' she asked, looking at me expectantly.

"I don't think he remembers." I replied, feeling stupid for admitting it.

"Did you talk to him about what you and Bec have decided?" she asked, referring to our agreement to stop making cakes for Sam and his friends. "You're not a bloody charity, Magnolia."

"I know mum. I will tell him." I knew that I would have to tell Sam about the cakes but he was due to arrive in a matter of minutes. He was bound to have a headache and I didn't want to stress him out. "I'll talk to him about it later."

"Make sure you do, Bub. Dad and I like Sam but I don't like the way he bullies you about the cakes. I know Dad is fed up with it too."

"I know, Mum. He just doesn't understand how much work they are." I replied. Sometimes I wondered what my parents would think if they knew about Sam's drunken antics. "Please tell Dad not to say anything!"

"You know he wouldn't say anything." she said, looking a bit annoyed. "We just want you to be happy sweetheart. I don't like that he screamed at you."

I appreciated my mother's concern but she had no idea how much worse things could be. I believed that Sam really was mostly a good guy. I was sure that he would never cheat on me or call me the kinds of names I'd been called in the past. If my parents knew my terrible secret, I was sure that they would understand my hesitance to cause problems with Sam. I genuinely didn't believe that I deserved any better.

When he arrived a few minutes later, I had my bag and keys, ready to head straight off. I knew that Mum was annoyed with him and I didn't want him to notice and question me about why. We went and had a delicious dinner down by the harbour. It was such a lovely clear evening that we went for a long walk afterwards. We held hands and talked about my itinerary in Melbourne as well as what we could buy for his friends who'd just gotten engaged. Sam was back to his usual, perfectly nice and calm self and the night before became nothing more than a bad dream.

I never told Sam that Bec and I had decided to stop making cakes for his friends, in case it caused more problems. Instead, I used my ever-increasing workload as an excuse whenever someone asked. I was relieved that Sam didn't question why I was knocking back his friends' requests. The accusations about ripping off his friends also became a thing of the past, much to my relief.

Chapter Five

Over the next few months, more of Sam's friends became engaged to their girlfriends. Most of his mates were guys he'd been playing rugby league with since his early teens. During the past couple of winters, I had religiously attended all of his games and so I became close with most of the other girlfriends. Sam and I had never talked about getting married but suddenly we were attending endless engagement parties and weddings. By the time our three-year anniversary loomed we were starting to feel the pressure to take our relationship to the next level as well.

I had always dreamed of my wedding day. As a little girl I was obsessed. I would get dressed up in the flower girl dress that I'd inherited from Hayley when it no longer fit her and walk down the aisle with my brother's friends and neighbourhood boys. I wasn't particularly fussy about who I was marrying, I just loved any excuse to put on that dress and throw the bunch of fake flowers that mum had given me. The flowers were pink roses that she had left over from one of my Easter hat extravaganzas. I got married every other weekend there for a while. It made sense, at least logically, that Sam and I should take the plunge and get engaged too. We had a good time together and we liked each other's friends and family.

But deep down I knew that Sam was not the wonderful, sweet and supportive guy that my family thought he was. Despite all the drama about Bec and my cakes, my family still thought he was a good, solid boyfriend and believed that he would make a good husband. I had been such a burden on my family as a teenager that I felt as though I owed it to them—as much as I owed it to Sam to start thinking about settling down with him—even though the thought of spending my life with Sam didn't fill me with excitement, in fact it even scared me a little bit.

The trouble was that the thought of being alone and unloved forever scared me more. I desperately wanted to have babies and be loved by a good man. I wanted to be able to erase the words that vile old man had said to me so many years before. I decided to ignore all the red flags because I genuinely believed that Sam was the only man who would ever want me, I was so sure that he was my one and only shot at the love that I craved.

I continued to justify Sam's excessive drinking to myself, even though it really bothered me. I hadn't been exposed to people drinking much growing up. My parents were often on-call with their jobs so anything more than a wine or beer when we went out or had people over wasn't common. I had gotten drunk a couple of times when I first landed in the US, despite not actually being old enough to drink over there. The restaurant I worked in had a bar and the owners were pretty relaxed about us helping ourselves to drinks when we were cleaning up after closing.

My friends and I would then head off to some party where we'd drink all sorts of god-awful concoctions out of those red plastic college cups that you see on TV. I had gotten so drunk a couple of times that I ended up too sick to go to work the next day. As a result of those nights, I soon realised that I wasn't cut out to be a drinker. I loved a glass of wine or two occasionally but most of the time I preferred to be the designated driver. Especially once I got home and got used to driving on the left-hand side of the road again.

But not Sam. His drinking habits were like nothing I'd seen before. It scared me to think of how out of it he often became. The urinating on the floor was bad enough but the stories his friends would tell about him ending up in hospital after a wild weekend completely blew my mind. Sam had been so eager to start Mad-Monday celebrations after his team won the Grand Final that he'd gotten dressed without showering first, despite having sustained a nasty gash to his leg.

By Monday afternoon Sam had been in the same clothes for two days. He had wet himself and even slept on a footpath for a few hours. When he arrived home and told his parents about how much his leg hurt, they were horrified to see the nasty gash that now looked infected. Sam was so drunk that his parents needed to bathe him before taking him to the hospital where he spent three days on IV antibiotics to fight the infection in his leg—sepsis.

The incident had happened a couple of years before Sam and I met but the story had become legendary among his mates. The guys would have a wonderful time recounting every disgusting detail about that weekend, laughing as they did so. Even a few of the other women would smile and tut along affectionately as their husbands and fiancées retold the story.

But I didn't see the joke. I couldn't understand why anyone would find the story funny. Their friend had been so intoxicated that he didn't notice the life-threatening infection developing in his leg. He had chosen not to bathe for an entire weekend, which in itself seemed gross to me with my obsession with cleanliness. I had to leave the room whenever the story came up in the end. If I didn't have to listen to him and his mates laughing and joking about it then I could pretend it hadn't happened.

Another thing that worried me was a little four-letter word that I'd become more and more conscious of. Not the one you might think. It was the L word. Sam and I had never actually said that we loved one another. Of course I loved him, everyone did but I never had the courage to say it out loud because he'd never said it to me.

I didn't know a whole lot about love. My previous experience with it had ended in disaster. I didn't think for one moment that I was worthy of great love but it didn't stop me from wanting it. I wanted what my parents had, somebody who screamed it from the rooftops, and told me every chance they got, that they loved me. Sam's nastiness about me ripping his mates off often made me wonder if he even liked me. He never admitted to having screamed at me during his mate's party but he had at least apologised—wasn't that worth something? Surely Sam wouldn't be talking about marrying me if he didn't love me? If we got engaged then maybe he would stop drinking so much. Maybe he would finally tell me how much he loved me and I could still have my fairytale.

That's why I said yes when Sam agreed to buy the ring I'd seen and fallen in love with in the window of a local boutique jewellery store. Bec and I had chosen our dream engagement rings on a lunch and shopping trip a few months earlier. Mine had a half carat diamond in the centre with smaller round stones set on a decorative platinum band.

When Sam and I walked into the jewellers his initial reaction to the ring was that, at four thousand dollars, it was far too expensive. My soon-to-be fiancée was noticeably annoyed with me for expecting such an expensive ring. His reaction reminded me of how worthless I often felt. I knew friends and colleagues whose husbands had spent two and three times as much on their engagement rings. I knew that I needed to keep the peace because I hated to make a fuss but when the sales woman awkwardly asked if we'd like to see some smaller diamonds I politely refused. I had my heart set on that particular ring.

"It's okay, thank you." I was mortified by Sam's outburst. "Maybe we should just go."

"But I thought we were going to lay-buy a ring." Sam said, completely ignoring the look of embarrassment on my face. "Just choose another ring."

"It's okay, you don't have to get me a ring." I replied, wishing that we could just leave. "It was a dumb idea." I felt stupid for thinking anyone would actually want to marry me. I had never been so embarrassed in my life.

"I want to get you a pretty ring, babe." Sam held his hand out to me as he spoke. "I just don't understand why anyone would spend that kind of money on a stupid ring."

"It's fine. Can we just go and get some lunch please?" I asked, feeling desperate. I was thankful that the sales assistant had excused herself to go and help someone else but I didn't want to be there any longer. "We can just come back another day."

"I'll tell you what." he said, once again looking animated and excited. "Why don't you lay-buy the one you want and pay for half of it and then I'll pay the rest?" He looked so pleased with himself.

"I guess so. Sure." I didn't want to pay for my own engagement ring. I wanted him to think I was worth a few grand for a stupid ring but how could I expect him to believe that when I didn't believe it myself?

"Thank you." I said before taking his hand and walking over to where my beautiful ring was sitting in the cabinet, waiting for me.

As we ate lunch a short time later, I couldn't help but wonder if there could possibly have been a less romantic way to select an engagement ring. I had been so excited about our big outing.

I had jumped out of bed that morning like a kid on Christmas. I was full of anticipation as I bathed and dressed in the outfit I'd selected the day before. My outfit consisted of jeans and a white top paired with my favourite pink crystal-heart encrusted cardigan. I had chosen a baby pink colour for my manicure and pedicure the day before and even my lipstick was matching. I was so excited about whatever romantic gesture he was going to surprise me with when he gave me the ring. But there I was instead, having just put my own ring on lay-by, wishing I was good enough to get a big romantic gesture from the man I was going to marry.

As I sat there eating and pretending that I was fine with what had transpired that afternoon I thought back to the old man. The disgusting, scary old man who owned the newsagency where my friend had worked when we were just fourteen. I believed that old man when he called me terrible names. A slut and a good for nothing whore. I desperately wanted Sam to fix me, even if I didn't fully understand it at the time. I sat there, desperately wishing that I could tell him about what that old man had done to me, and to my friends and other girls. I had always been so ashamed—I couldn't explain to Sam why I so desperately wanted the big romantic gesture. I had always believed that my big love story would someday heal me but I couldn't bring myself to utter the words.

Anthony was the only person I ever told about the old man and that had backfired spectacularly. I believed that at his core, Sam was a decent man, or at least he tried to be. I knew that he would be so horrified by my admission and that he wouldn't call me the vile things that Anthony had but I was terrified that he would see me through my own eyes. I had spent so many years believing that I was a good for nothing slut and that I had let that old man do those things to me. I couldn't risk him rejecting me and so instead I plastered a smile on my face and tried to get excited about my beautiful ring and the fact that Sam was going to marry me.

For the next few weeks, I had a wonderful time researching and planning my dream wedding while I made the repayments on my ring. I didn't tell my family that I was the one making the instalments, simply that Sam and I had chosen and were paying off my dream ring. My family were excited at the prospect of me settling down with a good guy. I continued to hide Sam's troublesome and embarrassing drinking habits as well as the constant bullying. Sam wanted me to buy a property with him and invest the sizeable amount of money that I had saved into the property. Sam and I earned roughly the same salary but he already owned a couple of investment properties with his brother and wasn't in a position to contribute anything towards the deposit on our first home together.

I had worked so hard to save that money and the thought of having someone take it away from me terrified me. I grew up hearing about how my biological father had been such a deadbeat. My grandfather wholeheartedly believed that, given the opportunity, that man would have taken advantage of my mother and her generous family. I tried to reason with Sam, asking if he would consider living with my parents for a couple of years before we thought about buying a place of our own. I was hoping that we would become pregnant fairly quickly once we were married and so having the financial freedom to take a year off without having to worry about paying off a mortgage seemed like a sensible idea.

One day, about two months after our visit to the jewellers, Sam and I were at the engagement party of his close friends, Tom and Stacy. I had been looking forward to the party for weeks because of how much I liked those particular friends. Tom was not a huge drinker like most of the other guys that Sam played football with and so I had often found myself hanging out with him and Stacy at functions. Even when we went away to Melbourne one time with the whole team and their partners, I had found myself sharing a taxi with them back to the hotel so that the rest of the group could go out and get wasted. I always felt at ease when they were around and I felt honoured to be invited to celebrate their engagement with them.

Sam and I had only been at the party for an hour or so when he started to slur his words and shout at me. I didn't pay much attention to what he was trying to say at first because I assumed that he was just shouting over the loud music but when I looked at him, I realised he looked angry.

"What's wrong, Sam?" I asked, puzzled about his sudden outburst. "What's happened?"

"I'm sick of you accusing me of trying to steal your money," Sam shouted. "You don't even trust me!"

"What? Why?" I asked, recoiling from his words. "I'm sorry, what are you talking about?"

"Why would you want to live with your parents when we're married?" Sam demanded, following me as I began walking towards the door. I was conscious of several people who were staring at us.

"I thought we would have a baby first, that's all." I explained dumbly. "Of course I trust you."

"Bullshit! We've never even talked about kids," Sam said, his voice barely more than a whisper now that we were away from the noise. "You don't want a future with me! You just want to stay stuck in the same place forever."

"That's not true!" I pleaded desperately. "I love you. I want to be with you. I want to marry you." I reached my arms out, trying to calm him down.

"I don't want this." Sam said flatly, without an ounce of emotion in his voice." I'm sick of this mediocre shit."

"What are you saying?" I asked, dropping my arms to my sides. "Don't you love me?"

"Not really." he mumbled, the words barely audible.

"Did you ever love me?" I asked desperately. "You asked me to marry you."

"No, I didn't!" Sam shouted again. "You bullied me into lay-buying that ring, Magnolia. I didn't want to buy it. I don't want any of this!"

"What are you saying?" I already knew what he was going to say but I needed to hear it from his mouth. "That you don't love me?"

"For God's sake! No. I don't love you and I don't want to get married to you or anyone else." The look of hatred in Sam's eyes was real. I raised my hands and stepped back, trying to distance myself from his words.

"Okay," I said. I turned then and ran away from him. I ran as best as I could in my three-inch heels. I kept my head down as I grabbed my bag from under the table that Sam and I had been eating at happily not an hour earlier. I was thankful that no one noticed my chest heaving as I sobbed silently, or that if they did, they didn't say anything. I looked up just in time to see Sam walk back inside. For a moment I hoped that it was a bad dream, that he would come to me and tell me that his cruel words were some kind of mistake, a sick joke even.

But he didn't. I watched for a moment as Sam looked around the room. His eyes landed on me for a moment before he turned and walked towards the bar, shaking his head as he strode purposefully towards a group of his mates who were ordering drinks. My heart sank even further, if that was even possible, after his vile outburst. I knew that I needed to get out of there like my life depended on it and so that's what I did. I reached my car a minute later and somehow managed to drive the forty minutes home to the safety of my bedroom.

As I closed my door I headed straight over to my bed. There was only one way that I knew how to erase the pain. I sat down before taking the steak knife from my bedside drawer. I dug the jagged blade deep into the soft white flesh of my left forearm. I sliced at my arm half a dozen times before the stinging sensation took over.

The pain of those cuts was so much easier to cope with than the pain in my heart. I knew from experience that the shame of what I'd done to myself would come soon enough but in that moment I didn't care. I had learned a long time ago how to live with the consequences of my cutting episodes.

I had started slicing my skin as a way to try and cope with the shame of what the disgusting old man had done to me all those years earlier. It wasn't something I did often but when I felt myself falling, flailing out of control, I knew that I could catch myself with that steak knife. The thin white scars on my skin were a small price to pay.

I sat there on my bed for several minutes. Breathing slowly I closed my eyes, determined to see my new future. The future where someone would love me the way I wanted, the way I needed to be loved. When I opened my eyes, I looked down to see blood dripping onto my leg. I jumped up and grabbed the first aid tub from my wardrobe. As I pulled the tub out, I noticed a familiar box underneath. It was my photo box. Once I had cleaned and bandaged up my arm, I removed the lid of the box and walked back over to my bed.

At first the photos brought a smile to my face. There were pictures from family holidays, pool parties with Bec, Hayley, James and myself eating ice creams on the sunlounges in my grandparents' backyard when we were just little children. There was a whole pack of pictures from my time living in California and then, halfway through looking at the photos I found a print from a photo shoot that Sam and I had paid for early on in our relationship. We were dressed in 1920s costumes and we looked so carefree and happy.

I was so angry. I was angry at myself for thinking that I was ever worthy of a man like him and I was angry at him for leading me on. It didn't matter that I'd been so tolerant of his drinking or that I had let him bully me and accuse me of ripping off his friends when in truth Bec and I had barely broken even despite spending hours of our time meticulously crafting those stunning cakes. The cold hard reality was that Sam didn't want me, apparently, he never had.

Without a second thought I grabbed my knife and stuck it right through the middle of the photo before tearing it in half. I spent the next half an hour tearing up every photo of Sam and I that I could find. As I tore up the memories, I tried to convince myself that I could do so much better than him. I was going to find someone who would take the pain away and love me. I was determined to find my great love the way everyone around me seemed to have found theirs.

Chapter Six

When I woke up the next morning it was the stinging sensation in my arm that reminded me of the pain in my heart. I was dreading the conversation with my parents and James but even more so, I was dreading the conversation with Bec. I was still in shock about Sam's outburst and trying to make sense of his words. I didn't know how I was supposed to tell everyone that the guy I had spent three years with and then chosen an engagement ring with just weeks earlier had never actually loved me. Not only had Sam made it clear that he didn't love me, but his disdain for me was also palpable.

I grabbed my phone, foolishly hoping that there would be a message from Sam, apologising for his words, telling me that he didn't mean any of it. There was no such message though. I knew that Sam was probably still drunk. I placed my phone back onto my bedside table and hopped up. I knew that I needed to distract myself before his words infiltrated my soul any further.

I showered before applying new Band-Aids to my arm, careful to cover them up with a long sleeve top before grabbing my phone and heading downstairs to break the news to my family.

"Hey kid. Coffee?" Dad smiled at me as I entered the room. "I've just made a fresh pot."

"Thanks." I said, my bravado slipping as the tears started to fall silently. I turned away to try and compose myself.

"What's wrong, Mags?" James asked, walking into the room behind me just as I looked up.

"Bub, what's happened?" Mum asked a moment later, standing up from her seat and walking the few steps to where I was standing.

"Sam broke up with me," I announced, sobbing as I remembered his words again.

"Oh dear. What happened, sweetheart?" Dad's voice broke through the chaos of my thoughts. "Did you guys have a fight?"

"No. He said he didn't want to marry me because he doesn't love me." I admitted to the confused faces in front of me. "He was so nasty."

"Oh darling, I'm so sorry." Mum said as she wrapped her arms around my heaving shoulders.

"He's a loser, sis!" James said angrily. "Who the hell does he think he is? I'll kick his arse!"

"James, that's enough." Dad placed his hand on James's shoulder before wrapping his arms around me too. "I'm so sorry, Bub."

As my family held me up, I stood there once again trying to understand what was so terrible about me. I had been such a good girlfriend to Sam. I had ignored his horrible drinking habits, disappearing for whole weekends, and the urinating on my bedroom floor those few disgusting nights at the start of our relationship. I had put up with him bullying and humiliating me over those beautiful cakes to the point where I no longer enjoyed making them at all. I had put up and shut up so many times and I still wasn't good enough. I still wasn't worthy of his love. Deep down I knew that I wasn't worthy of the love I craved, I'd known it since I was fourteen but I needed it. I so desperately wanted and needed to be loved.

I told Bec that night on our way to grab an impromptu dinner. I had spent the day with my brother and my parents hovering nearby. We watched movies as we ate ice cream and chocolate. Being fussed over was something I had always struggled with, never quite believing that I was worth the fuss but I was thankful for the distraction. As the hours passed that day I found solace in their company. I was barely even allowed to go to the toilet alone.

As it turned out Bec had been debriefed by James already. We had barely made it out of our street before she turned to me and placed her hand on mine as I rested it on the gear stick of my beloved little car.

"I'm so sorry. You've always been too good for him, sweetheart," Bec announced, her voice so gentle and full of concern. "I wish you'd told him to go jump that night he screamed at you about the cakes."

"I really thought that maybe he loved me though." I replied, feeling stupid for thinking so. "He never said it but he acted like he did, at least sometimes."

"He never told you that he loved you?" Bec asked, I could see the confusion and then fury in her eyes. "Are you serious?"

"Yeah." I felt embarrassed by my admission. "I never said it to him until last night either though."

"And then he threw it in your face! He's not good enough for you!" Bec announced, her face softening again. "Everyone loves you Magnolia. It's his loss."

"I love you too, kid."

I didn't know what I would do without my family but I couldn't help but wonder if they would feel the same way about me if they knew the truth. I didn't believe that I was worthy of the way my family rallied around me over the days and weeks that followed but I needed and appreciated it so very much.

Mum, Bec and Hayley took control of returning the things I had collected from Sam over those seemingly meaningless three years. The gifts of perfume and an angora sweater among other things including CDs and a jumper I'd borrowed from him and kept because it smelled of his aftershave. Mum had tried to convince me to keep the gifts, if not his things but I couldn't. I needed to purge my life of every memory of him. I needed to tear him up just as I'd torn those photos to shreds.

When Bec and I went to cancel the lay-buy for the ring, I found out that the jewellers did not offer refunds for change of mind. I had already paid almost half the cost of my ring but I no longer wanted it. I explained the situation to the sales woman, hoping that she might refund my money but she refused to budge. I had no choice in the end but to choose other items. If I hadn't spent almost two thousand dollars I would have walked out of there on principle but instead I chose a beautiful diamond cross and necklace for mum and a stunning pair of pink sapphire earrings for myself. I was grateful to Bec for helping me choose the items. Without her help that day I doubt that I would have walked out with more than a credit note.

When I wasn't being coddled by my family, I threw myself into my work. I was grateful for the distraction of coordinating half a dozen events that were due to take place later in the year. Sam had never been a big believer in mixing work and pleasure, at least not where my workmates were concerned, and so keeping my heartbreak to myself was relatively easy, most of my colleagues had never actually met the mysterious Sam, I had sometimes wondered whether they even believed that he existed.

It was about three weeks after that soul-crushing night, just as I was starting to feel like my life could go on without Sam, or any man for that matter, that I got a text. It was Anthony. He had moved to Sydney for work and wanted to catch up. He said that he wanted to apologise for the way he'd treated me when we were together. It seemed like fate that my Hollywood star lookalike with the dreamy Californian accent should turn up at that very moment on his white horse to rescue me.

Anthony. I had spent years trying not to think about him before that text came through. He was my first big love, and he broke my heart. But before that he truly was like something out of a Hollywood movie. He was handsome, charming and so full of confidence. I had only been in America for a few weeks when we first met. I had landed in San Francisco to stay with Katrina, one of mum's best friends who was living in the Bay Area of Northern California. My parents had reached out to Katrina asking if she would take me in for a few months while I worked and saved enough money to travel around America for the rest of that year.

Katrina had always been like an aunty to me. She knew that I'd had a rough few years back at home before dropping out of high school and so she was thrilled at the idea of having me come to stay with her. She helped me line up a job at a local restaurant and I quickly made friends with a group of girls from work. Most of the girls were attending college at nearby Stanford, with the exception of me and another Aussie girl who was there for her gap year after graduating high school.

The parties that my new friends took me to were just like the ones I had grown up seeing on TV and in the movies. They were wild. There would be up to a hundred people stuffed into a small house with more spilling out onto the street. The drinking games, the people making out in bedrooms and kitchens, it was all so surreal but exciting. Some of the parties required you to buy your cup before you were allowed in. The surcharge would give you a cup and a number of drink tokens, usually two or three. Those tended to be the tamer parties.

But the night I met Anthony was definitely not one of those tame parties. I wasn't even planning on going out that night. I had pulled a double shift at the restaurant after one of the other servers called in sick. By the time I got home it was almost 10 pm. Katrina was away for a few days and I was ready to curl up on the lounge with a book and a glass of wine. But when I switched my phone on after work there were a dozen messages from the girls, begging me to come to a party with them.

I called them back, agreeing to pop over for just one drink before they went out. But then when I arrived, walking in the door to the sound of my favourite 90s rock and a bunch of overexcited and tipsy girls, I was quickly swept up in their excitement. Before I knew it, I had borrowed a cute pink mesh-top to go with the hipster jeans and boots I had changed into at home and was hopping into a cab, headed to what promised to be a great party.

My friends had this weird thing about not getting dropped right out the front of your destination. It was a safety precaution to make sure creepy taxi drivers didn't know where to find them later. It wasn't something that would ever have occurred to me back home but I quickly learned to go with it. That night was no different. As we hopped out of the taxi a couple of streets over from the party, we could already hear the fun that was waiting for us. It was a Valentines themed party which made sense since it was, in-fact, Valentine's Day.

As we approached the house there were guys running around dressed in cloth nappies with wings and toy bow and arrow sets. They would shoot the bows at people who were kissing, much to the annoyance of those young lovers. Almost everyone was dressed in pink or red and the girls and I were no exception. I wore my long blonde hair out with pink sequins stuck in it to match my top.

I didn't really notice him at first. He was just another one of the impossibly attractive guys I'd seen since I arrived. Aussie guys could hold their own but I'd only ever known guys my own age and they were kind of scrawny and awkward for the most part.

The guys at those parties tended to be in their early twenties. They seemed so grown up and mature. Anthony was one of those guys. He was twenty-three and had graduated college a year and a bit earlier. Anthony was tall with dark brown hair and the kind of tan you'd expect for a guy who surfed a lot. I found myself talking to him while my friends went on the prowl. I had no interest in meeting anyone. I was only planning on staying with Katrina for a couple of months before heading onto the next leg of my adventure in Vegas, so I was happy to just hang out with him until the other girls were done flirting.

He didn't ask for my number, and I didn't think twice about it as I left the party that night. But then the following day one of my friends admitted that he had given her his number and asked her to pass it on to me. I called him a couple of days later but only because I thought I'd met a new friend. I had no interest in him romantically, not at first anyway. We started to hang out as friends, and I quickly realised that he wanted more. I didn't realise that I liked him until I was making plans to leave for Vegas.

I realised that I didn't want to leave him behind. I'd never been in love before. I had convinced myself that I wasn't even capable of it and I certainly didn't think I was worthy of it but then I started to think I could fall in love with him. I was excited about the idea of my first love being a part of my big grown-up adventure. And so, I decided to stay put, at least for a while. Katrina was thrilled, as were my parents. They believed that the more time I spent with our dear friend, the more I would start to truly heal from those traumatic few years.

Sending me to the US had been a last resort for my family, a desperate attempt to get me away from the kids I had been hanging out with back at home, the group of teenagers I'd started hanging out with who had introduced me to all sorts of drugs. My parents had no idea about the pain I was trying to chase away every time I got high. I had never told them about the old man.

They believed me when I told them, honestly, that my new friends on the other side of the world did nothing more than drink alcohol at the parties we attended. I knew that they hoped I would stay with Katrina for the entirety of my year-long stay in America. I also knew that they liked the sound of the young man I had started talking about on our calls. The man who sounded like an angel, and he was, at least compared with the boys I had known at home.

My friends were excited when I told them about my change of plans and my boss was too. My boss was actually someone that Katrina knew through mutual friends, and he often commented to her about how much he appreciated my work ethic. He was happy for me to stay on for as long as I was allowed to.

So that was that. I told Anthony that I would change my plans. I figured that if things didn't work out, I could always continue my travels as originally planned. As it turned out, our new relationship was slow to develop. Anthony was working as a sales executive for a big tech company in Silicon Valley. His job required him to do a fair bit of travelling interstate. I still found it hard to trust men after what I'd been through a few years earlier and so I found myself with the best of both worlds. I had a spunky boyfriend but still had plenty of room to breathe and time to go shopping and on weekend adventures with Katrina and to parties and football games with my friends.

Before I knew it, I had been in the US for ten months. My visa would allow me to work and party for twelve months. After that, my plan had always been to come back home. It was around that time that he started to talk about wanting me to stay and live with him. At first, I didn't see how that would be possible but then he had an idea. A junior marketing role was advertised internally at his company. He knew that they had a sponsorship program where every now and then they would hire somebody from overseas who was on a Visa like mine and then sponsor their right to work for a period of a year or two.

It seemed like the perfect solution. My parents, brother, and Bec had all been to visit by that point. They had all met Anthony and agreed that he seemed like a genuine guy. When I told them that I was thinking about staying and beginning a real career, they all encouraged me to do whatever made me happy. They said that although they'd be disappointed about not having me home as planned, the job sounded like a great opportunity, and it wouldn't hurt to see where my relationship was going. Katrina assured them that if anything went wrong with my Californian spunk then her door was always open. My parents assured me that there was always a plane ticket home if I needed it. They were just relieved to see that I was getting myself back on track after what had been a difficult few years for all of us.

And so, with that I stayed. We moved in together and embarked on a wonderful adventure. We'd been together for over three years when I found out about what he'd been getting up to on those work trips. I chose to believe that he hadn't done it all along, that it was only a recent thing but deep down I knew that it wasn't. He had been so self-assured and confident from the moment we met, and I knew that he could charm his way into anyone's heart, or at least into their pants.

Chapter Seven

Thinking about what Anthony did to me back then should have been enough to remind me that he was bad for me. I should have told him to go to hell. But I was feeling so fragile about the whole Sam situation that, against my better judgement, I agreed to see him.

I hadn't so much as heard his name in years. I was still working for the same company where he had worked back when I met him but by then he was long gone. The sales team had always had a high turnover rate. As soon as a rep went two quarters without hitting their target, they were out the door. When he finally got the chop, it had felt like a little win for me. It was nice to see his name disappear from my email contacts. He told me that now he was living in Sydney and working, ironically, for our biggest competitor. Apparently they didn't get the memo about his selling skills, although that thought didn't occur to me at the time.

I agreed to meet him a few days later at a bar near my work. His building was only a couple of streets away as it turned out and so it worked out perfectly. In the days leading up to our catch up we ended up texting back and forth a lot. He even called once and it struck me how easy it was to talk to him, even after so many years. I didn't tell my parents or my brother and I sure as heck didn't tell Hayley or Bec.

My cousins were the ones who had arrived to pick me up from the airport when I got home from America. They had bundled me and my broken heart into the car and then spent the next few months helping me figure out how to put the pieces back together. They'd kill me if they knew that my Friday night work drinks were nothing quite so innocent.

For once in my life, I arrived late. Only five minutes but if you knew me and how punctual I always was then you'd understand what a big deal that five minutes was. It wasn't lost on him either. By the time I reached the bar he was standing up. He stretched out his arms and enveloped me in them. Everything about him was so remarkably familiar. He smelled the same and I could have sworn that he was wearing a shirt that I had bought for him shortly before we parted ways.

He looked the same, with the exception of his hairline which was noticeably further back than it was the last time I'd seen him, and his waistline, which was a bit thicker. We spent the next couple of hours talking about mutual friends in the US. A few of his friends had been so disgusted by his behaviour that they chose to dump him and stay friends with me. But life meant that I barely spoke to them anymore. Anthony explained that he was back in touch with a few of the guys. I was thrilled to learn that one of them was married and another of the guys was just weeks away from tying the knot too. They were both decent guys and I knew that they would make good husbands and fathers.

The mere presence of Anthony erased all thoughts of Sam from my subconscious. The night at that engagement party seemed like a lifetime ago. Anthony had been so vocal about how much he loved me when we were together, even if he was sleeping around. His outrage as I explained what had transpired with Sam was so validating.

"You're so beautiful. Any man would be lucky to marry you, Maggie," Anthony told me in that sexy accent I had always loved.

"Not really. I mean you didn't." I looked down as I spoke. The two glasses of wine I'd practically sculled giving me the courage to say things I'd never normally have been brazen enough to say but not enough to look up at his face.

"I wish I had married you." Anthony admitted, lifting my chin gently with his hand. "I loved you. I really never meant to do those things. I'm so sorry, sweetheart. I wish I could go back and do things so differently." His apology seemed so genuine that I couldn't help but believe him.

"Oh, really?" I asked, the last shred of commonsense flew out the window as I clung to his words, to the idea that someone could love me after all.

The look on my face must have told him all he needed to know because a moment later his tongue was in my mouth. It wasn't hot the way I remembered. I felt like I was being accosted by a lizard, sucking and licking my face. It was a bit gross but I didn't care. I was going to kiss Sam out of my mind once and for all.

Anthony had loved me once and in that moment nothing else mattered. I kissed him back, forcing myself to ignore the weird new goanna impersonation.

I spent the next six weeks ignoring it. My intention after that first night was to be careful of him. I wasn't going to let him break my heart again or anything dumb like that. When I was away from him, I had complete control of my emotions. I had all the common sense and insight to understand that he was just my rebound guy. I knew that he was a heartbreaking shit of a man. But then I would see him and that commonsense would fly straight out the window. It was like my fear of huntsman spiders. I was not at all fussed when they weren't around, convincing myself that I had outgrown my phobia. But then I would see one in my house, and I would be hysterical. I had spent weeks sleeping on the lounge once after spotting one in my room.

Anthony was so sweet and attentive when we were together that I was able to ignore that voice of commonsense and reason in my mind, especially after he once again declared his undying love for me. We were sitting at my favourite spot on Sydney Harbour eating dinner together one evening when he wrapped his arms around me and told me that he loved and needed me. I had no reason not to believe his words. When we were together, I was so sure that I was finally living my happily ever after.

Anthony and I were having such a wonderful time together. I was starting to think it was safe to tell my family that we had reunited. I had the speech all worked out in my mind about how much he had changed, how he was sorry and he loved me but then, less than two-months after our big reunion, my twenty-sixth birthday came and went without so much as a phone call from him.

I sat at dinner, surrounded by my beautiful, generous family. There were presents and a cake that Bec had made for me. Amy had bought me a helium balloon and a single red rose, a tradition our group had started in high school. I tried so hard to have a good time but instead I sat there all night, obsessively checking my phone as I tried to hold the tears at bay.

I knew that my strange behaviour didn't go unnoticed, but my family ignored it. Instead, they put all their energy into making me smile. And it nearly worked. I ignored the sick feeling in my stomach as the evening went on, telling myself over and over, that he must've been caught up with work or some emergency. But by the end of the night, I had no choice but to admit to myself that he had done it again.

I didn't bother to call him again after that, I told myself that I was cutting off contact, but I knew that the truth was; he had ghosted me. On my birthday. As the weeks went by, I tortured myself, wondering how the hell I was going to raise the little baby growing in my belly without his help.

I had always been able to tell Hayley, Bec and my closest friends everything, just as they could tell me anything. but things were different. I hadn't told anyone that I was seeing Anthony, how

                                                    Unlovable

was I supposed to tell them that he'd convinced me not to bother with protection. How was I supposed to tell them that I was carrying his baby?

That's why I eventually messaged his mate instead. He was one of the guys who had chosen me as his friend after the first breakup. I knew that they had patched up their friendship so I figured that if there was something wrong then he would tell me. And did he ever.

Anthony had told me at the bar, on that first night, that he had recently broken up with some woman he had been seeing since arriving in Sydney. But that wasn't true, not by a long shot. I listened as his friend told me about how Anthony and his wife of two years, an Australian woman from a small country town near Canberra, were pregnant and just weeks away from meeting their first child, a little girl.

Chapter Eight

I had been having an affair with a married man. Not just that, I was twenty-six years old, single and pregnant to that married man. I'd been fighting the urge to vomit for weeks but the news that I had been doing something so vile sent me running to the bathroom. I managed to lift the toilet seat just in time. I heaved, over and over until the contents of my stomach were completely expelled.

I had met guys in pubs and at music festivals over the years. I'd flirted with men, only to realise that they were married before turning on my heels and all but running. I had dumped friends a couple of times after finding out that they were knowingly having affairs with married men. It was against everything I stood for but now I was no better. Actually no, I was worse. I had been playing around with someone who had, not just a wife, but a pregnant wife.

I realised that I needed to tell Hayley and Bec. I knew that they would be disgusted by what I had done but I couldn't bear the weight of it by myself. But when I told them my terrible little secret that afternoon, they weren't appalled, well they were but not by me. My cousins knew me well enough to know that I would never have intentionally carried on an affair with a married man. Plus, they already knew what kind of person he was. After all, he had done the same thing to me, and with multiple women. The girls weren't surprised that he was still doing the same things, which made me realise that I shouldn't have been surprised either.

I told them that I'd accidentally gotten pregnant too. I had initially made the decision on my birthday that I would raise the baby alone but how could I have a baby that had been conceived like that? How on earth could I do that to another woman? Anthony's wife was the one who deserved to have a baby, not me. It broke my heart but I knew that I couldn't go ahead with having my baby, our baby, not like that.

I booked in the next day to have an STD check and then made the heartbreaking call to book in for a termination. I had only known about my pregnancy for a few weeks at that stage. But I'd already made so many plans. I already had so many hopes and dreams for the tiny life that was growing inside of me but everything changed when I found out about the woman who was already carrying his baby. His wife. My feelings of joy and excitement turned to shame and disgust. The weight of it was almost more than I could bear.

The clinic couldn't get me in for over a week, I rang around to other clinics that performed the procedure, determined to do what I needed to before I lost the courage altogether but I was told the same thing each time. Somehow, I was going to have to walk around for another week, knowing that I had to do something devastating in order to make things right.

It was three days later, when I was cleaning my bathroom, that my plans changed. I was scrubbing the shower door when out of nowhere the most terrible pain tore through my abdomen, sending me crashing to the floor. It took me a minute to drag myself over to the toilet. The blood was everywhere, and I knew that I was losing the baby. My tiny baby knew that they weren't going to meet me. Instead of letting me do something that I would never forgive myself for, they had decided to take the decision out of my hands.

I sat on the toilet for the longest time, sobbing and apologising as I held my stomach, wondering if I'd willed it to happen and feeling guilty that there was a part of me that felt relieved. I was relieved to realise that I no longer had to walk into that clinic and end the life that I so desperately wanted to be able to bring into the world. I never could have expected the devastation that followed.

I was relieved that the miscarriage happened on a Friday night. For the next day-and-a-half I told my parents and anyone else who asked that I had a cold. I needed to wallow in my misery alone, so I ordered pizza's, ate ice cream and binge watched my favourite romantic comedies. I slowly convinced myself that I would be ok. I convinced myself that I would meet one of those handsome romantic guys on my screen. They were going to find me and make it all better.

And I prayed, something I had never been too good at. I wanted my baby to know that I was sorry. I had so desperately wanted them but I didn't see how I could let my happiness overshadow someone else's. I prayed because I so desperately wanted that little soul to know how much I loved them. I would never forgive myself for what I had been planning to do. I had never despised myself as much as I did then.

By the Sunday afternoon I knew that I needed to share my burden, that's why I called my cousins. I was relieved to see them walk in the door not half an hour later. Bec and Hayley came to rescue me, just as they had done so many times before. Those two women, my brother and my parents could fix almost everything but I couldn't bear to break Mum and Dad's hearts with my news and I was worried about what James would do to Anthony.

I didn't want my sweet but overly-protective brother getting himself in trouble so instead I let the girls help me tidy up the food containers in my room before showering and swapping my track pants for a sundress. I walked outside for the first time in two-days and breathed in the sweet smell of jasmine in the air as I carefully manoeuvred myself into the back of Bec's car.

Food had always been my family's love language and so we picked up some takeaway before driving down to Greenwich pier. The late afternoon sky was so clear and bright, making me feel, for the first time since my birthday, that maybe the world was not going to end.

For the first time in what seemed like forever, I sat down and had a huge heart-to-heart with the girls. I told them that I couldn't understand what was so bad about me. No matter how nice, kind and agreeable I was with them, the men I dated still treated me like shit. I kept the part about the old man to myself though because deep down I knew exactly what was wrong with me. I knew that what he did to me all those years earlier had made me dirty and unlovable. It was the only explanation. I laughed when I spoke about how my mum tried to tell me that it was because I was too pretty. That the men were actually intimidated by my looks. I loved her for saying it but I knew that I wasn't anything out of the ordinary. I knew that my nan, mum, and two aunties were such special women and that they would do anything to make me feel better, just as Bec and Hayley would.

I was relieved that the girls didn't seem to think anything of the denim jacket I'd thrown on to cover up the fresh bandage on my arm. I had prepared a story about the bandage that was hiding the fresh wounds that ran horizontally along my forearm. It was a lie that I had formulated many years earlier but had never needed to use. Something about burning myself on the oven door. Everyone knew I was a bit of a klutz so I figured it would be believable enough.

Nobody knew about how deeply damaged I was. Nobody knew quite how much I despised myself. From the outside I was such a high functioning, successful professional woman who everyone assumed was just a bit unlucky in love but my internal reality was very different. My personal reality was so much more complex. My smile hid such a dark and shameful secret.

Chapter Nine

had always blamed myself for going along with it. My friend worked at a nearby newsagency on the weekends. The old man who owned the shop with his wife was always cranky and I was a bit scared of him. One day my friend told me that some of the other girls she worked with were making an extra fifty dollars a couple of times a week by letting their boss practice his massage skills on them. I was disgusted at first, but she reassured me that there was nothing untoward about it—he was looking for new girls to practice on.

I didn't have a job back then. My parents were insistent that studying was more important in high school. I got money for chores but at fourteen, fifty dollars just sounded too good to be true. I decided to give it a go. What harm was a little back massage after all? The shop closed at midday on Sundays, so the arrangement was that I would get there at 1 pm when the staff had all left.

I walked up to the shops; it was a fifteen-minute walk that I'd done dozens of times before but I had no understanding of the significance that each step in his direction would have on me. I walked into that newsagency completely oblivious to the evil that was lurking inside. When I got to the back room there was a massage table set up. My instincts told me to turn around and run. But I didn't. I stayed. I walked over to the table as instructed, stripped down to my underwear and laid down. The feeling of his hands on me was utterly repulsive. The sound of his voice was so scary.

For some reason I didn't stop him when he moved the electronic massager down between my legs and started to massage me in the most intimate way. I knew that it wasn't ok, what he was doing. I had never done so much as kiss a boy. I didn't want him to do it but he told me that it was okay. He told me that no one would believe me if I told them what had happened. And I believed him. He was a well-known—well-respected—member of the community and I was just some little slut, he said. And the strange waves of pleasure that hit me over and over, as he held that massager against my underwear made me believe him.

I wanted to get out of there but I was frozen with fear. He was a big fat man of about sixty years old, and I was only a small fourteen-year-old girl. Well, I was a regular sized teenage girl but compared to him I was tiny. When he started to unzip his pants, I burst into tears. He had already stolen my innocence. I had never had an orgasm before but I had read enough articles in my Dolly magazine to understand what had just happened. The disgusting way that my body had responded to that man filled me with so much revulsion, disgust and shame; I knew that I had to somehow get out of there.

I wasn't going to let him be the person I had sex with for the first time as well and so I begged. I asked if we could leave that for next time. I was relieved to see him zip himself back up and walk over to a drawer. He removed a cash box and counted out fifty dollars in five dollar notes and walked over to hand them to me. I quickly put my clothes back on and grabbed the money while he unlocked the glass sliding door.

And then finally when I was back on the footpath, I realised that I was free. I ran away as fast as my legs would carry me. I ran all the way home, relieved to find that the house was empty. I jumped in the shower in my ensuite bathroom and scrubbed myself until I was red raw. I didn't stop until I saw the blood bubbling from the places where he had touched me. I was so confused. I hated myself for the way my body had responded. I was sure that he was right, that I must have been some disgusting lowlife for what I'd let him do to me and for the fact that I'd enjoyed it. I so desperately wanted to tell my parents or my cousins, but I was too ashamed. I thought that I would get in trouble. I was convinced that my family would think I was all of the things he'd called me.

I had tried so hard to bury that experience over the years, but it was always there. The voice in my head reminding me of that weekend. I went from a regular, carefree and happy teenage girl to a gym obsessed, obsessive compulsive nightmare who hated herself overnight. And then I started wagging school. I started to hang out with a group of older teenagers who hung around a big nearby shopping centre. At first, I resisted their offers to smoke pot with them.

I had never been exposed to drugs before, my parents barely even drank and so I was scared. But then one day I gave in to the peer pressure. And for a little while the pain and the memory of that man disappeared. And so did the disdain and the self-hate that I carried with me everywhere. It didn't take long before I was using anything I could get my hands on. Pot, LSD, even heroin. I lived to get high. And I got high because deep down, I wanted to die.

For three-and-a-half years after the shameful day I did everything I could to escape my vile new reality. My parents could see that I was on a path of self-destruction and I knew that they blamed themselves but I was so far gone that I didn't care. It never occurred to me that they would still love me if they knew the truth—how could anyone love such a monster? And so, I continued down that dangerous path until they had no choice but to step in.

My parents sending me to live in the US literally saved my life, and then Anthony came along and saved my soul. By the time he ripped my heart out a couple of years later I had come so far. I was working and enjoying being a normal twenty-one- year-old. I hadn't touched drugs since before I left Australia and I knew that I never would again. But Anthony's betrayal plunged me back into that feeling of self-hate and shame. Meeting Sam filled me with so much hope, making me believe for the first time in such a long time, that someone might love me and prove once and for all that the old man was wrong.

When Sam admitted that he had never loved me, the cuts from his words were so much deeper than anything I could do with my little knife. I blamed him, in a way, for leaving me so vulnerable. Sam's rejection had such a profound impact on my self-esteem that when Anthony came to me, my desperation to be loved was so strong that I fell for his lies again without question.

As I sat there with Bec and Hayley, mourning the loss of that little person that I'd already known I could never meet, I desperately wanted to entrust them with my shameful secret. For the briefest moment I knew that doing so would finally set me free but as I opened my mouth to speak, the words just would not come. It didn't matter that I was an expert wordsmith. My ability to craft sentences that could make people see software as sexy was something I was endlessly proud of but those three words, I was molested, were beyond me. I closed my mouth and took a deep breath, once again pushing the memory of that day down.

Instead, I exhaled and steered the conversation away from my situation. I knew that living vicariously through the girls' happiness was the next best way to regain my own inner peace.

Chapter Ten

By Christmas I was starting to feel better, both mentally and physically. I was enjoying work, and I was spending more time with my family than I had done in years. Hayley's husband, Ben, was an engineer. The previous Easter he had accepted a twelve-month contract in Western Australia. Hayley was not keen on pulling the kids out of school, nor did she want to leave her job as a primary school teacher. But the money was too good to say no, so off Ben went, by himself, to a small mining town several hours away called Kookynie. He came home for just five days each month. I found myself spending more time at Hayley's place than I did at my own house. Even Bec, who was still in her love bubble with Damian, managed to tear herself away a couple of times a week to hang out with us.

And my brother, James, got engaged. He and Amy had been together since they were seventeen. They both agreed that they would finish studying before taking the next step in their relationship. James had decided to specialise in obstetrics and gynaecology, which meant he was technically still studying but he was making money at least. They finally agreed that they didn't want to wait any longer and so James purchased the most spectacular diamond ring I'd ever seen and popped the question on New Year's Eve, as they watched Sydney

Harbour light up with fireworks and the promise of a magical year ahead.

2003 was off to a great start and I was even more excited to learn that Amy wanted me to be her chief bridesmaid. I had never been in a wedding party before but my obsession with finding someone to love me meant that I already knew what my duties would entail. Amy and James were planning a short engagement because after so many years together they wanted to start a family. Amy was happy to have a baby first but James wouldn't hear of it. My brother wanted the big pavlova love fest that he believed his beautiful fiancée deserved. I had never realised that my brother was such a romantic.

I knew I needed something to distract me and help me get over everything that had happened with Sam, Anthony and my pregnancy and so on top of the wedding planning, I started looking into holiday destinations near home. I had recently seen an ad on the TV about North Queensland, a short three-hour flight from Sydney. I could imagine myself lying around in the sun and drinking cocktails while I figured out where my life was going.

One night, just after Easter, I was having dinner with Bec and Damian at the pub when I had a wonderful idea. I was earning good money and had a huge amount of spare Qantas points saved from all my work trips. I asked Bec and Damian if they wanted to come away for a few days, my shout.

"Mags, don't be ridiculous!" Bec scolded. "You can't pay for us."

"I wouldn't be paying much. I have so many points from all my work travel and the taxes would be less than one hundred dollars each." I explained excitedly. "You guys have been so wonderful and supportive since I broke up with Sam and then through the whole Anthony shit-show. And besides, when was the last time you went on a holiday?"

I saw Damian exchange a strange look with Bec before he spoke.

"There's no way I'm crashing the girls' holiday but you both should go." Damian said, just as the waitress arrived with our meals. He thanked her before turning his attention to Bec. "I think you're overdue for a few days off babe."

"When are you thinking?" Bec asked me. I could tell she was warming to the idea.

"I was thinking of early spring. I've been researching Cairns or Hamilton Island," I replied, feeling hopeful. "I've lived halfway around the world and I've never been to the Barrier Reef!"

"If you can be flexible with dates then why don't you go when I'm in Melbourne in September?" Damian asked Bec and I. "I can check the dates when I'm at my desk later."

"That conference!" Bec exclaimed. "I'd forgotten about that. Boo!" I laughed as my cousin pouted at the thought of her boyfriend leaving, even for a few days. And I smiled when he squeezed her hand so sweetly in return.

"So, is that a yes?" I asked excitedly. "Are we going to drink cocktails and get our tan-on in September?" The three of us laughed at that, knowing very well that the suntan part was wishful thinking with our pale skin.

"Cheers to that then." Damian said cheerfully as he raised his beer in a toast. "To the girls' trip!"

Bec and I laughed, raising our glasses and repeating Damian's toast. I knew that my cousin would not agree to holidaying without Damian for anyone else but she knew how badly I'd taken the breakup with Sam and then Anthony and the baby. It made me happy to see how much my cousin and her lovely man adored each other. Bec's last boyfriend had been a womanising jerk. He'd cheated on her and ended up marrying the other woman after getting her pregnant.

Bec met Damian just a few weeks later and then spent the next couple of months refusing to go out with him, claiming that she was done with men altogether. Damian had been so smitten with the pretty little blonde named Bec that he persisted and seeing the way he looked at my cousin made me genuinely happy that he did. It gave me hope for the first time since becoming single. Maybe I would meet a good guy like him too.

Winter had never been my favourite season before but the winter of 2003, when I was twenty-seven, was an absolute blast. Hayley's husband, Ben, was home from the west coast, making it easier for her to come out for the occasional kid-free night out while Ben looked after the kids. Bec and I had a great time planning our North Queensland adventure. We were heading up to the Whitsundays, at the southernmost end of the Great Barrier Reef. Neither of us had been that far north before but a few people had told us to check out Airlie Beach, so we added it to our itinerary.

I was grateful that between work, wedding planning and the holiday countdown I barely had time to think about Sam, Anthony or my seemingly never-ending single status. Being around so much love made me feel like anything was possible, that maybe everyone was destined to find their soulmates—even me.

A few days before our trip I had an appointment to try on dresses with Amy and her other three bridesmaids. I caught public transport into the office that day, so James would pick me up at nearby Chatswood station on his way home from work. The bridal party were all meeting at our place and then heading into the city to try on the dresses before going out for dinner.

For once I managed to get away from work early and so I arrived at Chatswood almost an hour early. I happily wandered around the shops for forty minutes or so before heading back down to the bus stop outside the station where we'd agreed to meet. There were no seats near that particular bus stop, so I pulled my book out of my bag and started reading as I leant on the wall of a nearby shop. I'd been reading for a few minutes when a man's voice snapped back into the moment.

"Excuse me, do you have the time please?" It took me a moment to realise that he was talking to me.

I recognised him as soon as I looked at him.

"Hey. Is your name Harry?" I asked, feeling clever.

"Ah no!" he exclaimed, seeming freaked out by my question. "Harry is my brother. My name is Zac."

"Oh, I've heard of you." I said, amused by the confused look on his face. I realised that he was Harry's younger brother. He had gone to school with my brother. I had seen both of the brothers around Lane Cove many times. Harry was taller and more boisterous but Zac was much better looking. I explained who I was. And then right on cue James drove up next to us.

Seeing me chatting with his old schoolmate prompted my brother to get out of the car. He walked over and shook hands with Zac. They talked for a minute or two, I could have stood there watching him talk for hours. He had the smoothest voice. He stood there confidently in his polo shirt and chinos. I had a giggle to myself as I noticed that he was wearing boat shoes too. He was such a North Shore preppy guy, not at all my usual type. As James and I said goodbye to him I realised that he was wearing a watch. I couldn't believe he had used such a brazen line on me. No one had ever done that before. I blushed at the thought.

Of course, James claimed to have no idea how to contact my new crush. He told me that he didn't want me chasing Zac up. He didn't feel comfortable with his sister dating someone he'd gone to school with, especially a bad-boy like Zac. I didn't believe for one second that my new crush could possibly be a bad guy. He was so well dressed and polite. And anyway, it was pretty rich that I couldn't date someone from his school considering that Amy was one of my best friends before she was his girlfriend or fiancée. I decided there and then that I was going to see him again, I didn't know how but I was going to make it happen—just not until after my holiday.

Bec and I finally boarded the plane up to Daydream Island in the last week of September. It had been a full two weeks since I'd met Zac, albeit briefly. I had made a point of getting off the bus near Lane Cove Plaza every day, instead of going the extra few stops to the end of my street. I saw his brother twice but realised on the first occasion as I started to approach him that he was kind of scary looking. He had a pierced eyebrow and a bit of a mean face. Before I knew it, I turned and awkwardly walked away. I started to think I would never see Zac again so I flirted up a storm with the pool maintenance guy at Daydream Island instead. Bec and I wandered around the resort, feeding stingrays and snorkelling during the day and drinking cocktails at dinner each night.

The trip was wonderful and it was over far too soon. We arrived home on the Saturday morning of the October long weekend— the first weekend in October. That night Bec, Damian, James, Amy, my parents and I ordered pizzas for dinner to go through some wedding details. James had stopped at the bottle shop on the way home to grab a few bottles of wine. The evening started off as the quiet night we'd intended it to be but by the time my parents went to bed at 11 p m the rest of us were in the mood to party. By midnight we were dancing to the beach boys as they crooned about California girls as we drank the cocktails that Bec and I had invented in our desperation to keep our holiday vibe alive for a bit longer.

The following morning, I drove up to Lane Cove with Bec to grab a few groceries. It was still chilly of a morning and in the evenings, so I threw a jumper and a pair of leggings on. It was far too early to be heading out into the world after the late night we'd had but we needed supplies to make French toast and bacon. My mum had always been a health freak and only bought whole grain bread so off we went in search of some nice thick cut white bread and other goodies. We drove out of our street at 10 am, looking like sunburnt zombies. Once we had collected most of the things we needed for our big breakfast from the supermarket we decided to go and grab a coffee and a cheeky pastry from a nearby bakery as well as the bread. And that's when I saw him.

He was just as nicely dressed as he had been a few weeks earlier. I had thought about the mysterious Zac with his nice clothes and sexy voice a lot since that day in Chatswood but I'd given up on ever actually seeing him again. He looked up, almost instinctively, a matter of seconds after I spotted him and immediately his face lit up. I remembered that he was good looking but holy cow, he was gorgeous! As he said hello, I felt something on my arm. It was Bec nudging me. I remembered my manners and introduced them.

"Oh Zac, this is my cousin Bec." I said self-consciously.

"Nice to meet you, Bec." Zac responded, thrusting his hand out to shake her hand.

"Hi. Nice to meet you" She replied sheepishly. Despite Bec's sunburn, I could see the familiar flush in her cheeks. I was sure mine must have looked the same.

Hearing him speak again reminded me of why I'd so desperately tried to bump into him a few weeks earlier. I remembered my messy hair. It hadn't been brushed that morning, just thrown into a messy bun. And I wasn't wearing a scrap of makeup. I knew that I must have looked like absolute rubbish but it didn't stop him from talking to me. He spoke so beautifully and confidently. My mum had always been obsessed with good grammar, as had my grandparents and my aunts. No one in my family would dare to drop a "youse", unless we were doing it to intentionally annoy our parents.

I had never met such a well-spoken man outside of my own family. I guess it was my habit of going after tradies when I got home from California. They were always attractive but a bit bogan too. Zac's voice sounded like Russell Crowe's. Sexy, smooth and buttery. The more he talked the more I started to realise that he looked a bit like the Gladiator actor too. Our coffees were ready far too quickly. I stood there awkwardly for a moment before saying goodbye. I was conscious that there were hungry savages at home, awaiting our arrival with the breakfast supplies. As I was about to turn and walk away, he stepped over and squeezed me in a huge hug.

The hug only lasted a matter of seconds but it was delicious, if not totally unexpected. He smelt like soap and sandalwood. I swooned—Yep, swooned!—For the first time in my life, I was absolutely dizzy. I was smitten. When he pulled away, he asked me, ever so confidently, if he could have my number. I didn't have any paper or a pen and so he asked the guy behind the counter who he knew by name. A minute later Bec and I turned to take our leave. When I turned to get another sneaky look at him, I realised that he was doing the same. He was nothing like Sam. As I walked away, I crossed my fingers and hoped that he would call. I wondered if he was the one I had been waiting for? Maybe he was the one who was finally coming to rescue me. From the past. And from myself.

And he did call. As I sat at the table eating with my family, not an hour later while Bec teased me mercilessly about the random hottie who had so casually hugged me and then asked for my number, my phone rang. Everyone at the table stopped talking and eating. I knew that I wasn't going to be able to talk to him with everyone sniggering and acting like rowdy preschoolers, so I grabbed my phone and raced into the house and up the stairs to my bedroom.

Somehow, he sounded even sexier over the phone. Lying on my bed chatting with him on the phone was surreal. I listened as he told me that he'd been trying to figure out how to see me again. I didn't tell him that I had tried to bump into him in the plaza, just that I always seemed to see his brother around but never him. We spoke for a good half an hour or so before Amy popped her head into my room to ask if I was coming to Newtown to go shopping and have lunch. Explaining that everyone else was keen for an impromptu adventure.

As I excused myself to reply to my friend turned sister-in-law-to-be, Zac apologised for keeping me for so long. I wanted to go to Newtown with the others, but I could have happily talked to him for hours too. It must have been my lucky day because before saying goodbye he asked me what I was doing that night. I could have been planning to meet Pink herself that night, my all-time favourite celebrity, and I would have cancelled in a moment for him. But thankfully I didn't need to blow off my queen because it just so happened that I didn't have any plans.

I told him that I didn't have any plans yet and asked what he was thinking. He told me that he wanted to see me and suggested drinks at our local pub, the Longy. We agreed to meet at 7 pm before wishing each other a good day in the meantime. And so, a casual wander around the shops in Newtown with my crew turned into an all-out first date preparation shopping trip followed by a pub lunch.

As I walked out the door just before 6.45 pm I had been puffed, sparkled and prettied up within an inch of my life. I'd never been one to do the full-face make-up thing, purely because I was really bad at it. A friend had given me a book, actually an encyclopaedia, about make-up application a few years earlier but it lost my interest pretty quickly when I realised that the end results looked more like something you'd see at a drag queen bingo night than on an almost twenty-seven-year-old woman. But thankfully, Amy and Bec had worked their magic, and I was impressed.

As I walked through the side doors of the pub ten minutes later, I could see that the place was bustling as usual. The Longy had always been a popular gathering spot for locals. My brother, cousins and I loved it because it was within walking distance of our street. As I approached the bar, I jumped at the sound of everybody screaming and it took me a second to realise that there was a football match happening. And then I saw him. Zac laughed as he held his hand out, clearly amused by my reaction to the rowdy guys near the TV. He wasn't to know that the sound of strange men screaming made me nervous.

And then he did it again. He wrapped his arms around me. It only lasted a few seconds, but it was long enough for me to notice that he smelt even better than he had that morning. At that moment I realised that I had never been so attracted to a man I barely knew. Or anyone for that matter. Like the perfect gentleman he paid for the drinks and then we wandered out to the back patio to find a seat. The night went far too quickly. We talked and laughed. I was surprised to learn that he worked as a carpenter. I couldn't help but laugh when he told me that, much to his confusion. I explained that he didn't strike me as a tradie, he looked more like the kind of guy who got up and put a different suit on every day. I couldn't imagine him being covered in sawdust but I knew that somehow, he must still smell divine.

I also knew that I wasn't imagining the incredible chemistry between us. Even with the total lack of self-esteem that plagued me I could see that he clearly liked me. I found myself making excuses to touch his arm or his hand. It hadn't been immediately clear, but I realised at one point, when I squeezed his arm that he had some pretty impressive muscles hiding under his preppy clothes. I wondered how long it would be before he kissed me.

Somehow, the pub emptied out around us while we sat there, mesmerised by each other, or at least me by him. Eventually, an annoyed-looking barmaid came over and told Zac, by name, that it was time to leave. I shouldn't have been surprised that she knew his name. He had told me earlier that he often stopped by for a drink after work before heading home. If I were one of the barmaids there, I sure as hell would have known his name too.

We soon found ourselves standing outside the pub awkwardly. I knew from my brother that he lived down at Riverview, a suburb of Lane Cove that was about a five-minute drive away. Zac hadn't brought his car and so I offered to drive him home. We continued to chat easily as I navigated the familiar streets. It still felt strange sometimes, driving back on the left-hand side of the road, even though I had been back from the US for several years by that stage.

We pulled up outside of his house far too soon. For the first time that night, I started to feel nervous and self-conscious because I was sure that I was so far out of his league. I took a deep breath, trying to calm my nerves. And then he leaned over and kissed me like I'd never been kissed before. The combination of his delicious smell and the taste of beer on his lips was intoxicating. At that moment, I didn't care about anything else. As long as he kept kissing me like that, I thought I could do anything. I could burn the skeletons in my closet and conquer my fears.

I wasn't sure how long we were kissing when he abruptly pulled away, exclaiming that it was too late for a girl like me to be sitting in some dark street, kissing a guy that she barely knew. I laughed nervously before grabbing his face and kissing him again. We both laughed. But he had a point. I didn't want to, but I knew that I needed to get home. There was more wedding prep to be done the following day, and I had a family lunch at my grandparents' place that I needed to help cook for.

I wasn't normally so brazen but I was desperate to see him again, so I asked if he was free the following Tuesday. I wasn't sure that I could wait that long but I didn't want to come across as desperate. He was free and eager to see me.

Chapter Eleven

nd so it began. The strange, almost-relationship with the hot preppy carpenter named Zac. We quickly developed an intimacy that I'd never shared with anyone before, not Anthony and certainly not Sam. When Zac and I were together, when it was just the two of us in those early weeks and months, it felt like everything was finally right with the world.

One night, a few weeks after our first date, I was driving back from a night out in the city when Zac told me to pull over into an upcoming driveway. I had no idea where he was taking me but I trusted him and so without hesitation, I did as I was told. And I was so glad I did. When I parked the car and followed him down the narrow grassy hill between two apartment buildings, we were greeted by the most spectacular view. The city skyline twinkled in front of us like a million fireflies dancing. If I didn't know better, I would have believed it was all done just for me.

I didn't even realise that I was crying until his voice cut through my thoughts.

"Are you okay, babe?" Zac asked, his voice full of concern.

Baby Number Three

"Oh god, I'm such an idiot. Sorry." I said, feeling embarrassed. "It's so pretty. It's breathtaking."

"It's stunning." Zac responded matter-of-factly. "Best view around."

"I love it. Thank you for bringing me here." I smiled up at him, sure that it was a sign. A moment later his mouth was on mine. It was the first time he'd touched me that night and it was worth every minute I had been forced to wait. I was sure that I was finally with the man who was going to kiss all my trauma and self-hatred away. He was going to kiss away the memories of that old man forever.

That beautiful lookout point became our favourite place to hang out together. We would walk down that hill, hand-in-hand, watching in awe as the beautiful lights of the city came into view. When we were at our magical park, with the stunning lights shining over us, the rest of the world disappeared. When we were there together, I felt like I was good enough. I felt like it was finally my turn to be part of something special. Maybe even love.

The time we spent closed away in my bedroom was the same. The moment the door was locked behind us he would gently but passionately take me in his arms. He was a generous and skilled lover, more so than anyone I'd been with before. On those nights I was able to imagine a future where we were together for the world to see.

But those nights were few and far between because Zac had no particular interest in spending time around my family. He was polite and friendly if he happened to pass my parents on his way out the door but as a rule he would only come back to my house if my parents were away or working. Every so often, when dad was working on a Saturday night, my mum would call to let me know that she was going in to work for an emergency consultation. If I was out with Zac when she called, I would use it as an excuse to drag him away, eager to once again feel his lips on my mouth, his hands on my skin and the love that I was delusional enough to believe he had for me when we were alone in the dark. He always obliged, happy to leave the world behind for a couple of hours.

The time we spent around other people however, was very different. I quickly came to realise that Zac was not a fan of any kind of PDA. Not only did he refuse to hold my hand or kiss me when we were around his friends or mine, anyone looking from the outside would have thought we were nothing more than mere acquaintances, new friends at best. In those early weeks and months there were several occasions where Zac would take my hand to lead me into whatever pub we were going to that night, only to let go of me the moment he spotted his friends. Every now and then he would come up behind me and nuzzle my neck, like a tiny little taste of what was to come later but even that was only if we found ourselves alone for a moment.

But after a few months even those fleeting moments of hand holding and neck nuzzling stopped. It was so confusing. Zac's friends knew that he and I were dating. He had a small group of close friends that he spent most of his time with. I liked them and I genuinely felt that they liked me too. When we hung out with Bec, Hayley, James and their assorted partners he was always friendly and personable but still showed not an ounce of affection towards me. It made no sense to me that Zac could go from one extreme to the other.

One night, about six months after we started dating, Zac and I were at a local pub with a few of his mates as well as Bec and Damian. I had been away on a work trip for the past ten days and was feeling on top of the world. I'd had a wonderful time coordinating a big event in New Orleans. I'd spent my days running around organising all the logistics of the event and my nights enjoying some unbelievable festivities, including a Mardi Gras inspired street parade for my company only, with fire twirlers and stilt walkers chaperoning us as we marched along to the sound of jazz music. My trip was a great success but I was glad to be home. I had missed Zac and had spent that Saturday afternoon getting my hair and nails done to make sure I looked good for our big reunion.

When I walked into the pub with Bec and Damian I felt good. My new dress was sparkling and hid the new lacy underwear that I was looking forward to showing off to Zac later that night. I walked confidently over to him, ready to wrap my arms around him, sure that the combination of us not seeing each other for so long and the subtle addition of his favourite perfume on my skin would surely make my advance a welcome one.

I was within arm's reach when he moved to the side, dodging my embrace and instead raising his hand in a strange half wave, half stop gesture before speaking.

"Hey" was all Zac said before taking the pool cue from another guy I didn't recognise.

"Hi." I said, feeling completely crushed by his blatant rejection. I turned away quickly, embarrassed about the tears that threatened to ruin my carefully applied mascara. I was used to feeling like an afterthought when we were out with people but he had never physically recoiled from me like that before.

As Zac walked off to take his shot in his pool game, completely unphased by the way he'd made me feel I stood there, surrounded by dozens of strangers, feeling like I might drown. And I might have, had Bec not taken my hand and led me silently away from everyone. My tears began to fall as my cousin strode toward the bathroom, never letting go of my hand. Relief washed over me as the door closed behind us.

"What's so bad about me?" I cried. "Am I that repulsive, Bec?"

"Oh babe," Bec said, wrapping her arms around my shoulders as she spoke. "Did you guys have an argument or something?"

"I've barely spoken to him since I left." I said, confused. "He said he was looking forward to seeing me tonight but then it's the same shit."

"I didn't realise you felt that way?" She asked gently as I grabbed a tissue to dab my eyes. "Last time Damian and I hung out with you guys you said that you were fine with his weird no affection thing?"

"I mean. I'm not really." I admitted, my voice barely more than a whisper. "I like him so much. And he's so different when it's just the two of us."

"Then you need to tell him how you feel." Bec said, sounding annoyed. "You deserve someone that wants to kiss you after two weeks apart. Hell. Even after two hours apart!"

"Maybe." I mumbled. How could I possibly demand that he kiss me in front of his friends? I wasn't some wonderful, wifey material girlfriend. I wasn't the girl that men wanted to take home to meet their parents. If I demanded more than he was willing to give I was terrified that he'd dump me. I loved Bec but she couldn't possibly understand. Bec had found Damian because she was worthy of a guy like him. My cousin was worthy of love, affection and the realness that she shared with her lovely boyfriend. I had learned long ago that I wasn't particularly worthy of any of those things, no matter how much I wanted them.

Zac may have been unwilling to show me affection around other people but in my mind, he still made up for it when it was just the two of us. When we were tangled in my sheets on those delicious nights, I was able to pretend that I was in the real, loving relationship that I so desperately craved. The promise of what lay ahead later that night was enough to snap me out of my funk.

"I'll talk to him later." I lied, knowing that I would do no such thing. "We'd better get back out there."

"Make sure you tell him, okay?" Bec said sternly, hugging me again. "You deserve your fairytale."

"I will. Let's go and have fun. The wedding is going to take up the next month of Saturdays!" I said gleefully, referring to James and Amy's upcoming wedding. I couldn't believe that the big day was only a few weeks away. Thinking about the wonderful time I'd had with Amy and the other bridesmaids over the past few months of wedding, kitchen tea and hens night planning immediately cheered me up. I was sure that if I just gave it more time things would change with Zac.

I couldn't wait to have him there as my official plus one. He hadn't wanted to come along at first but eventually gave in when I told him how much James wanted him there. It was a bit of a white lie but I didn't care. Zac may not have cared about letting me down but there was no way he was going to knock back my brother.

And so, we walked back out to Damian, Zac and the random assortment of people in that pub and proceeded to eat, drink and play pool just like I did most weekends. Zac pretended not to notice that I had been crying but I didn't care. At the end of the night we went back to my place as planned and just like so many evenings before, I managed to convince myself that Zac did have real feelings for me, and that I wasn't just some nuisance that he hung out with at the pub on the weekends, followed by a roll in the hay before he snuck off back to the home he shared with his father. To the part of his life that I wasn't welcome to be a part of.

My parents were away that night and so I had the extra treat of Zac actually staying with me for the whole night, rather than his usual habit of leaving after an hour or two of fun. As we laid there that night, chatting about life I thought it would be a good idea to remind him about Amy and James' wedding. Zac wasn't one for planning things too far in advance and so when the invites were first sent out a few weeks earlier he had told me to ask him again a couple of weeks beforehand. James had been annoyed when the RSVP date passed without a response from my plus one so in the end, I decided to add him as a yes and just hope for the best.

When I cheerfully broached the subject again that night I was thrilled to hear Zac's response.

"Sure, babe. I don't have any plans so I should be able to come "Zac said. "What are you wearing?"

"Oh, I've got my dress!" I exclaimed excitedly, jumping up from my bed and walking the few feet to my wardrobe. "Amy picked it up when I was away."

"Put it on for me, "Zac demanded in that sexy drawl that I loved. "Then I'll help you take it off."

"I can't." I blushed at the thought of him taking the dress off. "Amy will kill me if anything happens to it."

"Well then you'd better leave it and get back over here." I didn't need to be told twice. By the time Zac left the next morning I had once again managed to convince myself that he must surely have some kind of feelings for me. How could he possibly rock my world the way he did when we were alone otherwise? And surely, he wouldn't have agreed to attend my brother's wedding with me if he didn't see me as his girlfriend? I spent the rest of that day feeling on top of the world. The memory of the previous evening's rejection was replaced by anticipation as I imagined us finally taking our relationship to the next level. I couldn't wait to finally introduce him to the rest of my friends and family properly.

The next few weeks passed in a blur of work and the final wedding preparations. Between myself and the other three bridesmaids we arranged a huge kitchen tea for Amy at my house. The original plan was to hold the party at Amy's parents' place but their kitchen remodel was delayed and in no state to host almost forty tipsy women drinking champagne and playing ridiculous games.

My parents and I had agreed that I would build a granny flat in their huge backyard, since, at twenty-seven years of age, the chance of me ever being able to buy a home nearby, was depressingly slim.

I resisted the previous summer when my parents first suggested the idea. I was sure that things with Zac would become serious, leaving me with a mortgage on a granny flat that I knew Zac would never agree to move into because of the close proximity to my parents. The fact that my boyfriend snuck out during the night to avoid having to speak with them wasn't lost on my mum and dad. It was the morning after one of those nights that the subject of building the granny flat first came up.

Mum was getting a start on that evening's baked meal, a Sunday night family tradition that she had continued from her own childhood. Dad was reading the paper and I was drinking my coffee and making toast. I was happily daydreaming about the fun night I'd had with Zac when mum's voice cut through my thoughts.

"Dad and I have been looking into building a granny flat in the backyard."

"Okay. Why?" I was confused.

"So that you can have your own place." Dad said, looking up from his paper. "We're worried that you'll miss out on having your own house at this rate."

"But Zac will never agree to move in with me if I do that." My reply was automatic. As much as I hated it, I knew even then, just a few months after meeting my preppy boy that he was in no rush to settle down, at least not with me.

"What on earth is that about Magnolia?" Mum asked. I looked up to see that she was watching me expectantly. "Why does he sneak out of here in the middle of the night?"

"It's nothing against you guys. He doesn't really have any family except for his dad," I explained, making excuses for him. "His mum died when he was a little boy and his brother and sister don't talk to him. I don't think he knows how to act."

"Have you already talked about moving out with him?" Dad asked, I could hear that he wasn't happy about the idea.

"We've only been together for a few months, dad." I snapped back, immediately regretting my reaction. "I'm sorry, I didn't mean to be rude." I saw the look that passed between them.

"Will you have a think about the granny flat?" Mum asked. I was thankful that she didn't say anything about me being short with Dad a moment earlier. I hated it when my parents were annoyed with me because it further amplified my feelings of not being good enough.

"I'll look into it. I do like the idea of having my own kitchen with pink appliances." I said, hoping that they would drop the subject so that I could get back to daydreaming about the boyfriend I was sure Zac was going to become.

After a few weeks of researching and discussing how everything would work, I finally came to realise that my parents were right. There was no way I could afford to buy so much as a unit on my own, let alone a standalone house, not if I wanted to stay near my family and friends anyway. I wasn't ready to give up on the idea of my happily ever after with Zac but I knew that I needed to think about the future. I agreed to sink my savings into the deposit. The building work was due to begin the week after the wedding and so the kitchen tea ended up being our last big lawn party before the majority of our backyard was gone forever.

The party was fabulous, we played games, ate scones, little quiches and cakes, drank mimosas and watched on excitedly as Amy opened her gifts. I even managed to sneak away afterwards to meet Zac at our magical park for half an hour before James, Dad, Ben and Damian arrived to help us clean up and eat the rest of the food. Of course, Zac was invited to join us but as usual he had no interest in joining my family for what he claimed, "wasn't his kind of thing."

I chose to ignore the alarm bells that Zac's refusal to join us set off in my mind, just as I had done a dozen times by that point. I wondered how he was going to make it through a wedding, surrounded by my entire family and so many of my friends, not to mention a number of guys that he and James had gone to school with, if he couldn't bring himself to hang out in the casual setting of my parents' messy kitchen.

If there was one thing Zac knew how to do better than just about anyone else though, it was to shush my inner voice. Somehow, during that half hour rendezvous, I let myself be convinced that he was staying away so as not to make the day about us. Zac reminded me that it was Amy's kitchen tea and she didn't need us making it about our relationship. His suggestion that I was being selfish by inviting him at all really hurt. I had spent weeks planning a party that my friend would love and had no interest in taking the spotlight from her.

My initial reaction was annoyance but the more he insisted, the more he convinced me that he was right. When I walked back in the door to a house full of my rowdy family that afternoon, I didn't think twice about telling everyone that my boyfriend had a prior engagement that I'd forgotten about.

I swallowed my disappointment over the next few hours as I once again spent an evening surrounded by loved up couples and wondered whether I would ever have that same kind of love. I tried to convince myself that everything would work out with Zac, we just had to get through my brother's wedding first.

The following weekend, just two weeks before the wedding, was Amy's hens' night. Just like the week before myself, the other bridesmaids and the women in my family and Amy's had spent countless hours organising every last detail. From cocktails and finger foods, in the downstairs private bar at the pub to the vast buffet followed by a show at a casino in the city. The evening was one that I was sure we would talk about for years to come. The matching pink T-shirts that we all wore attracted far more attention than any of us could have expected and made the occasion even more fun.

I lost count of the number of attractive men who insisted on buying Amy drinks. I was even able to let my hair down and drank far more than what I normally would. Being surrounded by so many women that I loved and so many cute guys that I wish I had the guts to talk to helped me keep my mind off Zac for most of the night but as we piled into cabs in the early hours of Sunday morning, it once occurred to me that everybody else in that taxi was going home to a man that loved them. It was a sobering thought and by the time I closed my bedroom door quietly behind me, aware that Mum had gone home to bed several hours earlier and would likely be asleep, I had already messaged Zac half a dozen times.

We had only spoken twice since the previous weekend. I hadn't seen him again since our brief meeting at the park after Amy's kitchen tea. If I was completely honest with myself, I knew that

I did not even miss him that much. Deep down, in the place where I kept my deepest darkest secrets buried, I knew that there was probably no future with Zac. I wasn't stupid enough to think that he loved me, most of the time I suspected that he didn't even like me, I didn't particularly like myself either. I suppose that's why I hid from the truth about what we had. In my mind Zac's cookie crumbs were all I was worthy of.

Eventually, after sending a couple more messages, I fell into a drunken, dreamless sleep. When I woke up the next day I had completely forgotten about the texts until I looked at my phone and saw the messages from Zac asking if I was drunk. As it turns out he'd still been out himself despite my messages coming through at almost 3 am.

I was confused by his last message which read simply.

See you at the wedding.

Was he really not going to talk to me until the wedding? I couldn't understand why he would want to go for another couple of weeks without seeing me. The voices in my head, telling me I wasn't worthy of him, the insecurities that I'd managed to ignore since meeting him, started to bubble back up to the surface and threatened to spill over. I'd spent so many years trying to get my life back, trying to forget about all the stupid things I'd done in my teens. The drugs, the booze and the old man. I had my dream job and I was so desperate to have everything with that dream guy. I didn't want to wait until the wedding to see him, so in a brazen move I messaged him back, desperately hoping that he would be receptive.

"Can you spare an hour tonight? Maybe at the Vista?"

The vista was the name we had given to our secret little rendezvous spot. The park with the magical lights where anything felt possible, even my happily ever after. Zac agreed that he would meet me before going to his mate's house and so we hung out briefly that night and the following Sunday night, both times at the vista.

On both occasions we met there and spent barely an hour together before he had to race off. I didn't mind since I too needed to get home to help with last minute arrangements for the wedding the following Saturday. I was so excited about being part of James and Amy's big day that I didn't notice how distant and strange Zac's behaviour was in the week beforehand. When we parted ways on the Sunday night, I kissed him with my usual amount of enthusiasm before driving away full of excitement and hope for the future.

Chapter Twelve

I opened my eyes on that Saturday morning in April and saw that the sun was already shining brightly. I jumped up and flung open my curtains to expose the stunning, cloudless autumn sky before throwing a jumper on over my pyjamas and bounding excitedly down the stairs. I was excited to see James and my parents already drinking coffee and nibbling on some of the pastries I'd picked up from a local bakery the previous afternoon.

"Hey boofhead! How are the old cold feet doing?" I asked as I flung my arm playfully around James's shoulders.

"Very funny, sister. I saved you the cannoli like you asked." James replied, pointing at the pink box in front of him on the kitchen island.

"Coffee Bub?" Dad asked, already pulling my favourite mug out of the cupboard.

"Yeah, probably a better idea than champagne at this hour." I said, laughing. I was in such a great mood and enjoying myself. I was looking forward to being part of the big day. And I was looking forward to Zac seeing me in my dress. Thinking about my spunky boyfriend seeing me in my beautiful blush pink bridesmaid dress with the sequined bodice was exciting enough but knowing that Zac was finally going to come and meet my family properly meant that I couldn't have been more excited if I was the one walking down the aisle that day myself.

"What time are we going to the hotel Mum?" I asked, referring to the Harbourview hotel room that Amy, her mum and cousin had stayed in the night before. It was the same room that Amy, her bridesmaids and our mums would be getting ready in and where the newlyweds would then spend the night before jetting off on their honeymoon the following evening.

"We're due there at 11 am" Mum checked her watch as she spoke. "So, we have a couple of hours before the car gets here."

"Okay nice." I said, jumping into planning mode. "We have the food to take. And when are the boys getting here? Remember not to drink more than two beers each before the church, okay?"

"Calm down, buddy." James laughed." It's not one of your big conferences, silly."

"I promise I'll keep them in check, kid." Dad responded, knowing James' old school mates well enough to understand my concerns.

"Thanks. Make sure they eat, okay? There's plenty of food and Ida is coming in to help heat it all up," I said, referring to our lovely neighbour, before slapping James playfully and heading back upstairs. I knew that James and Amy both appreciated all of my fussing. I was thrilled to know that I'd been able to help with so much of the planning for their big day. One of the things I loved most about my job was the large events that I got to plan around the world. The Sydney-based contacts I had made over the years were all thrilled to help me make my twin brother's wedding day as wonderful as possible and I couldn't wait to see it all come together.

The morning flew by and before I knew it mum and I were pulling up at the hotel with a boot full of food, champagne, and our dresses, ready to be spruiked and coiffed to perfection for the big day.

I thought about Zac many times over the course of the morning. I couldn't wait to see him dressed in the grey suit he was planning on wearing. I thought about my first impression of him all those months ago, when I first met him. I was so sure that the preppy guy must practically live in suits but the reality was that, seven months into dating I had not yet seen him wearing one. As I stood there, happily tipsy, thinking about how excited I was for him to see me all done up too, I realised how much I wanted to hear his voice.

I knew that we were due to head downstairs in a matter of minutes so I quickly grabbed my phone and a passkey for the room before walking out to the hallway. I hit Zac's name in my recent call list and was surprised when his phone clicked straight over to voicemail.

"Hi, it's Zac. Leave a message."

"Hey it's me." I chirped. "Just thought I'd say hi before we head to the chapel. See you soon!" I was disappointed about Zac not answering his phone but I didn't want to make a big deal out of it. I physically shook it off, remembering that my boyfriend often turned his phone off if he was busy. I walked back inside the room happy in the knowledge that Zac was probably with Dad, Damian, Ben and James right at that moment. I was sure that he just didn't want anyone to interrupt him while he got to know everyone finally. He was such a guys' guy and I could imagine him already being part of the gang.

My thoughts were interrupted by Amy, standing in the doorway of the bedroom, looking beautiful in her ivory lace dress. I laughed with everyone else as Mum let out the loudest wolf whistle I'd ever heard. I thought fondly of all the hours I'd spent with Mum as she tried to teach me her little party trick as a child. I thought about how easily James had picked up that new skill and how, no matter how hard I tried, I just couldn't get the hang of it. My mother rarely practised her skill outside of our home but whenever she did it made me smile. For a moment I was transported to a time before the old man, before the heartbreak of losing my baby and boyfriends who didn't answer their phones, when I was just a carefree child, oblivious to the dark realities of the world.

The sound of a phone ringing snapped me back to the present. I looked down to the phone in my hand and saw a familiar name. The call was coming from the limousine and town car hire company I've been working with for years to transport the big executives from work to and from events. We had hired

Peter and his drivers to transport the wedding party to and from the church and then to Luna Park.

"Hi Pete! Are you downstairs?" I asked my friend excitedly.

"We will be there in two minutes Mags." Pete answered, calling me by the pet name that so many of my close family and friends used.

"See you in five!" I ended the call and proceeded to round everybody up. All thoughts of wolf whistles and Zac temporarily forgotten as I raced around, grabbing flowers, bags and a dozen other necessities before herding everyone out the door.

We arrived at the little chapel at James and Zac's old school not twenty minutes later to a flurry of activity. As we pulled up in front of the beautiful little sandstone building there were a few people standing outside but the sight of three black Mercedes adorned with white ribbons quickly did the trick to send them hurrying inside. I couldn't see Zac amongst the stragglers but I didn't think anything of it. In the months that we had been dating I had always known him to be punctual. I knew that he would have been one of the first people to arrive and assumed that he had wandered inside with James and Dad.

The sound of Christina Perri's 'A Thousand Years,' one of my favourite songs, and Amy's all-time favourite, filled the air to tell us it was time to start our procession down the aisle. As I walked behind Hayley's two older children who had been recruited as the flower girl and page boy, I smiled back at the familiar faces in the pews as I searched for Zac.

By the time I reached the altar, followed by the other bridesmaids and then Amy and her dad, I was starting to feel panicked. I reminded myself that the chapel was bursting with people and it made no sense that Zac wouldn't be there. And then I realised that Zac would probably not know about wedding seating etiquette. I had been looking to my right, assuming that Zac would be sitting on the groom's side of the church. It made perfect sense that he was probably sitting somewhere behind me, admiring my dress from a distance and waiting for me to notice him.

I spent the next forty-five minutes watching the ceremony and helping to distract Hayley's kids with snacks and toys as they became more restless by the minute. I managed to take a quick look behind me a couple of times but for the most part I had no choice but to wait until the bride and groom were walking back up the aisle before I could have a good look and locate Zac. Finally, it was time for everyone to applaud the newlyweds before following them towards the back doors. As I walked slowly behind Bec and James, to the sound of applause and another beautiful love song my heart sank more with each step as I realised that Zac was nowhere to be seen.

I felt sick. I couldn't comprehend anything that sinister. I refused to believe that my boyfriend was capable of standing me up at my brother's wedding. As soon as the photographer was finished shooting us from a hundred different angles in front of the chapel, I excused myself as I grabbed my phone and tapped Zac's name on the screen. Once again, the call quickly clicked over to voicemail.

"Hey Zac. It's Magnolia. I um ... I just wanted to make sure everything's okay? Call me when you can please? If you're on your way just go straight to Luna Park" I said calmly, feeling anything but. As I started back towards the happy couple who were surrounded by so much love, I looked up to see a statue of an angel next to one of the stained-glass windows. I walked the few steps to her and placed my hand gently on her cold, grey stone foot before looking up at her face. "Please make him come." The words were barely more than a whisper as they left my mouth.

For the next two hours the bridal party drank champagne and nibbled on all sorts of sweet and savoury treats as we were driven to half a dozen stunning locations around the northern shores of Sydney Harbour. Each time we arrived at a new spot, everyone would pile out for yet another round of photos until finally we arrived at Luna Park, ready to join the assorted friends and family who had gathered after the ceremony and were now eagerly awaiting our arrival at the reception.

I held my breath as I walked into the stunning ballroom with its huge crystal chandeliers and hanging vines. The room had been decorated with beautiful blush-coloured roses that matched our bridesmaids' dresses. I searched the sea of faces hopeful, just as I had done in the chapel a couple of hours earlier, but it was no use. The heartbreaking reality that Zac hadn't turned up was impossible to ignore. I wanted to run home as fast as my feet would carry me. I wanted to feel the searing release of my knife as it sliced through my flesh. But I didn't.

I swallowed the hurt and self-destructive thoughts, wiped the tears carefully, so as not to ruin my perfectly applied makeup, and took my seat at the bridal table. As the entrees were served, I made small talk with my friends and family, hoping that no one would notice the absence of my plus one. Just as I was starting to think no one had noticed I caught Bec's eye across the crowded ballroom.

"I'm so sorry." she mouthed at me sadly.

I nodded back, knowing that even a whisper would set me off.

By the time the speeches were finished I had sculled several glasses of champagne in my attempt to take my mind off Zac's no show. I headed toward the toilets as a matter of urgency, not noticing that Hayley, Bec and Mum had jumped up and followed me. I walked out of the cubicle a couple of minutes later and looked up to see the three of them staring at me. I could see the concern on their faces but more than that, I could see pity.

"I don't want to talk about it now." I said. Holding my hands up defensively, as though I could protect myself from what he had done.

"Did he at least have the decency to call or text you sweetheart?" Mum asked, reaching her hand out to me.

"No." I couldn't say any more. I was so scared that the tears might drown me if I let them fall.

"I'm so sorry, Bub,." Hayley said. "We love you."

Bec said nothing, instead wrapping her arms around my shoulders. As my chest heaved and the tears fell, silently but for the sound of my sniffles, my mum and my two best friends held me. I heard the sound of the door swing open and a moment later another pair of arms was wrapped around me. I stood there for several minutes, desperately wondering what was so wrong with me. I tried to absorb the energy of those beautiful, strong women who were keeping me afloat when the sound of Amy's voice cut through my thoughts.

"Tomorrow, we march to that fucker's house with our pitchforks!" I laughed as my new sister-in-law raised her fist in defiance. "But right now I urgently need to pee."

Chapter Thirteen

When the five of us walked back out of that bathroom a short time later it was with a sense of purpose. We were all in agreement that we didn't need that dumb guy there anyway. I barely spent another moment alone after that trip to the bathroom, even Amy and James seemed to hover nearby at times. I didn't understand at the time why they were so worried about me. I was so used to shitty behaviour from my boyfriend, and the boyfriends before him, that I had learned to cop it on the chin. It was no big deal, or at least that's what I tried to tell myself.

That's not to say that I was okay with it. I hated that I meant so little to Zac that he could ghost me on such an important day. I wondered what was going through his mind right then. Was he sad about not coming? Was there a genuine reason that he hadn't shown up? Did he feel indifferent or was it all some big joke? By the time I threw my shoes off, ready to help gather the gifts and leftover cake and sweets to be brought home it was almost 11 pm and I had almost convinced myself that I could do better. I was going to forget about Zac just like everyone had told me to do but by the time I hopped into bed a few hours later, after drinking even more champagne, my resolve was completely forgotten. Thankfully I was exhausted and fell asleep quickly.

✧ ✧ ✧

I managed to sleep until nearly 10 am the next morning. I lifted my head off the pillow and groaned, remembering the amount of champagne I'd guzzled the night before. And then I remembered the reason for my drinking. I grabbed my phone instinctively. There were messages from Bec and Hayley, both wanting to check in and a few messages in the group chat that Amy and I had with our school group where some of the girls had shared photos from the ceremony, the speeches and then the first dance. I was thankful that no one mentioned my boyfriend's mystery absence.

The only thing missing was a message from Zac, explaining that something terrible had happened that stopped him from making it to the wedding. I knew it was ridiculous but I so desperately wanted to believe that he had a genuine reason for not coming. Because if he had just not bothered to turn up then surely that would just once again confirm my fears? That I simply wasn't worthy of a man who cared enough about me to show up when I needed him to.

I pulled myself out of bed and into the bathroom to shower and get dressed before heading downstairs. The smell of bacon cooking filled the air and straight away my stomach started to grumble in protest. I hadn't eaten since sneaking some of the leftover chocolates from the reception when I arrived home the night before so I was relieved to see Dad and Damian cooking a big fry up while Mum and Bec sorted the dozens of gift boxes that were piled haphazardly on the dining table.

"Nice of you to join us!" Damian joked, clicking his tongs together. "Bacon?"

"Yes please. You guys know how I like it." I replied before turning towards my mum's voice.

"Have you heard from him, Bub?" She asked, worry etched clearly on her face.

"No," I looked from Mum to Bec and then back to the toaster as I waited for my breakfast to finish cooking. "I'll try calling him again later."

"Why, Magnolia?" Bec asked. I could see she wasn't impressed by the suggestion. I looked away as I swallowed fresh tears.

"I need to know why he didn't come." I said, trying to explain myself through the tears.

"Oh babe, I'm sorry. I'm not angry at you." Bec said as she held her hand out to me. "We're furious at him for thinking he can treat you this way."

"I don't understand what I could have done to make him not come," I said, feeling pathetic. I knew that I wasn't good enough. I had known for such a long time but my family always had this idea that I deserved better. It made me feel uncomfortable so I did what I did best. I changed the subject. "Anyway. It's fine. Where are the rest of the cannoli's?"

"Because the guy is an idiot who doesn't deserve my girl's sweet little cousin," Damian said, ignoring my last question and sounding like a protective big brother.

"That's right, Bub," Bec said, walking over and wrapping her arms around her seemingly genuine and wonderful boyfriend. "He's made an enemy of us. He's not treating you like this and getting away with it."

"Anyway! I appreciate the concern guys but let's not let my drama ruin the weekend, okay?" I ignored the looks on everyone's faces as I took a bite of my bacon. "Has anyone heard from the lovebirds yet?"

"James sent me some pictures of their breakfast spread earlier." Mum responded as she sat down next to me with her phone. "They should be back here to open the gifts in a few hours and then Dad and I will take them to the airport.'

For the next hour or so I sat at the kitchen bench, eating my breakfast, drinking coffee and reminiscing with everyone about what a beautiful day we'd all had celebrating with Amy and James. I was just starting to feel like I might just have the strength to delete Zac's number from my phone when a message came through from him, and then another.

ZAC
Hey. What time do I need
to be there today?

I'm leaving soon.

What was he talking about? I was confused. We had nothing planned. Where did he think we were going? And then it hit me. Was he talking about the wedding? Surely not? I grabbed my phone and muttered an excuse before racing up the stairs and back to my bedroom without looking back. I could only imagine what everyone was thinking but it didn't matter. I needed to know what his messages meant.

As soon as I was behind my closed bedroom door, I unlocked my phone and started to type a reply. I was desperate to know if he really had mixed up the days but every time I typed a response, I realised how stupid I sounded. How could anyone possibly get the date mixed up for such an important event? What about the voicemails I had left him the day before, asking why he hadn't turned up? I sat on my bed, staring at Zac's messages, not knowing what to do. Eventually I wrote back.

> Magnolia
> Hey. Sorry, what do you mean?

I didn't want him to think I was angry or feeling hurt in case it genuinely was a mistake on his part.

> Magnolia
> The wedding was yesterday.

I crossed my fingers that he would call and apologise. I was so sad and disappointed that he had missed the big day. I sat there, eyes glued to the screen for almost ten minutes before my phone finally lit up.

"Hello." I answered tentatively.

"Yeah hi. What do you mean it was yesterday?" Zac asked. I could hear that he wasn't happy. My heart sank again.

"The wedding was yesterday." I said quietly, repeating what I'd written several minutes earlier.

"Why did you tell me it was today?" he hissed. "I could have gone to play golf down the coast but I didn't go because of this wedding," He barked down the phone.

"I-I'm sorry," I stammered. "James sent you the invitation, Zac." I said nervously, trying not to cry. I couldn't understand why he was angry with me.

"I didn't look at the invite because you said it was today."

"Okay well I'm sorry. I tried calling you yesterday to see where you were'" I said, still fighting back tears.

"Well, I was busy yesterday," Zac said, sounding calmer. "I didn't have my phone turned on."

"I guess these things happen." I was relieved to hear that Zac sounded calmer. "Maybe we can still hang out today?" I asked.

"If you're dressed up, why don't we go somewhere swanky this afternoon?" I asked hopefully.

"No. I'm going to go and play golf with the guys after all. I've already messaged, and they'll meet me there."

"Oh, I understand," I said, trying to hide my disappointment. "I'll make it up to you I promise."

"Ok. I'll talk to you later," Zac said before ending the call.

I sat there staring down at my phone in my hand feeling like a complete idiot. I couldn't understand how Zac could possibly get the days mixed up. I had been carrying on about the wedding from the day we met. James and Amy had sent a copy of the beautiful paper invitation to Zac's home address with the date clearly printed inside. Logically I knew that there was no reason for him to have mixed up the dates, but he was so convincing. He had nothing to gain from lying and so as I sat there tracing the scars on my left arm with my finger I decided that he must be telling the truth. Somehow it must have been my fault that Zac didn't turn up to the wedding. I wasn't sure how but I knew that I needed to make a big gesture to show him how sorry I was.

I raced downstairs a short time later to find Bec and Damian gathering their belongings. As I explained the situation I saw the look they exchanged with my parents.

"Oh dear, how could he possibly have mixed up the dates?" Bec asked. "Did he not get the invite?"

"I don't think he's very good at keeping track of things like that," I lied. I knew very well that Zac was a stickler for planning out his time. I just desperately needed to believe that his no-show from the day before genuinely was because of an oversight and nothing more. I didn't want to hear any more about him from my family.

" I don't know honestly, I just don't want to think about it or talk about it anymore," I said, looking around at the worried faces in front of me. "I have to go out so I'll see you guys later. I'll be back in time to see the present opening." Without a second thought I grabbed a slice of cake, my handbag and car keys from the dining table and raced out the door. Fifteen minutes later I found myself sitting at the little park I loved next to Woolwich Pier, eating cake and googling flashy hotels as I stared out at the majestic harbour in front of me. I was determined to make it up to Zac and prove to my family once and all for all that he really did care about me.

Chapter Fourteen

It took me a couple of weeks to find a date that suited us both but finally I managed to organise what I was sure would make up for the misunderstanding that had resulted in me attending my brother's wedding alone. Zac ended up playing golf with his mates on the Sunday just as he said he would. By the time he got home that night he was too tired to see me but finally the following Saturday he managed to come and see me after his workmate's birthday drinks. It was only a brief meeting at our special little vista but I was thankful to see that he was back to his usual happy and friendly self. When I first suggested a night away, I could see that he wasn't particularly keen on the idea but eventually, when I offered to pay for the whole thing, he came around and agreed.

I had a wonderful time choosing a hotel an hour up the coast in Terrigal that Bec and I had stayed in a few years earlier for a friend's hens' weekend. By the time our night away finally rolled around it had been a month since the wedding. For mid-May the weather was still unseasonably warm. I was looking forward to spending time at the beach and even packed a swimming costume, just in case we had time to spend at the sauna before we came home the following afternoon.

Baby Number Three

When I arrived at Zac's place at midday that Saturday, he seemed happy to see me. We spent the hour-long drive up the coast chatting easily and before I knew it, we were driving along next to the lake and then the beach. I began to feel the anticipation of having my boyfriend all to myself for a whole day and night. I couldn't wait to finally spend some quality time together for the first time in what seemed like forever.

We were able to check into the room straight away and it didn't disappoint. It was sleek and sophisticated with a chandelier positioned directly above the huge king-sized bed. The moment we put our bags down he gently laid me on the bed and started kissing me in that way that only he could. We hadn't been intimate in weeks so I could feel the anticipation of what was coming when he suddenly stopped and announced that we should go and explore the beach first, since the weather was so glorious. I liked the 'first' part and so was happy to oblige.

We headed across the road and took our shoes off before walking down the soft white sand to the water's edge. Zac took my hand and led me in the direction of the well-known lookout point to the south of the main beach. I felt like things were finally looking up. Zac didn't let go of me all the way up the hill. When we finally reached the lookout almost forty-minutes later, he dropped my hand, looking around, as if to make sure no one had caught him in that rare PDA moment. I swallowed my disappointment and forced myself to enjoy the breathtaking view of the ocean instead.

We spent another couple of hours wandering along the beautiful coastline, with him talking about his friends and job while I waited and hoped that he would take my hand in his again—he never did. We arrived back at our room with enough time to shower and get dressed for dinner.

The restaurant within the hotel had a great reputation. It was the other reason I'd chosen that particular hotel for our big night. The food was even better than I expected. He had a steak whilst I stuck with a salad. I was conscious of the new lingerie that I'd changed into excitedly after my shower. When we finished eating, we were both happy to skip dessert and instead we headed back to the room. I liked the idea that there was something much yummier about to happen and the look on his face as I paid the bill suggested that there was too.

But there wasn't. When we got back to the room, I slipped into the bathroom to freshen up before opening the door to see that he'd turned the telly on. Um okay, I thought to myself. He was sitting on the bed so I brushed the strange feeling away and walked confidently over to join him. We kissed and I was lost once again in his delicious taste and smell. We started fooling around a bit more. Finally, clothing was being removed and I was in heaven. And then he stopped.

Right as things were finally heating up, he jumped off the bed and started getting dressed as he announced that he wanted to go down and try out the sauna. And then he kissed me on the forehead before walking out. I was confused. It took me a minute or two to register what had just transpired. And then that inner voice started again. The one that had been telling me for years that there must be something wrong with me. Maybe the things that the gross old man had said were true.

I sat there on the bed for what seemed like forever, I was frozen, confused about why his demeanour had suddenly changed. Zac had been hot and cold from the moment he jumped in my car but he never usually knocked back an opportunity to admire me in my little lacy numbers. I had lost count of the number of lingerie sets I had bought since we started dating.

Finally, after about twenty minutes I forced myself to get up and get dressed again. I gathered my dress from the ground and put it back on. I knew that Zac could easily spend two-hours in the sauna so I decided to use the time to try and take my mind off the heavy feeling in my chest and do some work.

I pulled my laptop out of the tote bag that housed it and my purse. I was about to login when Zac walked back into the room.

"Hey," I said hopefully. "How was the sauna?"

"It wasn't working so I went for a quick beer downstairs." Zac answered ever so casually.

"Oh," I said, trying desperately to hide the disappointment in my voice. "I would have come for a drink too."

"Why?" Zac's voice was no longer calm. "Why are you constantly trying to push yourself onto me?"

"I didn't mean it like that." I hung my head as I spoke, feeling that familiar feeling of shame wash over me again. "It's just that we've been together for eight months but we never really do anything anymore."

"You're always chasing after me," Zac said, his nose turned up in disgust as he spoke. "I'm sick of you always being there."

"But ... I- You're my boyfriend and we never see each other," I admitted pathetically.

"What?" he laughed. "Since when am I your boyfriend?"

"You were going to come to James's wedding." I reached my arm out as he took several steps away from me.

"Yeah, because you nagged me for weeks," Zac laughed again. "Why do you think I didn't turn up?"

"You told me you'd mixed up the dates though?" I asked, not understanding what he meant. I had stood up for him for weeks against my better judgement when Bec and James accused him of not bothering to show up.

"Of course I knew what day it was, I'm not an idiot, Magnolia," Zac said, laughing again. "I was going to come but you were so obsessed with the whole stupid love thing that I was worried you might declare your undying love for me, so I changed my mind."

"Oh my God," I said, feeling like I might fall and never stop. "Why?" I looked down at my feet. My last question was not intended for him but for myself. Why was I so stupid? Why did I think that such a good looking and charming man could possibly have feelings for me? Why the hell did I believe his lame excuse about not remembering what day the wedding was being held?

Everyone had told me to trust my instincts but I ignored them all. I ignored myself, all because I thought someone might actually have feelings for me. I wanted to be sick. I wanted to ask him what was so bad about me but I was far too ashamed and so instead I sat on the bed, tears streaming down my face as he packed his belongings into the duffel bag he'd brought away with him.

"You're desperate and pathetic." His words took me back to that back room, the back room where the old man had called me horrible things too. "Lose my fucking number." And with that he walked out, the door slamming shut behind him.

Chapter Fifteen

I began gathering my belongings soon after Zac left. I had every intention of leaving and running back to the comfort of my family but as I looked around the empty room, I realised something. I always seemed to be running back home and burdening my family with my problems. I did so every time I had my heart broken. Every time a man had said nasty things or broke up with me, I ran home expecting everyone to fix me. I didn't want to be a burden to them anymore. I so desperately wanted to be the strong, capable woman that everyone assumed I was, rather than the trainwreck with the long sleeves that covered a multitude of sins, and so I decided to stay.

I went for a walk along the beach to try and burn off some of the nervous energy. The calming sounds of the waves crashing helped to ease the urge to cut my arm. Once I felt more in control of my emotions I walked down to a nearby convenience store, bought a block of chocolate and a tub of ice cream. I returned to the room, hopped into the bed with my sugary treats and proceeded to binge-watch romantic comedies to try and take my mind off the shitty things Zac had said. I knew that somehow, I had to try and accept it once and for all. The old man, Sam and Zac were right, I was unlovable.

$$\diamond \; \diamond \; \diamond$$

When I got home the following day, my bravado almost went out the window when James and Amy teasingly asked how my romantic weekend away had gone.

"Hey Mag's," Amy began. "How was the dirty weekend?"

"Babe! I do not want to hear about my sister's raunchy night away." James playfully scalded his wife. "Let's keep it G-rated girls."

"It's fine. We broke up." I said bravely, determined to make them believe that I didn't care. "He left last night. His loss."

"Oh man. I knew he'd do something shitty, Maggie. I told you not to go out with him," James reminded me needlessly. "He's a bad guy sis."

"Yeah, it would appear that he is." I agreed, deadpan. "I should have just stuck with Sam.' I had been thinking about Sam on my drive home that morning, wondering if things would have been okay, had I not gotten carried away with my silly fantasy about us getting married.

"He was a jerk too, Amy reminded me. "There is someone out there for you, honey. I promise."

The look on my sister-in-law's face was almost the end of me. "I think I'll just live vicariously through you lot for a while." I joked before walking towards the door. "I'll see you guys at dinner."

As I went to shower and get changed for the BBQ that we were all attending at my grandparents' place that night, my thoughts once again went back to Sam. I knew that me pushing him to buy my dream ring was the beginning of the end of our relationship. I often wondered whether things would have continued if I hadn't gotten carried away with the notion that he might want to marry me. But then I remembered something.

As it turned out, just nine months after Sam and I split up, he was already married to somebody else. I met her once. It was about four months after that horrible night at his friends' engagement party. My cousins, Ben, Damian and I were at a pub not too far from where Sam lived but I'd never have expected to bump into him there. He was with a woman. She had fiery-red hair and was obviously several years older than him. My first thought was to turn and walk away before he noticed me but then he looked up and caught my eye.

Before I could escape Sam raced over to say hi like we were old friends or something. It was strange and awkward, especially when the woman walked over to stand by his side. When Sam cheerily introduced the woman as his new girlfriend. I stuck out my hand to shake hers, trying to act like I didn't care but seeing that he had moved on so quickly just further amplified my belief that I must have been the problem in our relationship, not him.

A few months after that chance meeting in the pub Sam and his girlfriend got married. The woman had two young children, something that Sam claimed to have no interest in but that didn't stop him from wanting her in a way that he never wanted me. I had tried so hard to put the past behind me and move on from the devastation of his words but then Zac came along and reopened so many old wounds. I couldn't understand what was wrong with me—did men sense that I was messed up? Did they somehow know my dirty little secret? I started to wonder if I wore it like a neon sign, my shame and disgust. Was it written on my face that I was damaged goods? That I was dirty and not worth loving?

Chapter Sixteen

s I raced around my bedroom, getting ready for the family BBQ, it suddenly occurred to me that I didn't have a single item of Zac's. We hadn't exchanged Christmas gifts or Easter eggs; we hadn't borrowed CDs from each other and he'd never lent me a jumper with his delicious smell on it. The jarring reality was that whatever we had, it had never been real. I had ignored his attempts to show me, on so many occasions, exactly how he felt about me.

I knew that I would not cope if I had to spend the night justifying his absence to my family yet again. I knew that the BBQ had been organised by my parents so that everyone could see the pictures from James and Amy's wedding but I suspected that they were also making a fuss so that I could finally introduce my boyfriend to everyone. I didn't want everyone questioning me about his absence like they had at the wedding and so I picked up my phone and sent Bec and Amy a text:

Hey, can you please make sure everyone knows that Zac and I broke up? I wrote. I'm not in the mood to have the Spanish Inquisition about why he's not there tonight.

Bec
Oh, bloody jerk.
Are you okay?

Amy
Are you sure you're okay?

I'm okay, I promise.

I wrote back, only half telling the truth.

Magnolia
I just don't want anyone fussing about me tonight. I want to see wedding pictures and drink mimosas. I'll see you guys up the road soon.

I sat down on my bed, grabbed my iPod and turned it on shuffle before throwing it down in front of me. Once I'd put my earphones in, I reached down and pulled the box of wedding magazines out from under my bed. I had bought them excitedly the day that Sam and I agreed to buy my dream ring. In the weeks that followed I had so much fun pouring over the pages of my magazines. I excitedly picked out dresses, jewel encrusted heels and of course my dream cake.

When Sam broke up with me, I wanted to tear those magazines to shreds just as I had done to the photos but something stopped me. I didn't want to tear up my dreams of a fairytale wedding. I didn't want to throw away my dream of being rescued by my prince and so instead I had stashed them, in the hope that I would need them some time in the future.

As I flicked through the dog-eared pages, I smiled as I listened to cheesy love songs and read some of the notes and comments that Bec and I had added throughout one magazine in particular. There were arrows and love hearts drawn on the pages we'd bookmarked. So many details that I'd long since forgotten about. It occurred to me, not for the first time, how much I loved blush pink and lace. Reminiscing about the wonderful time I'd had with those magazines made me more determined than ever.

I was happily looking through the dreamy images of happy couples posing in tea-lit gardens when the familiar sound of Chad Kroeger's voice played through my earphones, reminding me that there must surely be someone out there who would love me. I took it as a sign, surely Nickelback were right? I had no idea how but I was determined to meet that somebody out there, waiting to hold me—and heal me?

When I looked down at my phone I realised with a start, that I'd gotten so engrossed in my little wedding and love fantasy that I'd completely lost track of the time. I bundled up my magazines and carefully placed them back in the box before pushing them under my bed, grabbing my bag and racing down the stairs.

✧ ✧ ✧

Fifteen minutes later, I was standing in my grandparents' kitchen, making the salad with Amy when I heard the familiar sound of Hayley's kids laughing excitedly. It didn't matter that the weather had turned cold, even when the pool was covered up the kids knew that their great-grandparents' place was filled with the promise of adventure. As the kids ran upstairs Hayley and Ben walked in, bundled down with bags and food.

By 6 pm the house was full of music and laughter. In typical fashion Dad, James, Ben and Damian were gathered around the BBQ with Amy's dad, my uncles and grandad with beers in hand as they talked about football while the women stood around in the kitchen, chatting and prepping the rest of the food. It often occurred to me how stereotypical my family dynamic was when we were all together, but I didn't care. I looked around at the people who meant the most to me and it occurred to me for the first time that Zac's refusal to meet my family really was his own loss. I might not have been good enough but my family was far too good for him.

Dinner was as loud and hectic as you would expect with twenty people, spanning four generations of one family. By the time dessert was ready to be served it was getting late. Once James gave the green light we piled into the living room, cheesecake and ice cream in hand, to watch the wedding video and slideshows on the huge projector screen.

For the next hour we laughed and cried as the images of my beautiful sister-in-law and dapper but ever-dorky looking brother appeared on the huge screen in front of us. Seeing everyone in their stunning formalwear was strange. It was as if I was seeing them for the first time. Especially when I saw my own image up there. If I didn't know better, I would have looked at that twenty-something woman and assumed that she was just a regular, happy woman. But I knew better, I could see the pain on her face. I could see the tint of red in her eyes, and the smile that didn't quite curve the way my mouth did when I was genuinely happy.

I was relieved to hear how happy everyone was with the photos, especially the ones I was in. I was so worried at the time that my sadness had dampened the day for James and Amy but hearing their excitement and delight as they reminisced about the day made me realise that everything was fine. I hadn't ruined their big day. I was also relieved when no one mentioned how I'd been stood up. Just like on the wedding day I didn't want to take the spotlight away from the people who deserved it.

I needn't have worried about stealing the spotlight though because, as the slideshow wrapped up, James and Amy once again stood in front of the TV, thanking everyone again for their love and support. As everyone started standing, James spoke again.

"Hold on everyone," James called out. "We have another topic we need to raise."

"Oh my gosh," I whispered to myself, wondering if there was a baby on the way. I hated myself for the feeling of jealousy that overcame me.

"You're joining the parent trap?" Ben called out a second after the thought occurred to me. "Honeymoon is over guys."

"Ben!" Hayley scalded her husband, elbowing him playfully before asking. "So, are you?"

"Um, nope!" Amy replied, holding up her champagne happily.

"Ok Bec and Damo, you guys had better get up here before we start any more rumours!" James laughed, tapping his beer against Amy's glass before taking her hand and leading her back to the lounge.

I turned back to the front of the room just in time to see Bec thrust her hand out. There on her ring finger a stunning ring, similar to the one she had chosen on our shopping trip a few years earlier. Within moments Bec and Damian were surrounded by a dozen excited family members, all scrambling to get the first look at the huge diamond ring. I sat back, taking the opportunity to breathe and register the news.

I forced myself to remember that my younger cousin's engagement was not about me. Bec and Damian had been together for a few years after all. It filled me with joy when I saw them together because it was clear that Damian adored my sweet little cousin. I had been hoping to see them make their relationship official for the longest time. I thought about that Nickelback song again and realised that Bec had found that "someone". My job at that moment was to get over myself and celebrate her.

I looked up to see Bec looking at me, worry etched across her face.

"Congratulations, beautiful," I mouthed, holding my hands over my heart as my smile reached all the way to my very core.

"Thank you," Bec mouthed back, holding her hands on her chest, her relief palpable.

Chapter Seventeen

Over the next few weeks, Bec and I wasted no time in pulling the box of bridal magazines back out from their hiding place beneath my bed as we began the exciting task of planning her and Damian's dream location wedding.

Bec had always dreamed of getting married on a tropical island. When Damian proposed, as it turned out, two days before Amy and James's wedding, he did so down at one of our beloved Harbourside picnic spots. Damian paid his younger sister, Isobel, and her boyfriend David, to pick up pasta from our favourite restaurant while he set up the faux Hawaiian picnic for two.

Bec arrived at the park under the guise of having dinner with Isobel. It took her a minute to figure out why one of the picnic tables was decorated with tiki torches and frangipani flowers. When Damian walked up the hill, dressed in fawn-coloured pants and a white button-down shirt she realised she had been duped and that she wasn't there for a quiet takeaway dinner with her boyfriend's sister. Damian walked up to Bec, took a lay from a box on the ground and laid it gently around her neck before dropping to one knee and producing the stunning diamond ring from his back pocket and slipping it on her finger as he asked her to marry him.

Apparently, Damian had been planning to propose after Isobel and David were finished serving their dinner and pina coladas and left the lovebirds to it but seeing his girlfriend standing there looking confused in her blue, floral dress and wedges was simply too much. Damian decided that he had already waited too long and needed to ask her straight away.

Bec and Damian both agreed that they would keep their news a secret until after James and Amy's wedding. Their original plan had been to break the news to everyone the following morning but then Zac went and stood me up. Bec and Damian both agreed to hold off on sharing their news until the family BBQ a few weeks later, assuming that I would be feeling better by then. When I texted Bec just before the BBQ to tell her what had happened, she tried to convince Damian to hold off on sharing their news again, in case it upset me but, in the end, Bec realised that I seemed fine and agreed to announce their engagement after all.

Damian's family already knew about the engagement, since they had helped to organise the whole thing. From the Hawaiian decorations, to the pre-made cocktails that Damian's mum had packed in ice and then of course Isobel and David helping to pick up and serve the food. The idea that my cousin needed to hold off on telling her own family in case it upset me was upsetting in itself but eventually Bec convinced me that it wasn't a big deal. My joy and excitement about their impending nuptials were real and a wonderful way to distract me from my own mediocre and now non-existent love life. I tried to ignore the nagging feeling, telling me that everyone I knew was lovable

   Unlovable

but me, instead putting all my energy into helping wherever I could. Maybe I would meet a tall, dark and handsome stranger in Hawaii that would sweep me off my feet once and for all?

Bec and Damian were renting a unit just a few minutes away from our street and my parents' backyard was finally being torn up in preparation for the slab to be poured for my granny flat. My initial reservations about building the separate dwelling gave way to excitement when I realised that I was effectively going to be able to completely design my very own two-bedroom home. The granny flat was expected to take about four months to build, meaning that all going well, I would be moved in by my twenty-eighth birthday in mid-November.

I often found myself at Bec and Damian's place on the weekends for dinner or pre-drinks. I was almost able to convince myself that spending so much time with them was all in the name of wedding planning or because of the noise and mess at my own house from the granny flat construction. I told myself, like a mantra, that third wheeling had nothing to do with my fear of putting myself out there into the dating world again. Being with my cousin and her charming fiancé made me feel safe.

Watching the way Damian treated Bec made me crave the same thing all the more, while at the same time I wondered how I could possibly find my own perfect guy if I wasn't willing to take a chance on someone new. I decided that the wedding really was going to be the perfect opportunity to meet someone.

Bec and Damian were getting married a few days after Christmas in Maui, one of the Hawaiian Islands. What had started off as a tiny ceremony with just immediate family had blown out to a fifty-person affair. In terms of a destination wedding, it was going to be huge.

Our family were all planning to fly over to Hawaii on Boxing Day. We were going to spend a few days enjoying the peace and quiet of the resort they had chosen before Bec and Damian's friends arrived for the wedding on December 30th. Most of the preparations for the actual wedding were to be handled by the hotel. Bec had asked me to be her chief bridesmaid and so was excited about planning her hens party and kitchen tea with the other bridesmaids.

Bec was obsessed with all things VW because her and Hayley's dads had grown up restoring kombis with their dad. I had tried to keep that in mind when we were planning the hens night. My cousin also loved dancing and so she was delighted by the 1950s theme of the evening. Everyone had made such an effort with their costumes. Some of the girls had even coordinated and dressed as the Pink Ladies. The evening started at Bec's parents' place, where we served tequila sunrises with aperitifs to get everyone into the party spirit.

At 6 pm the sound of horns outside told us that the next part of the adventure had arrived. A mate of Hayley's dad had a wedding-kombi business and was willing to give us three of his vans for an hour. We piled out of the house, twenty women squealing and cheering at the sight of the cute pastel-coloured vans as we all hopped into our allocated vehicle. The rest of the night was spent in a fifties themed diner in the inner-city suburb of Annandale. We ate burgers, drank cocktails and did the twist. It was the most fun I'd had in a long time, and I was over the moon when Bec and several of the other women said the same thing. I couldn't wait for the relaxing holiday—wedding—a few weeks later.

Christmas and then Boxing Day came soon enough. We would normally have done a huge baked meal on Christmas Day but with everyone flying out the following day my mum wasn't keen to leave food in the fridge. She couldn't freeze the turkey since they actually came frozen to start with and so for the first time ever, we decided to get with the times and do a seafood lunch. We polished off the rest of the food on Christmas night while we finished packing so that we'd be ready to leave when the maxi-taxi arrived early the next morning.

The ten-hour flight to Honolulu went quickly. I had been travelling to the US for work for years so I wasn't fussed by the turbulence we experienced as we flew across the Pacific Ocean. I felt a sense of purpose as I calmed some of the other people in our travel party, especially the kids who were not seasoned fliers and quite scared by the dipping and falling of the big aeroplane. I may not have been fulfilling my own dream of flying to Hawaii to marry the love of my life but at least it was reassuring to feel needed at that moment, just as I had throughout the months of planning parties and the big day itself.

When we landed in Honolulu, there was another fifty minute flight before we finally landed on the island of Maui. I hadn't been to any of the other islands besides Oahu in the past, so I was excited to look out at the scenery as we made our way to Wailea on the western side of the island. The contrast between the lush green mountains and hills and the sparkling ocean was spectacular. By the time we reached our hotel I knew that we were in for a magical holiday.

We spent the first few days kayaking and swimming in the crystal-clear waters of Kea Lani beach. One morning we hired a bus to take us up to Lahaina for some shopping and spent the trip there and back watching the humpback whales frolicking not far from the shoreline with their new calves. We enjoyed watching green sea turtles swim right past us while exploring the ocean in the hotel's kayaks most afternoons and then drank far too many of the island's traditional Mai Tais afterwards. It was amazing to share those lazy sun-soaked days with my family. By the time Bec and Damian's wedding day arrived we were all feeling rested and energised. My whole family was excited about chipping in to make the day as special as possible. And I was ready to meet one of Damian's single mates that I had heard about.

When Bec walked down the aisle behind myself, Hayley and Damian's sister just after 4 pm, there wasn't a dry eye in the house. Her dress was simple but stunning with a million jewels sewn into the long princess skirt. I looked at Damian as he tried desperately to hold it together and smiled, so thankful again that my cousin, and one of my very best friends, had found someone who adored her so completely. The ceremony was over too quickly and before we knew it everyone was mingling on the grass outside the chapel, waiting to congratulate the newly-weds and taking photos with the stunning Hawaiian sunset in the background.

By the time the bridal party arrived at the reception, which was being held in the form of a traditional Hawaiian Luau, the party was well and truly underway. I had seen Damian's single mate Steve several times throughout the afternoon but it wasn't until I found myself standing next to him in line at the buffet that I finally got the chance to talk to him.

"Hi there, you're Steve, aren't you?" I asked, feeling confident thanks to one too many of those delicious Mai Tais.

"Hey. You're one of Bec's cousin's, right?" he asked cheerily, not taking his eyes off the bowl of prawns in front of him as he spoke.

"Yes, I'm Magnolia," I said, sticking my hand out to him awkwardly. "Nice to meet you."

"Hi Magnolia," he laughed before taking my hand. "Steve. Nice to meet you too."

We chatted about the beautiful island for several minutes while we piled our plates high with food. As we walked back towards our tables, I scrambled to find an excuse to keep talking to him. Steve and I were seated at separate tables, but I had an idea.

"Hey, it was lovely talking to you," I began. "Will you be on the dance floor later?"

"You too." Steve smiled as he spoke. "I can't dance but I'll probably still end up there."

"Okay, we can be terrible together." I laughed, feeling excited about spending more time with the good-looking Steve. "Enjoy your dinner."

"You too." he said before walking back to his table.

I ate dinner with a renewed sense of enthusiasm. As much as I had enjoyed the relaxing few days and magical evenings spent lazing on that stunning island with my beautiful family, it didn't stop me from feeling alone. Everywhere I looked, I was surrounded by loving couples. My parents, brother, cousins, aunts and uncles. Every adult in my family was loved by a wonderful partner. Everyone except me.

I had tried so hard to swallow my feelings of inadequacy since Zac's cruel outburst a few months earlier. I'd thrown myself into work, like I always did. The short engagement meant that Bec and Damian needed all the help they could get with planning the wedding and the parties beforehand. I was so busy that I was able to successfully ignore my blatant inability to find someone to love me. Being the third, fifth and even the ninth-wheel on that glorious island just reminded me again of how desperately I wanted that same validation of love. I looked over at Steve and was thrilled to see that he was looking at me too. As our eyes locked, his face lit up. My heart soared.

Chapter Eighteen

As I ate my dessert and continued to play Googly-eyes with my new spunky friend, Amy joined me at the bridal table. I hugged my sister-in-law, realising that I hadn't seen her since the reception.

"Hey!" I exclaimed. "Where have you been?

"I'm not feeling great." Amy replied. I realised that she was looking a little green around the gills.

"Did you drink too much?" I asked, feeling confused. "You've been a bit off all week though."

"I've been a bit off for the last couple of months." Amy admitted sheepishly. "I'm hoping it calms down soon."

As Amy looked down and instinctively cradled her stomach it suddenly dawned on me. "Oh my gosh!" I said, suddenly understanding what was happening. "Are you guys pregnant?"

"Shhh!" Amy scalded as she hugged me. "We're not telling anyone else for a few weeks because it's still a bit early but I wanted to tell you. We want you to be the baby's godmother?" She looked at me questioningly.

"Oh, I would love too." I said as I hugged her again. I swallowed the lump in my throat as I thought about my own little baby. I had never told my parents or Amy and James about that baby. No one but Bec and Hayley knew about the affair with Anthony that had resulted in the pregnancy that I had all but wished away, despite my desperation to become a mother. "I'm so excited." And I meant it. Perhaps I was about to get my own shot at happiness. Maybe I was going to ride off into that beautiful Hawaiian sunset with the cute guy. Maybe I would even get another chance to become a mother myself?

By the time everyone hit the dance floor I was feeling great. Maui was the most beautiful place for a wedding. I was just months away from becoming an aunty for the first time and I was swept up in the idea of Steve being the mystery man I had dreamed about meeting at the wedding. It didn't matter that he was blonde and kind of short. He seemed nice, he was handsome and from what I'd heard, he was also single. And perhaps most importantly, at least in my mind at the time, he seemed genuinely interested in me.

As everyone danced and clapped along with the hula dancers on the stage Steve and I had a wonderful time chatting and dancing with a large group of other people. I was so sure that we were making some kind of lasting connection that I completely missed something. One of Damian's other mates seemed to be hanging around. I was desperately hoping that he would get the hint and leave us to get to know each other. By the time the newly-weds had finished their first dance and kicked off their shoes, a lot of the older guests had started to disperse, retiring back to their rooms after a long afternoon and evening of celebrations.

When Bec and Damian finally said their goodbyes, it was almost 11 pm. I was looking forward to finally getting a minute alone with Steve when I noticed that the other guy, who's name, as it turned out, was Daniel, was saying his goodbyes before walking away. I had come up with the perfect plan earlier in the night, to take Steve down to the beach. I had it all planned out in my mind, that we could go and sit on the beach and talk while sharing one of the pieces of cake I had taken to share with Hayley and the kids the following morning. Once we finished the cake, we would go for a moonlit walk along the beach to look for shells. At some point I hoped that Steve would kiss me. I noticed that he was heading in the direction of the men's toilet and so I decided to take the opportunity to do the same thing.

As I raced over towards the women's bathroom, in the same block, I heard the familiar voices of Steve and Daniel talking. I stopped outside the window, shocked as I realised that they were talking about me.

"What's with Bec's weird cousin following you around all night babe?" Daniel asked. "I think she has the hots for you." he laughed.

"I'm sure she was just being friendly." Steve responded kindly. "Damo said she's had a pretty shit run with guys. Maybe she just finds gay men to be safer at a wedding than some predatory and drunk straight guy."

"Darling, she has the hots for you. Plain and simple." Daniel laughed again. "She's a bit desperate if you ask me."

"Don't be a bitch. Come here." Steve responded with a laugh before the voices became muffled.

I was thankful that I'd removed my shoes already, making it easier to sneak away without alerting the two men to my presence. I turned and ran as fast as my legs would carry me. I felt completely humiliated. I couldn't believe that I had spent the whole evening flirting with a gay man who was in attendance with his boyfriend. Had I really become that desperate and pathetic in my quest for love that I would spend my time at my cousin's wedding trying to pick up another man's boyfriend? As I reached the safety of a nearby pool cabana and stopped to catch my breath, I slumped onto one of the pool loungers.

"What the hell?" I screamed at the universe. "Why?"

I knew that people back up at the reception were likely to have heard me. The last thing I wanted was for anyone to come looking for me. I grabbed my shoes and the carry bag with the cake and my cardigan in it and continued down towards the beach. I thought back to that night after Zac had walked out on me. The sound of the waves lapping at the shore was the only thing that kept me from doing something stupid that night.

I knew that I needed to be down there on the beach again. Even if I couldn't see them, I knew that the creatures swimming peacefully nearby—the turtles, whales and tropical fish—would take my mind off the mortifying embarrassment of what had just happened, if just for a minute.

I stood there for a moment, taking in the beauty of the ocean and the sky in front of me. I had been marvelling at the stunning sky every night of the trip. I hadn't been to Hawaii in several years and I'd forgotten about the brilliant sunsets and how different the stars were, compared to what I was used to seeing at home. The reflection of that beautiful starry sky on the ocean was a sight to behold. I stood there looking up for a few minutes before walking down closer to the water, staying far enough from the gentle lapping of the waves to keep my feet dry.

I wondered how I had let myself get to a point where I was chasing a man who was, at least in hindsight, so obviously not interested in me. Was I really that desperate and pathetic that I would spend my cousin's wedding day obsessing about a man who was not only not-single but gay? My desperation to find love was turning me into a person I no longer recognised. The contrast between my professional life and personal life had become so great that I was no longer sure which one was even the real me. I knew that something needed to change but I had no idea of what, or indeed how.

As I sat there, lost in my own thoughts, the sound of something being dragged along the sand, not two-metres away from me, snapped me back to the present. A cold chill ran down my spine and my first instinct was to grab my bag and run from whatever danger was looming but something stopped me. I realised as I watched in wonder, that the sound was coming from a huge, green sea turtle making her way up the beach right next to me.

I looked around me, not quite believing what I was seeing, wondering if I was being tricked but there was no one else around, just me and that majestic mother turtle. For the next couple of hours, I watched on in delight as the turtle dug her nest before laying her eggs inside. I had seen a dozen or more turtles during the course of my time on the island but it had always been from a distance whilst they glided past me in my kayak. Each sighting before that evening had been fleeting, lasting a matter of seconds before the creatures swam out of sight in the dark blue waters of the Central Pacific Ocean.

As I watched the beautiful mother giving new life, something in me changed. I had been searching for a sign for the entire night. I had been looking from the moment the plane landed on that spectacular island, and for so many years. Almost from the moment I walked out of that newsagency as a teenager I had been looking for something, or more accurately, someone, to come along and save me. As I contemplated the significance of that mummy turtle, I had what I could only describe as an epiphany.

Suddenly everything made sense. For the first time in my adult life, I saw a real, beautiful, love-filled future laid out clearly in front of me. The serene animal in front of me had chosen me as the protector of her treasured eggs and future offspring. As she painstakingly covered her eggs to protect them from the elements and predators, I finally understood my purpose. I didn't need a man.

I was going to become a mum.

Chapter Nineteen

By the time I gathered my belongings and dusted the sand off myself it was almost 2 am watching the once-in-a-lifetime scene unfold in front of me was such an emotionally charged experience. I was so lost in the moment that time became irrelevant but as reality seeped back in, I remembered that I had to be at brunch in a matter of hours. As I climbed the steps, I took one last look back down to the beach. I vowed to bring my own child back to visit those hatchlings.

I tiptoed into the apartment I was sharing with Hayley and her little family a short time later. I wanted to stay up so that I could start researching how to find a sperm donor. I wanted to figure out what questions I would need to ask the doctors, and what physical and other traits I would want in a donor. I was so excited about my new plan but I knew I had a huge couple of days planned before I was due to fly home. So instead, I cleaned my teeth, removed my makeup and changed into my pyjamas before sliding between the fresh, cool sheets. I closed my eyes tightly and drifted off to sleep watching my mummy turtle and her future babies in my mind's eye.

I woke up the next morning to the sound of Hayley sneaking around in the ensuite bathroom off my room. I looked at my phone to check the time and groaned when I realised that I was going to have to get up.

"Sorry, did I wake you?" Hayley asked as she appeared next to my bed.

"It's okay." I groaned, stifling a yawn. ""It's lucky you did. It's nearly 9.a.m.

"Yeah, I know. I'm just going to give Amelia a quick bath then we're pretty much ready."

"I'll have a shower then I'll come down." I groaned again as I lifted my head off the pillow.

"That's what happens when you disappear with the cute single guy till all hours." Hayley teased.

"Oh dear." I mumbled, more to myself, as I sat up.

"What happened?" Hayley sat down on the end of my bed. "We saw you guys dancing. He seemed to like you.

"Um no." I laughed, determined to forget about the humiliation of hearing David mock me for chasing after his boyfriend. "He's gay. His boyfriend was there last night."

"No!" Hayley shouted. A look of confusion crossing her face as she did so. "I'm sorry. I thought he liked you."

"It's fine." I said, waving away her concern. "I can't believe I didn't realise, it was so obvious!"

"If you weren't with him then where were you for half the night, Magnolia?" Hayley asked, in her best mum-voice. "Who were you with?"

"I just went for a walk." I replied, smiling as I remembered my time on the beach just a few hours earlier. "It was nice."

"By yourself? " I could see that Hayley wasn't impressed. I knew how much she worried about some of my choices. "Please call me if you feel the need to go wandering around at night again!"

"Okay, I promise." I held my hand over my heart before picking up my phone to check the time. "Oh crap, we've got to get moving. I can't believe we get to spend New Year's Eve in Maui!"

Hayley hugged me before picking up the towel from the bed and walking back into the hallway, closing the door behind her. I felt bad for not telling her about my experience with the mummy turtle. I had every intention of sharing what I'd seen but then something stopped me.

The more I thought about the way that beautiful creature had entrusted me with her secret, the more I came to believe that she needed me to be the keeper of that secret. I had never been part of anything so huge, yet intimate, in my life. In my superstitious mind, I believed that the universe would reward me for keeping the experience to myself.

I showered and dressed in record time, conscious that we were due at brunch by 10 am As Hayley, Ben, their kids and I made our way towards the same lawn area where we had celebrated the wedding the night before I spotted Steve and David walking towards us. My first thought was to avoid eye contact after the humiliation of overhearing their conversation but then I realised something. There was no way for them to know I'd overheard them. I decided that it would be far more dignified to face my mistake head on, so Instead of averting my eyes, I thought again about my mummy turtle. Her trust and bravery filled my heart with the same, giving me the courage to smile before greeting the men as they stood in front of my little group.

"Hey, how did you guys pull up this morning?" I asked, beaming as I spoke.

"Hi. Good." Steve laughed. "How's your head?"

"Yeah, I'm feeling great actually." I laughed in response, thinking about the number of cocktails we'd all consumed the night before. "I think it's going to be pretty tame tonight though." I laughed again.

"Hey guys, we're going to be late." Hayley said, tapping her watch. "Should we walk and talk?"

"We'll catch up." I told her, knowing that I had to apologise to Steve and David first.

"Okay. See you in a sec." Hayley smiled at me knowingly before she and Ben walked off after their hangry, children.

I turned to face the two confused faces in front of me. "Okay so I just want to apologise." I began. "I had a strange idea that you were available yesterday." I said to Steve.

"It's okay, honestly." Steve replied graciously. "I had fun hanging out with you."

"That's nice of you to say." I said before looking at David directly. "And I'm so sorry for hogging him."

"Darling it's fine. I don't blame you really." David joked, squeezing Steve's hand. "Your gay-dar isn't working too well though is it?"

"I've never been great at knowing who's who in the zoo." I admitted, realising that I could really see myself getting along with both men. "Should we get over there before the kids eat all the food?"

"Let's go, Princess Magnolia." David said, hanging his long, lanky arm over my shoulder casually as the three of us walked towards the lawn. We arrived just in time to intercept a waitress carrying a tray with three Mai Tai's on it before putting our belongings down at the table where James and Amy were enjoying their breakfast with Bec and Damian. I hugged everyone before hitting the buffet.

That afternoon I went for a hike with my parents followed by an early dinner back at the resort. Most people were flying home the next morning so we spent the next few hours toasting everything from turtles to Mai Tais and the sunset and as we counted down to midnight, we toasted to the year ahead. I cheered excitedly as fireworks lit up the night sky, their dazzling reflection over the ocean was almost as magical as the stars had been the night before. It was crazy to think that it was 2005. I couldn't wait to see what the year was going to have in store for me.

Chapter Twenty

I was delighted to learn that Steve and David were staying on the island for another couple of days before heading back to Oahu to go surfing and see friends for a few days. With a day left before I was due to fly home, I realised that I was nowhere near ready to leave yet. I wasn't due back at work for almost two weeks and so on a whim, after a cocktail too many, I decided to extend my stay for another week as well.

I had been travelling for work for years. With the exception of my trip with Sam I had always travelled to America alone but I had never gone on a holiday alone. A week earlier the thought of a solo vacation in Honolulu would have filled me with dread but that was the old me. That was the woman who thought she needed a man to validate and save her. But I was determined to leave that woman on the beach in Maui, with the turtles and the glorious sunsets.

By the time I touched down at Sydney Airport on the morning of January 10th I had it all figured out. My time in Hawaii had been truly transformational, both the time spent with my family in Maui, and the week in the fancy hotel on Waikiki Beach.

Baby Number Three

I spent my days in Honolulu shopping and lazing on the soft, warm sand and my evenings eating takeaways in front of my laptop as I researched the steps that I would need to take in order to realise my dream of having a baby.

I read dozens of articles and reviews about different fertility clinics and eventually booked appointments with specialists at two of them. Several of the articles I read talked about how important it was to stop drinking alcohol long before you planned to get pregnant, so I made a point of leaving the Mai Tais alone for the remainder of my trip. I knew that once I started the process, I was going to want to move fairly quickly so I decided to book a couple of doctors appointments for the end of April. The building work on my flat had been delayed by several weeks with one thing or another and my move-in date had been pushed out to February. I wanted to be completely moved in before I found myself in a position where I couldn't lift heavy furniture and besides, I loved the idea of having a Christmas baby.

When I walked into the kitchen an hour or so after landing, I was excited to see Amy baking a cake with Mum while James and Dad sat screaming at some boxing match on the TV.

"What are you two carrying on about?" I joked as I poked my head into the living room.

"Hi Bub, how was the flight?" Dad called out as he punched the air in the direction of the two sweaty guys on the screen. "Did you bring us any souvenirs?"

"Yeah, I bought you some more cookies but then I ate them."
I replied, joking about our shared obsession with those little
pineapple shaped cookies that we had both hoarded from the
Wailea shops on our daily mission to get coffee. "Nah I saved
you some."

"Speaking of baked goods, is that the cherry ripe mud I can
smell cooking?" I recognised the smell anywhere, even though
I hadn't baked in years. "What's this in honour of?"

"I was cleaning the cookbook cupboard yesterday and found
your old recipe folder so we thought we would give this a go."
Mum opened the oven as she spoke. I could tell just by the
smell that the cake was just about ready.

"How are you, Aimes?" I asked my sister-in-law, noticing that
she looked noticeably less queasy than she had just a week
earlier. "You're looking great." I winked.

"It's okay, Magnolia. You don't need to wink, we know." Mum
scalded, flicking the tea towel in her hand at me playfully.

"What do you know?" I asked, feigning ignorance. I didn't want
to blow the surprise in case she was talking about something
else.

"That I am going to be a grandfather despite the fact that
I am far too young!" Dad called out from the lounge. A moment
later he and James were standing in the kitchen. "We found out
yesterday." Dad said, as he flung his arm proudly around James,
patting his back in the process.

I could see the pride on my father's face. I had often wondered if he felt ripped off about not having his own biological children. I knew that he and mum had tried to have more children several years after they were married but to no avail. I had always known that he loved us like his own children but the look on his face at that moment, and the tears that welled in his eyes told me that there was no prouder grandfather in the world than him. I couldn't wait to share the same news when the time came. I smiled as I imagined our family home, full of adorable babies being spoiled by their nan and pop, just as James and I had been so thoroughly spoilt by ours.

As the weeks passed, I was excited to put the finishing touches on my design choices as my granny-flat finally neared completion. I chose a fairly neutral palette throughout most of the house with the exception of my kitchen and lounge room, both rooms boasted a feature wall painted in the blue-grey colour that I had become obsessed with over the years from watching my favourite home improvement shows. I spent my weekends combing through furniture stores with my parents, excitedly choosing a huge cream coloured lounge and a new bedroom suite, which included my first ever king-size bed. But my favourite item was the large sea turtle portrait that I had paid a small fortune for in Hawaii. The picture had been shipped home from Maui. I couldn't wait to hang my mummy turtle above my lounge where she could watch over me and my babies when the time came to welcome them into the world.

By the time the week of my first appointment with a fertility specialist rolled around I was all moved into my granny-flat and eager to decorate my spare room in pink or blue. I had spent a lot of time shopping with Amy who, much to everyone's delight, was expecting a little boy. My nephew was due in June and I couldn't wait to meet him. I couldn't wait for my own future child, or indeed children, since I had made the decision to try to have two children in close succession, to play with their big cousin.

I hadn't taken any personal time off since the Christmas break. My boss in the US was always telling me to take advantage of our unlimited leave policy and so I decided that I would take the Friday off so that I could go and see a movie and get my nails done after seeing the doctor. I had my whole day planned out and couldn't wait to meet the woman I'd heard so much about. But then at 6 pm on Thursday night, just as I was finishing a few things for work, I got a disheartening phone call. I never normally answered calls from silent numbers after hours, in case they were marketing calls ironically, but something told me to take the call.

"Hello. Magnolia speaking." I answered tentatively.

"Oh Magnolia. Hi. This is Sasha from Doctor Marcus' rooms. How are you?"

"Hi Sasha. I'm great, how are you?" I said, relieved to hear that it was not some telemarketer who hadn't done their research and assumed I was the CFO, instead of a marketing person myself. "Is everything okay for my appointment tomorrow?"

"Unfortunately, Doctor Marcus is going to have to reschedule your appointment as she has to be in theatre tomorrow." Sasha explained. "I have a full schedule for her for the next couple of months so let's get you re-booked and I will put you on the cancellation list since you've already waited for so long."

"Oh, what a shame." I said flatly, my heart dropping. Of all the fertility specialists I had researched, Doctor Marcus was the one I was most interested in meeting. She had gone through IVF in her early forties to have her youngest son and from the reviews I had read about her, she sounded so kind and knowledgeable. I swallowed my disappointment before speaking.

"Thank you. I really would like to see her as soon as possible so if a cancellation comes up, I can be fairly flexible with work as long as I'm not travelling." We agreed on a new appointment date in early August instead. I had hoped to be well and truly pregnant by then but I reminded myself that a couple of months' delay wasn't going to be the end of the world. I also had the appointment with Doctor Allen, the second doctor that I had found while researching my options. Maybe she would end up being a good fit. That second appointment was happening the following Friday at 6 pm. I thought about cancelling my annual leave for the following day so as not to waste a day that I could be working but I knew I was overdue for a me-day and so I decided to keep it. The appointment the following week was only two blocks from my office, meaning that I could just wander down there after work.

My long weekend was lovely and relaxing. I spent time with Amy and James as well as Bec and Damian. Bec had just announced a few weeks earlier that she too was expecting her first baby and so I was really in my element. I couldn't wait to join the mum-to-be club as well. The week flew by and before I knew it, I found myself sitting in the large waiting area of the CBD clinic while I waited to meet Doctor Allen.

When a heavy-set, cranky sounding woman called my name half an hour or so after I sat in the waiting room with my book, I was full of excitement and anticipation despite the doctor's apparent bad mood. As I followed Doctor Allen down the long hallway to her room, I took note of the framed pictures of parents with their babies. I was excited to see that those pictures included photographs of gay and lesbian parents, and more importantly for my situation, pictures of single women with their tiny miracles.

I took a seat across from Doctor Allen and was about to ask her some of the questions I'd prepared when she spoke first.

"So, you don't have a partner I see." It was more a statement than a question. "Why not?"

"I guess I just ... I've never met anyone that I wanted to have children with." I said, caught off guard by her strange question. "I've decided to have a baby as a solo mother by choice."

"Well, you're not even thirty yet. You still have plenty of time to meet someone." I watched her as she spoke, writing on her notepad. She seemed determined not to look at me. "We need to freeze your eggs before they're no good but I don't think you need to have a baby alone".

"Oh." I was speechless. I didn't want to wait. I didn't want to try and meet someone. I was exhausted and fed up with trying to find a good man. I had come such a long way in the time since that special night on the beach in Hawaii. I had spent months getting my little house furnished and decorated, ready to welcome my own baby. I was excited about having my nephew and my own child close in age.

My first instinct was to listen to that woman with the food stuck in her teeth and the weird mouldy aroma wafting from her clothing. I thought that surely, she must know what was best for a woman my age. She helped people become parents every day after all.

But then I remembered my mummy turtle. I remembered how empowering it was, knowing that she trusted me enough to watch over her eggs. That wonderful mother had no idea that I would be long gone before her tiny hatchlings made their perilous journey to the water's edge. All she knew was that I was worthy of sharing in the magical experience on that beach.

I had been through so much in my quest to find love. I had beaten myself up so many times, wondering what was so bad about me. I had been so full of self-doubt and hate for myself that I'd let men convince me that I was some wile, unlovable freak. How dare some woman sit there, with no idea about the hell I'd been through and the dragons I still slayed every day, and tell me that all I needed was a man. Something in me snapped. As she opened her mouth and started talking about the process of freezing eggs, I pushed out of my seat and walked towards the door, opening it as I spoke.

"I didn't come here to be lectured about not having a man or freezing my eggs." I said, trying to keep my voice neutral as I spoke. "I want a baby now and if you won't help me, then I will go and find a doctor who will."

As I closed the door behind me, I felt a sense of power. It was invigorating. I held my head high as I walked past the reception desk and out into a waiting lift. I knew that I was going to have to pay that woman for wasting my time but as far as I was concerned, she could send the bill in the post. As I stepped out onto the street, I took a deep breath before turning and looking up to the third-floor windows that housed the fertility clinic I'd just walked out of, raised my arms in the air and gave that stupid woman a middle finger salute before heading for the bus stop.

As I stared out the window on the bus ride home, I thought about the way it felt to stand up for what I wanted. I had never so blatantly stood up for myself before, at least not in my personal life. I thought about Sam, Zac and Anthony. I had never had the courage to stand up for myself with any of them. I had let that filthy old pervert do a terrible thing to me because I was too scared to stand up and run away. Standing up for myself seemed so easy all of a sudden and made me believe, more than ever, that I could do it.

When I caught up with Amy and Bec that weekend, to help plan the final details for Bec's upcoming baby shower, I was more determined than ever to become a mum. I once again kept my plan to myself though. I was determined to keep the focus on the babies that we were already waiting to meet. It wasn't ideal that I was going to have to wait another couple of months before I could meet with Doctor Marcus and finally start my own family but I knew I had plenty on my plate to keep me busy in the meantime.

I was thankful when the ultimate distraction presented itself the very next weekend. We were playing the dirty nappy game at Bec's baby shower. Each of us took turns trying to figure out which chocolate bar had been melted and poured into each tiny nappy. As we laughed, acting repulsed by the appearance of those nappies, Amy suddenly clutched her tummy before announcing quietly to Mum and I, who were seated either side of her, that her waters had just broken.

My first thought was to panic but thankfully Mum jumped into action, calling James to come and pick up his wife and get her home. By the time James arrived at the party Amy was starting to feel extremely uncomfortable. James decided that it would be safest to grab the hospital bag and head to the hospital and it's lucky he did because, just three hours later, baby Joshua Gregory made his way, kicking and screaming into the world.

Little Joshua instantly captured the hearts of his parents, his grandparents, and of course his aunt. From the moment Joshua arrived in early May 2005, time seemed to speed up. Before I knew it, late August had arrived and with it, the day of my long-awaited fertility appointment. All going well I hoped to be pregnant by the time Bec was due in November.

Chapter Twenty-One

When the Saturday morning of my appointment finally arrived I felt nervous but I tried to take the bright sunny weather as a good sign. The weather was already warming up for late August—spring was definitely on its way. As I made my way to the clinic for my 11 am appointment, I wondered if I was going to find myself faced with the same response from Dr. Marcus as that of the last Doctor I'd seen a few months earlier but, thankfully, the moment I walked into the reception area of the new clinic, I felt completely at ease. There were so many obvious differences between the two clinics. From the lovely pink velvet chairs to the floor to ceiling windows that lit the room up beautifully.

The tiny lady who walked out and shook my hand a few minutes after I arrived was also a stark contrast to the heavy-set woman from my last appointment. Doctor Marcus was vibrant, with her bright pink linen dress and matching heels perfectly displaying her sunny and cheerful personality. I felt at ease as soon as we started our conversation. She had clearly read the notes that her receptionist had taken during our initial conversation several months earlier. Right from the start her attitude was so different to that of the last woman as well.

"So, Magnolia. Thank you for coming in. I understand you want to have a baby using a sperm donor?" she asked matter-of-factly but with kindness etched on her face. "And you're twenty-eight according to my notes?"

"Yes. I turn twenty-nine in November. I haven't had the best luck with men." I began. "I don't want to wait any longer."

"You're not alone you know. So many women are choosing to go down this path now and we have several sperm banks we work with, assuming you don't have a known donor?" Dr Marcus asked. "If not, we don't have a waitlist like a lot of other clinics."

"I don't know anyone that I'd feel comfortable asking to help." I explained. "So, I would like to use one of your donors.'

"Okay great. You don't need to make any decisions about the actual donor yet. I see here that you've had one pregnancy before that ended in a loss?" The empathy in her voice was another thing I noticed that was so different to that last doctor.

"As heartbreaking as it is, we take it as a sign that your body can get pregnant which is half the battle. We will need to run some tests and do an ultrasound as well so that we've got an idea of what we're dealing with".

"Okay well I guess that's something." I didn't want to tell her about what my plan had been that last time. I knew it wasn't relevant anyway. "So what tests are there?" I knew from what I had read that there were all kinds of tests that could predict a woman's likelihood of getting pregnant.

"We will test to see what your egg reserves look like, and I'll do a full blood count." Dr. Marcus explained. "We will do an ultrasound to check how many follicles you have sitting in your ovaries as a baseline as well, I can do that now or you can come back in a couple of weeks once the blood test results are back."

"I think that I might do the blood tests first just to give me time to process everything if that's okay?" I asked, feeling a bit overwhelmed by everything.

"Of course. Please don't apologise, I know this is a huge amount of information." my new fertility specialist explained. "Let's get your blood tests sorted out now to start things off."

A nurse came into the room a few minutes later and expertly drew several vials of blood from my arm before telling me to apply pressure over a small circular band aid for a few minutes. Once the nurse was finished, she wished me well before leaving the room. A moment later Dr. Marcus walked back in.

For the next twenty minutes the lovely little doctor with the bright pink dress, and the personality to match, answered a multitude of questions about the difference between In Vitro Fertilisation, or IVF for short, versus Intrauterine-Insemination, or IUI. The two different types of fertility treatments were vastly different; with IVF being the more invasive of the two procedures, requiring an operation to retrieve eggs from a woman's ovaries before being sterilised in a petri dish and then transferred back as an embryo. I was told that most women my age opted for the more straightforward method of IUI as a starting point. I knew that I wanted to have more than one child though, so it was likely that the IVF option was going to give me a better chance of doing so. It was important to me that my children shared the same donor.

By the time I walked out of the clinic and into the warm August afternoon I was feeling overcome with nervous excitement. Dr. Marcus had cautioned me that the process was likely to take a few months in total which was disappointing after how long I'd already had to wait, however, once I got past that I realised something. Getting pregnant in the new year meant that I might just get to have my spring baby after all. I had always dreamed of having a spring baby and then taking the whole summer off to hang out with my newborn. I was thoroughly enjoying being an aunt and Bec was a matter of weeks away from meeting her baby girl. I figured that by the time it was my turn to become a mum, the girls would have an abundance of advice and experience to impart on me. It was such a wonderful thought.

With the new lead time on my fertility journey I realised that I was going to need another distraction. As much as I was enjoying cuddling little Joshua, he was more interested in sleeping and pooping whenever I saw him. Bec was suffering from morning sickness that lasted from dawn to dusk and most of my other friends and family were tied up with work and their own kids and so I decided to do something crazy. When I became friends with David and Steve in Hawaii, after the wedding, I discovered that not only were they avid surfers, they were also into karate. I still caught up with the guys for after work drinks at least once a month and they had been trying to recruit me to give martial arts a try.

I had been tempted to give karate a go when Steve first told me about it a couple of months after we all got back from Hawaii but then I brushed the idea off, assuming that I would be pregnant before I had a chance to get the hang of it. I was clumsy at the best of times and I knew that no one would accuse me of being the most graceful woman on the dancefloor but Steve liked to tell me that none of those things mattered. When I caught up with my friends the week after my appointment with Dr. Marcus I decided to finally say yes and give it a go. Who knew, maybe even clumsy old Magnolia could learn how to kick someone's arse. I had fantasised about doing something terrible to that old man so many times over the years. I had dreamed about what might have happened, had I known how to defend myself against that old man. Maybe I would have had the courage to beat him up instead of cowering and letting him lay his repulsive hands on me.

I decided that the next man who tried to hurt me was going to feel my wrath. From the first time I put on my gee, my white karate gear, I was hooked. The feeling of power that I got when I was in the dojo was unparalleled. The sense of camaraderie as other women, men and even kids learned how to protect themselves against the evil world outside really gave me a sense of validation. I knew within the first few lessons that I had found a new passion. I couldn't wait for my own future children to start their lessons too. The thought of my children being able to protect themselves, if they ever found themselves in a situation like the one I had found myself in as a fourteen-year-old kid, really fuelled my desire to learn even more.

On top of the twice-weekly karate lessons I signed up for tap dancing classes. As a little girl I was obsessed with trying to tap. My mum finally gave in and booked me into classes when I was about six. Getting my first pair of tap shoes was one of my favourite childhood memories and I had always wanted to give it another try.

Trying on my new, grown-up tap shoes took me right back to that place. Back to when I was the little girl with big dreams. The innocent little girl who loved love and didn't know that monsters were real. I hurried off to my first class with the same level of enthusiasm as a child searching for chocolates on Easter morning. I wasn't even bothered when I realised how absolutely terrible I was. I tapped my heart out every week for the next few months and I loved every moment of it.

I had never believed older people before when they claimed that time seemed to speed up as you got older but my attitude changed that spring and summer. Before I knew it another birthday had passed, my twenty-ninth, followed three days later by the arrival of Bec and Damian's sweet little girl, Madison. Somehow the month between Madison's birth and Christmas flew by. The newest members of our family brought so much joy and excitement. For the first time in years, Hayley's children were more interested in their big new, cousin status than the pool or even Great-Poppy's cool video game collection. Especially Amelia who, at three, had finally graduated from the baby of the family, to one of the big kids.

By the time mum and I served dessert that afternoon I felt sure that I had never spent such a wonderful and carefree

Christmas before. I had enjoyed my family without the stress of some jerk treating me like an afterthought. I had been spoiled by every single person I loved, just as I had spoiled them in return. I laughed with delight as the children opened all their gifts, especially enjoying their reactions to the gifts I had so carefully selected for them all.

I realised that it was the first Christmas since I was thirteen that I was genuinely at peace. The realisation was so empowering, just like that night on the beach in Hawaii and so many experiences since that night, including my Karate grading two weeks earlier. I was so proud of my promotion to an orange belt. I knew that I still had a long way to go before I would be wrapping the coveted black belt around my waist but it was still a huge achievement. Steve and David were already teasing that I would be joining their senior classes before I knew it. As much as I hoped they were right, I knew that I had another, far more important task to tick off my to-do list first.

Chapter Twenty-Two

My appointment with Doctor Marcus, to kick off the IVF process, finally arrived in early February 2006. The tests she had conducted on the day of my first appointment showed that my egg reserves were on the low side for my age, meaning that IVF would be the most practical option for me, regardless of the number of children I planned to have. The trouble was that those tests also showed that I had a moderate case of endometriosis, or endo for short. I had always had extremely heavy and painful periods which I assumed were normal. Apparently, the diagnosis of endo meant that getting pregnant may be more difficult for me than it would be for a woman without the condition, for several different reasons.

I learned that up to ten percent of women suffered from the condition which caused a buildup of endometrial tissue in parts of the body other than just the uterus but I was relieved to hear that there was still every chance I could conceive with the right medications and care. By the time I found myself sitting across from Dr. Marcus to discuss the medication I was about to start using, I had undergone two minor procedures to remove the endometriosis from inside my uterus and fallopian tubes. The 'cleaning out' of my uterus was performed to increase my chances of becoming pregnant once an embryo was transferred.

And speaking of embryos, when I walked out of the clinic that day, it was finally with the plan for my IVF cycle. I had to wait for a week or so until my period was due. On the first day of bleeding, I would start taking the medications to help grow lots of follicles. When the time came to have my egg retrieval procedure, those follicles would hopefully contain mature eggs that the clinic would fertilise. According to a scan I had that day, there were a total of nine follicles before starting the hormone injections, which Dr. Marcus was very happy with, all things considered.

As I drove home after my appointment I tried to imagine what my child, or indeed children, would look like. In the months since Baby Joshua and Madison were born, I had begun to think about what it would be like to have twins. Dr. Marcus was hesitant to agree when I first raised the idea with her but then, before my most recent procedure, I took her through my list of pros and cons of having two babies. I could tell at the time that she was amused but also impressed by the time I'd spent considering everything. In the end we agreed that I would have two embryos transferred, assuming I had at least three. That way, if the double transfer failed, I would have one more try. I was sure that I'd have far more than that.

I arrived home shortly before 4 pm more excited than ever about the life I was building for myself. I couldn't wait to become mum, dad and protector of my own beautiful babies. I couldn't wait to announce my upcoming pregnancy to my family and friends. As I raced around getting ready for dinner, I thought about my wonderful friend, Page.

I was excited to think that Page was going to be in Sydney for a couple of weeks. Page was the sister of Anthony—my American ex-boyfriend. She was a year older than Anthony and from the moment we met, we were like sisters. When things had gone sour between him and I all those years ago I was relieved to hear that she wanted to stay in touch and we had maintained our friendship, despite the distance. She had even been to Australia a couple of times to visit her brother and meet the two daughters he'd gone on to have with his wife. Each time she came to Sydney we would go out for a meal, just the two of us. I couldn't wait to see her that night.

It had been a few years since I'd seen Page but when she walked into the pub a couple of hours later, on Valentine's Day as it turned out, it felt like no time had passed. We wasted no time catching up on each other's lives. I already knew that Page was officially divorced after separating from her second husband a couple of years earlier but I was thrilled to hear that she'd been dating a new guy for a few months. The new guy was a wealthy Wall Street trader who was several years her junior. He lived the high life in New York. They had met when she was out there for work and hit it off instantly.

Page hadn't had much luck with men either. It was something we had bonded over throughout the years. We would often share our dating disasters to cheer each other up. She had three children, all boys, from her first marriage and she was determined not to bring them up to be like their two-timing father. The new man had never met the boys and she was planning on keeping it that way. 'Mr Wall-Street', as she had nicknamed him, was her little bit of fun. They were both far too busy to want anything more than a hot weekend here and there. He was exactly what she needed.

I shared my news too. I hadn't spoken with my dear friend at length in months so when I told her that I was planning to try for a baby she assumed that I had met someone too. As I explained my plan, without going into detail about just how far along in the process I actually was, Page interrupted me. There was an urgency in her voice. I listened in disbelief as she explained that Anthony had separated from his wife almost a year earlier. He had decided to stay in Australia for the sake of his daughters, of which he now had three. The youngest of his girls was only 16-months, she had been conceived by accident after a few too many beers shortly before they'd separated. Page had told her brother that she was seeing me for a Valentine's Day dinner, only to have him ask after me.

Apparently, he'd realised long ago that he had made a mistake when he'd cheated on me. It made me feel smug to hear that particular news but I wasn't sure what I was expected to do with it. So much time had passed. I'd had so many horrible experiences since Anthony and because of him. I had done so much healing since the night on that beach in Hawaii, more than a year earlier. I was a different woman to the one Anthony had lied and cheated on, and then, as it turned out, with.

The time for apologies had long since passed and besides, I knew that a leopard didn't change its spots. and so, it made no sense to me when I asked questions about Anthony. I wanted to know where he lived and how often he saw his children. It made even less sense when I found myself punching his number into my phone later that night. The fact that it was Valentine's Day was not lost on me. It had been such a significant day when I was in America. All of that love everywhere had made me believe, for the first time since I was a child, that even I might be lucky enough to find it. And of course it was the date we met, at that party so many lifetimes ago.

Anthony had been the one who made me believe in fairy tales again back then, after I'd told him, one boozy night, about what had happened a few years earlier. He made it all better, at least for a while. I dialled his number when I got home that night convinced that it was fate. All common sense went out the window. Maybe he was being sent back to me for a reason?

It was a few days before we caught up. As I walked into that cafe the years fell away. I was surprised to see that he'd gone almost completely bald. He had aged considerably in the years since I'd last seen him but his smile was the same. The moment he saw me his face lit up.

And—once again—it was like all the bad things had never happened. Sam, Zac, even the terrible things that Anthony himself had done. And the old man. All the pain and trauma that had made me believe I was a terrible, unlovable woman.

Even our baby, the one I had never told him about. I had always blamed him as much as I blamed myself. After all, he was the one who'd put me in that position with his lies about being single. When I first walked into that cafe it was more out of curiosity but as soon as I saw him, I wondered, could Anthony and I at least be friends?

Chapter Twenty-Three

I ignored all the voices screaming in my head, reminding me of how far I'd come since my encounter on Kea Lani beach in Hawaii, because suddenly all that mattered was that he was there. Anthony was the only person who really knew me.

When I first met him, it had been three-and-a-half years since that day in the newsagency. To say that the experience had turned my world upside down would be a massive understatement. My grades went from above average to atrocious. I became reserved. After a lifetime of being a social butterfly I started to dread being around people. Girls at school, well, the mean girls anyway, started to sense a vulnerability in me that hadn't existed before. They honed right in on it. It was like I suddenly had a neon sign on my forehead telling everyone that I was an easy target—a freak. They bullied and teased me no matter how obscure I tried to be. I tried so hard to fly under their radar but nothing worked.

By the time I was seventeen I was a complete train wreck. I had started hanging out with those kids that fed me drugs like they were lollies. And that was when I first started cutting myself. I hated myself for what I'd let that filthy old pervert do to me. I discovered that the physical pain was so much easier to cope with than the mental pain and trauma that I carried around with me every day.

My parents were beside themselves with worry, wondering what they had done wrong. But the more they pushed, the more I pulled away. The more they tried to help, the more destructive my behaviour became. I dated guys purely based on their looks and I developed a strange obsession with hands. If a guy didn't have soft, almost feminine hands, I would instantly be turned off. I had never forgotten the feeling of that disgusting old man as he pawed at me with his huge, paddle-like hands. I would inspect their hands, claiming that I was reading their palms. Of course, no one thought twice about my strange little obsession. It was the 90s and naughties, it would be weird for a young woman not to be obsessed with astrology and palm reading in those days.

But the cute guys with the nice hands never lasted long. As soon as one of them tried to feel me up, I would run for my life. It would take me straight back to that dingy back room. I would delete their numbers. I would ghost them, not caring about the reputation that it was giving me. They'd call me a prick tease and a slut. And of course I believed them. I was convinced that they knew what I'd done. That they knew I was damaged and dirty, despite the scrubbing brush that I still used each day in the shower, to try and clean the filth and shame away.

By half way through year 11 I had dropped out of high school. I did odd jobs at fast food places, but I had no real interest in anything other than taking drugs and sleeping. Completely bewildered by my growing lack of interest in my future, my parents hatched the plan with Mum's wonderful friend Katrina. Mum and Dad agreed to pay for my airfares and anything else I needed while I saved some money over the first couple of months in the US.

I'd always been mesmerised by the thought of going to America and so I happily obliged. That was how I found myself, at eighteen years of age, at that party. I had never really met any Americans before I arrived at San Francisco International Airport. It was love at first sight. My new life, so far away from the trauma and the memories of that day. It was just what I needed to finally start healing from my horrible, shameful experience. When I first met him all those years earlier, it was the first time I was able to let myself trust a man. He brought me back from the brink. Somehow, I forgot about the way he could destroy me just as easily.

I walked out of that cafe with Anthony and forgot all about my new life. I decided to cancel my IVF cycle or postpone it at least. I immediately fell back into that comfortable and familiar place that was Magnolia and Anthony. A few weeks after our post Valentine's Day coffee date I met his daughters and I was instantly smitten with them, especially the littlest one. Spending every second weekend with the girls was fun, at least at first.

When Anthony told me that he loved me, after I jumped back in my car after filling it with petrol one morning, just a few weeks after Valentine's Day, I believed him. He seemed to understand why I wasn't able to say it back. I wanted to, so desperately, but the years really had taken their toll on me. He simply put his fingers to my lips when he saw the look on my face. I felt like I was finally home. He was my harbour, my safe haven and shelter from the storm. It was the kind of cheesy shit that I'd always sniggered about in movies but my Californian had shown up, as usual, when I needed him. He was back to save me from being alone after all.

I know I shouldn't have been surprised when my family freaked out. Especially Bec. She couldn't believe that I had fallen for his lies again. I tried to convince her that he had changed. He had grown up. She didn't believe it for a second but she didn't know my dirty little secret. No one in my family did, not even my mum or my cousins. Those three women were my confidants, as were my dad, my brother and Amy. I had tried to tell them about that filthy old creep so many times but his words, the names he'd called me, had stopped me. I was so terrified that my family would see me the way that he had and the way I still did. Even after so many years had passed, the thought of telling anyone still terrified me.

Anthony was the one person who had always known my secret and still said he loved me. I was thankful that most of my family seemed to come around slowly. For the first few months, things were good. I didn't care that he didn't pay his way. I knew that he had been laid off in the December before we got back together, so I was happy to shout dinners out and occasional weekends away. I figured that you couldn't put a price tag on the happiness I was feeling. I was finally living the life I'd always dreamed about with a loving partner.

But then one weekend I was sitting on the front porch of the house he shared with a woman named Tash, or TJ for short. Anthony had his children for the weekend and their mother arrived to pick them up. It was Sunday afternoon and I was enjoying a glass of wine with TJ, chatting with her happily when the woman pulled up out the front. As she got out of the car, I realised that I had never seen her in the flesh before. She had short black hair and was a lot bigger than she looked in the photos I had seen but I didn't care, I wasn't there to judge anyone. And so, with that I waved.

That weekend Anthony's middle daughter, Michelle, had repeated some of the horrible things her mother had said about me, saying that I was ugly and looked like a horse. I thought that maybe if she met me, she'd realise that I was a nice person. But apparently that wasn't the way it worked with unhinged people.

The moment she saw me wave she started screaming, not at me but at Anthony. TJ made a couple of comments that made me realise it wasn't an isolated incident. I'd heard plenty of things about her previously but up until that moment I assumed that it was just because of their nasty break up. Once the children were all secure in the car she drove off. I assumed that the strange outburst was the end of it but as Anthony walked over to join us on the porch, he told me what the screaming had been about.

Apparently, my attempt at friendliness had gone down like a lead balloon. Assuming that I was being smart she had lost it, screaming that she was going to bash my head in. I guess that she had looked at my size and decided that she could take me. Or maybe she was just letting off steam but either way, Anthony knew that I was still attending karate lessons a couple of times a week. He seemed to think it would be funny to tell her to drop the kids at her parent's place and come back to fight me. He'd told me often enough that she had never stepped foot in a gym in her life and so he knew that I would come out on top.

I couldn't believe what I was hearing. I was learning karate so that I could learn how to protect myself from bad men, not so that I could punch on with my boyfriend's ex-wife. I was relieved when she didn't return that afternoon but I demanded answers. They had been apart for over a year. He'd had another relationship between her and me. I didn't understand why she hated me so much. Their relationship ending had nothing to do with me and I was kind and respectful to her children. What the hell could possibly make a total stranger hate me that much that she wanted to try and beat me up?

Chapter Twenty-Four

And then he finally came clean. Anthony and his ex were talking about getting back together until I came along and ruined things. I couldn't believe that he hadn't told me earlier. The comments from the girls about my appearance started to make sense, as did the home-wrecker comments. I felt sick. As far as that woman was concerned, I had stolen her husband and she was hell-bent on getting him back. I know that I should have walked away. I should have restarted my IVF journey and ridden off into the sunset with the last shred of my now almost forgotten independence and dignity.

And I tried to. I told him to go back to his family. I would never have gotten involved with him had I known that he was planning to get back together with her. But he told me that her craziness reminded him of why they'd split up to begin with. He insisted that there was nothing that would make him go back to her. And so, against my better judgement, I stayed. And she used the kids as a weapon. If she couldn't have him then she was going to hit him where it hurt, by taking his daughters away from him.

Anthony tried reasoning with her, he pleaded with her, and he threatened her with court. But she called his bluff. He hadn't worked in months. He had sold his car soon after we'd gotten together and used the money to pay his rent and bills for a few months until he found another job. He'd given her a few hundred dollars at the time but she knew as well as I did—he couldn't afford a barrister. By the time she pulled that trick with the kids we had started talking about having a baby together. I had told Anthony, soon after our reunion, about my plans to have a child of my own. I explained how much I wanted a baby and was thrilled when he told me that he wanted us to have a baby together.

We had only been together for about three months when we started talking about trying to get pregnant. Ever the planner, I quickly had everything figured out down to the letter. Our trip to Melbourne with a group of my friends was coming up in July. It was a yearly trip that we had been taking since I returned from living in the US. Every year we would plan it over a long weekend.

The girls and I would spend our days shopping and drinking wine while the guys attended football matches and played golf. Every evening, we would all get together for dinner in St Kilda or along Lygon Street to talk about our adventures while we ate oysters and drank more wine. There was no way I was going to miss out on being able to enjoy my wine and oysters on our trip, especially if it was the last time before I became a mum— so the plan was to try for a baby when we got back home.

Of course, nothing ever seemed to be that easy. For the weeks that Anthony's ex-wife had cut off his contact with the girls I felt constantly on edge, as though she might be about to pounce from behind a bush or something. She was utterly obsessed with him. It didn't matter how many times Anthony told her that they were over, she just refused to hear it. I had blocked her on social media after a barrage of messages over the course of a few days when he and I had first reunited.

She called me every name under the sun. A tip-rat, a horse and a pig, which was ironic really considering her own appearance, she was shorter than me but probably weighed close to twice what I did. She even called me "Bucky", referring to my supposed buck-teeth. The last insult always made me laugh, just as I'm sure it would have made my orthodontist laugh, after the impressive work he'd done several years earlier, on my perfectly straight, not at all buck-teeth.

Once I blocked her on Facebook, I assumed that her behaviour would stop and that I could get on with my life. But then, not long after the Melbourne trip, she somehow managed to get hold of my phone number. I was reversing out of my driveway one night when my phone pinged with an SMS, and then another, and another. I pulled the car over, wondering what was going on. No one I knew was likely to be messaging me constantly unless there was an emergency. I stared at the screen with utter confusion for a minute. And then I started shaking as I realised who it was.

I had never been scared of another woman in my life until that moment. I should have driven back up the road and gone back inside to the safety of my home, with my parents. But I didn't. I had plans to spend the weekend out in the Blue Mountains, a couple of hours west of Sydney. It was supposed to be snowing and so we had made last-minute plans to have a weekend away with a few of Anthony's friends. He had gone ahead with another couple because I knew that I would be at work until quite late. By the time those messages started it was 7 pm and already pitch-black outside.

I tried my best to ignore them at first but by the time I pulled into a petrol station a few minutes up the road from my house there were dozens of messages written in her own unique version of English that I had come to know all-too-well.

Ur a homewrecker

You R going to pay for what you done to my family.

My daughter's agree that u r an ugly pig.

They hate you.

I am gonna get my dad's shotgun and fukn shoot you.

You WILL pay.

I won't stop til ur dead.

The messages went on, and on. They were relentless and they were unbelievable. I watched in horror as she even tried calling me a couple of times. I felt like I had been transported into my worst nightmare.

I filled up my car and then moved it away from the bowsers before calling him. I didn't know what else to do. Anthony was furious. He told me that she had been calling him all day begging him to come back. When he refused, she had started ranting about making me pay for what I had done and that she was going to shoot me with her father's rifle. The very same things that she had started messaging me when she didn't get a reply to the messages about my appearance.

I had been planning to get rid of my baby for that woman. Back when I was pregnant and found out about her also carrying Anthony's baby. I had been planning to terminate my pregnancy for her. I was convinced that I had willed that baby to leave me because I was trying to do the right thing by her and that was how she was going to repay me?

Things escalated so quickly from there. I hadn't realised until that moment how much I was shaking. I was upset and I was angry—no, I was furious. I desperately wanted to turn around and go home but he convinced me to keep driving. He promised me that he would make her stop.

Anthony shot down my suggestion of talking to the police, insisting that she was harmless. And so, I continued to drive. For the next hour and a half, I drove towards what I perceived as my safe haven. To him. I was so desperate to see him and share the news that I'd been holding onto for the past few days.

I was nearly there when all of a sudden, I found myself spinning. It all happened so quickly. It was like when you're falling in your sleep. I felt like I was dreaming, the spinning seemed to last for minutes but it was probably only seconds. There was a loud sound, a woman's voice screaming. The kind of screams I had heard in horror movies as a teenager. Eventually my car slammed into a barricade and came to a screeching halt on the wrong side of the road. I found myself face to face with a truck coming up the mountain towards me and realised that the terrible screaming sound was actually coming from me. I imagined the truck slamming into me and ending it all but I wasn't going out like that. I wasn't going to let her win.

Somehow, I managed to get it together long enough to move the car over next to the barricade that I'd slammed into. I hopped out of the car and somehow, I wasn't injured. I grabbed my belly instinctively, praying that everything would be okay. I fell to the road, screaming, as cars started pulling over. An older woman and two men raced over to see if I was okay. My cherished little red car looked like a mangled piece of scrap metal. I desperately wanted my mum and dad but I didn't want to scare them and so, when the lady who'd come to check on me retrieved my phone, I called Anthony instead.

By the time I hit the call button I had started to calm down but his voice sent me right back into a spin. I screamed again as I collapsed back onto the ground, explaining through my hysteria what had happened. The police and fire trucks arrived a short time later and by the time the police were finished talking to me, Anthony had arrived. I knew that I had to somehow stay as calm as possible for the baby. I ignored the strange cramping feeling that had started, like a dull period cramping. As soon as I saw him, I lost it all over again. I was furious. I had endured so much for him, because of him. Why did loving him always have to be so full of pain and hurt? I wanted to run from him and his psychopath of an ex. To a life where it was just my baby and I, surrounded by my family.

Instead, I let him envelope me in those arms that had held me so tenderly, so many times. I was sure that I didn't know how to be happy without him. I had tried so many times to no avail, each time it had ended in disaster. He knew my dirty little secret and he claimed to love me anyway. I knew that dealing with her was just the price I had to pay for his love. And that's why I went back to the holiday rental with him.

I went back and lapped up the attention from his friends and I started to feel like maybe everything would be okay after all. And for a little while everything was okay. In fact, everything was great. An hour after arriving at the house I was sitting at the dinner table surrounded by more attention than I knew what to do with. I was halfway through a piece of chocolate cake when it all came crashing down.

Chapter Twenty-Five

knew before I even sat down on the toilet that it was happening again. There was blood everywhere. I had taken painkillers in the car, hoping that the cramps were a normal pregnancy symptom that I could somehow erase. Of course they weren't. How could any baby survive such a horrific car accident, let alone a foetus that was just a matter of weeks into its development? I had been planning to tell him that weekend. We had gotten pregnant on our trip to Melbourne. I had only stopped taking the pill a couple of weeks beforehand. When I told Dr. Marcus about my change of plans, she had told me it would likely take several months to conceive but by some miracle it had happened straight away.

As I cleaned myself up, I could feel the anger bubbling up from deep down within my belly. I was sad, I was completely devastated but more than that I was pissed off. My fairytale ending had been a horror story almost from the start. For some reason I thought that the little baby we had conceived would fix everything. I foolishly believed that we could somehow get past all the psycho shit from his ex. I thought that maybe he'd finally get off his lazy bum and get a job. I was sure I was finally going to have the life that I craved with a hardworking, loving partner and a sweet little baby of my own.

I couldn't believe that it had been within reach for the second time but now I was losing that chance again. I was so distraught about the messages that I had wrecked my car on the side of a cliff. I hadn't seen the black ice on the road. The police had shown up and told me how lucky I was that I'd been driving fairly slowly. But I wasn't lucky. I had been on my way to tell Anthony about our baby. As I sat there in the toilet, I was sure that I had finally reached my breaking point.

I had endured so much over the years. The filthy old pervert who stole my innocence, the horrible guys that treated me like nothing more than an inconvenience. I knew that I was the one who had allowed those men to treat me badly. I knew that I was, once again, allowing Anthony to treat me badly, which was bad enough but I wasn't going to tolerate another ounce of abuse from his ex-wife, a woman I'd never even met.

When I walked out of that bathroom it was with a new sense of purpose. I called Anthony into the bedroom we were sharing and told him that I'd had enough. Of her that was. I gave him two options. Either he told her, in front of me, that I was going to the police if her harassment didn't stop that night, or I would go myself the following morning.

I told him about the babies too. I wasn't going to but it was so heavy. I had never told him about our first pregnancy, instead suffering alone for years and blaming myself but I didn't want to bear the weight of it anymore, I couldn't. Realising that I had lost not one but two babies because of the crazy shit he'd pulled me into was all the motivation he needed. He called her number. I heard her voice on his phone. She sounded desperate as always but for once he didn't humour her. He screamed at her so aggressively that I even took a step back.

By the time Anthony ended his call a couple of minutes later I was certain that my troubles with her would finally be a thing of the past. A few seconds after he hung up, I realised that he was crying. I walked the few steps to where he sat at the end of the bed and wrapped my arms around him. I stood there for what seemed like an hour as the heaviness in his heart threatened to pull me under. I could never have anticipated his reaction—all that grief. I realised that I had only ever seen him in such a raw, emotional state once before, the night he told me about finding his godfather's body when he was a teenager. I had forgotten he was even capable of it.

I had been so ready to plan my revenge. To get myself pregnant again so that I could leave him and go it alone after all, thinking that all I cared about now was the baby that he owed me. But as I held him, and as he wept for what could have been, I believed, once again, that he was the only man who had the power to make me feel like I was good enough. He was the only man who had been able to erase all the bad things. I knew that I couldn't go ahead with it. If I left, who else would want me? I didn't want to be alone anymore.

Chapter Twenty-Six

And so, the following Monday I took the day off work. I should have taken a week off. Between my written-off car and the loss of my baby I was in no fit state to be at work. But that wasn't who I was. My dating life may have been a disaster over the years but my work life had always been a very different story. Even after so many years, I still loved my job. At work I was a strong, capable and confident woman. The skeletons in my closet didn't threaten to destroy me there like they did in every aspect of my personal life.

I had only ever taken a few personal days off over the years. I'd taken a week once because I had the flu and couldn't get out of bed. And I'd taken a day, soon after losing that first baby. It wasn't the car or the miscarriage that made me call in sick that Monday after the crash though. It was because I was moving Anthony's stuff into my little granny-flat. We made the decision that night, in our moment of heartbroken solidarity, that we wanted to live together. He promised to get a job and start contributing financially to our future together.

I bought a new car, a little white hatchback. And then I planned a snowboarding trip. I had taken up snowboarding after a work trip to New Zealand several years earlier. I had bought all the gear before the trip and the following winter my parents bought me a snowboard. Anthony had been an avid surfer, having grown up in California, so it was no surprise when he was a natural on the snow too.

When our snowboarding trip arrived, it was great fun. We spent a weekend in a huge cabin with the same friends we'd been to Melbourne with, this time with their kids as well. After a fantastic weekend of eating, drinking and playing in the snow, Anthony and I headed up to Thredbo to stay for a few days, just the two of us. We boarded during the day and dined out each night. Our getaway went too quickly but not quickly enough. You see, the night I crashed my car we sat down and made a plan. First, Anthony would move in with me, he would get a job and then we would start saving together. I had poured all of my savings, and then some, into the granny flat and he'd been out of work for so long that he had nothing to contribute.

We agreed that we would save for a few months, go on a little holiday and then, once we had $5k in the bank, we would try to get pregnant again. That's why, as much as I enjoyed our little getaway, I was eager to get home. I was keen to get back to working and saving so that I could top my bank account back up.

It took another month and a half to reach our goal and in early September we both agreed that we were ready to start trying for our little rainbow baby. By then Anthony was spending every weekend in Wollongong, a city an hour and a half south of Sydney. His ex-wife had taken the girls and moved there, to a house that her aunt owned. For the first couple of weeks after the accident she refused to talk to him or allow the girls to so much as speak to him either but in the end the girls were so distressed that she had no choice but to let him back into their lives.

At first it was just a phone call at night but by the time we were ready to start trying for a baby again he was allowed to go down and see them. I didn't begrudge him his opportunity to have his children back but there was no way I was willing to put myself in the path of that woman again, especially not once I was pregnant.

I assumed that it would take several months to conceive. I had circled the key dates on my calendar for ovulation, only to realise that I really needed him there on certain weekends. I would never ask him to miss seeing the kids though so, although it was a bit disheartening, I convinced myself that there was no rush, especially since I was still hoping for a spring baby. The thought of taking a spring and summer off work to hang out with my tiny little baby was always enough to cheer me up again when he was away.

And that's why I wasn't worried about it when we only had one chance to be together that first month of trying. And it's also why, when he joked a couple of weeks later, saying that my boobs were bigger and I must be pregnant, I brushed him off. At first, I thought that surely, he was imagining things but he insisted that I use one of the tests that I'd bought before that fateful car crash.

I obediently went into the bathroom and did one of the tests, checking it after a minute. There was a pang of disappointment when I saw the single pink line staring back at me but I swallowed it. I reminded myself that it wasn't even possible, we'd only had sex on the sixth day of my cycle. I knew enough about biology to know that it would have been far too early, even with my short cycle. I showed him the test before throwing it out.

The next morning was a Friday. It was the October long weekend. My parents were going away with my aunties and uncles. Anthony was heading down a day early to see his girls for three days. I got up at 6 am and headed into my bathroom for a shower like I always did on a work day, only to realise that I had left the box of tests on my vanity the night before. Before I knew what was happening, I had grabbed another test out of the box and dipped it into the first morning wee as instructed.

Imagine my surprise when it immediately showed up as positive. I remembered the test in the bin from the night before. Thankfully I'd thrown it in my bathroom bin rather than the one with food scraps and all manner of other disgusting things in the kitchen. I rifled through the empty toilet rolls and things until I found it. I couldn't believe what I was looking at. It was positive too.

I grabbed the tests and ran back to my bedroom. He was still in bed despite the fact that he was supposed to be leaving less than an hour later. At that moment I didn't have the words to tell him what was happening and so with happy tears streaming down my face I simply showed him the tests. I couldn't wait to see the joy on his face.

There was no joy though. There was no happiness or excitement of any kind.

"The lines aren't dark enough, you're not pregnant". That's what he said. It was confusing. I had read enough about pregnancy tests to know that false positives were almost unheard of. I wasn't taking medications that contained HCG, the pregnancy hormone. I knew that the test from the previous evening shouldn't be relied upon but the one I'd just done was clearly positive. Still, he brushed me off as he got out of bed and headed into the bathroom to take a shower.

"What just happened?" I said out loud to myself. What the hell had just happened? He seemed so happy about the idea the previous evening but all of a sudden, he was disregarding me like I was just some foolish, idiotic girl. I sat on my bed, stunned as I waited for the shower to turn off. When he finally came back into the room ten minutes later, he could not have made it any clearer that, not only did he not believe me, he couldn't have cared less about the pregnancy tests or how that made me feel.

"I thought this was good news." I said, holding the test up to him hopefully.

"Why the hell would you drop a bomb like this when I'm going to see my girls?" he said angrily. "The test isn't even positive, it's too light!" he said again.

"Of course it's positive. There's a second line," I replied desperately. "Can we go and have breakfast to celebrate before you go? Please?" I begged.

"I have three children you idiot! That is not positive and besides, how dare you interfere with my time with my girls. I'm already here with you most of the time when I should be with them." He was practically screaming now and suddenly so full of hate. I recoiled, sitting back on my bed. I hung my head, tears streaming down my face.

It was the first time I had ever asked him to put me first. I didn't expect him to miss out on seeing the girls but I was hoping that we could at least go out for breakfast to celebrate. Just for an hour or so. I didn't have to go into the office since I had a roadshow to finish planning. I had been working late all week and so I wasn't worried about logging on a bit later. I wasn't asking him to choose me over his children. I didn't understand why he had reacted so aggressively.

And then he left without another word, slamming the front door on his way out. I couldn't breathe. I was so confused. We were having a baby together that we had planned and both wanted. I had walked into the bedroom with those tests expecting him to be as excited as I was. Instead, he had treated me like some low-life. I was simply asking for a couple of hours of his time so that we could start planning for our very much wanted and longed-for little baby. I had never felt so insignificant and worthless in my life.

I started to spiral. I had to distract myself before I did something stupid. I knew that I couldn't work in that state and so I decided then and there that if he couldn't be excited about our little baby then I would get excited for both of us. I jumped in the shower and dressed in jeans and a long sleeve top before heading out to my car. I turned the key in the ignition but nothing happened. It took me a couple of attempts to realise what the problem was. Anthony had needed my car the day before. He often borrowed my car when the cheap shit box his mum had sent him money for was playing up. I had lent him the car with half a tank of petrol in it but somehow, he had managed to not only use all of that petrol, he hadn't even bothered to top it back up.

My parents had already gone away. I texted my aunts and my grandparents but none of them were going to be home until the afternoon. I knew that I needed to be somewhere loud and busy straight away. I didn't care that it was pouring rain. I grabbed a jerrycan out of the garage and walked the ten minutes to the nearest petrol station. I filled up the can and then walked back home, my tears destroying my perfect made-up as it mixed with the rain water. In my distressed state I'd forgotten to take an umbrella with me.

By the time I got the petrol into the car, showered again and dressed in dry clothes it was almost 10 am I was sad to think that there was no one I could call. I didn't want my family or friends to hate him. I knew deep down that it would be justified but I needed to try and make things work more than ever now that we were having a baby together. I should have called Bec and Hayley but we hadn't spoken in weeks, not since the morning after I wrecked my car on the side of that cliff.

Anthony had gotten angry about Bec's carefree response when I called the morning after the accident and told her about the crash. When I ended my call with Bec he ranted and raved about her being a selfish bitch, insisting that she didn't care about me. He convinced me that Hayley wouldn't care either so I agreed that there was no point in calling her to tell her what had happened. I found out a few weeks after the accident that my cousins were going away for a few days. Bec and Hayley had never taken a girls' trip without me and so once again, it wasn't hard for Anthony to convince me that they were scheming against me. I was sad to think that they wouldn't care about my exciting news but I was determined to pull myself out of that pit of despair. I needed to do something that made me happy and so instead, I headed for the shops.

Chapter Twenty-Seven

knew that it was far too early to be buying things for my baby but I couldn't help myself. I desperately wanted my own little girl. A little dolly that I could dress up in pink frills and bows. I had a wonderful time buying a sweet little Disney princess baby tutu and a couple of adorable green jumpsuits with turtles on them. And my favourite find of all, a book about a huge blue dinosaur who'd gone on an adventure and gotten lost before being reunited with her mum. I couldn't wait to share my love of books, among other things, with my sweet baby.

The shopping trip made me feel so much better. The rest of the weekend was spent cleaning and rearranging the house and binge watching some of my favourite movies. I almost managed to convince myself that Anthony was happy about the baby. It made no sense that he wouldn't be. We had planned to finally have a baby together. I had taken him into my home, supported him and spoiled his girls. I sent gifts for the girls whenever he went to see them. It didn't matter that he ignored my calls and messages on the Saturday, or that he didn't send his usual message to let me know he'd arrived safely on the Friday. By the time he arrived home on Sunday afternoon I just wanted to ignore the strange feeling in the pit of my stomach and hit reset.

I wanted my little family so desperately. I thought that I needed him to be with me—with us. When he walked in the door, I could see the surprise on his face as the smell of lasagne filled the air. He laughed as he saw me dancing to The Beach Boys, his favourite band. He dropped his bag next to the lounge and joined me. We danced around, laughing as he twirled me around. I didn't pull away when I noticed the smell of perfume on his skin. I swallowed back the tears that threatened. Choosing to ignore that familiar feeling, what choice did I have?

For the next couple of months, I ignored the sick feeling in my stomach. I convinced myself that it was just morning sickness kicking in. The late-night texts and his sudden unwillingness for me to so much as look at his phone. I believed him when he reminded me that he was the only man who had ever loved me, the only man who ever would. He had convinced me that even my family wouldn't want to deal with me. He knew that they had sent me to the US all those years earlier and that I'd felt like a burden to them ever since. He could have done just about anything to me at that point and he knew it. So, he quit his job. He sold his shit-box car and then decided that it was my job to look after him.

Even my thirtieth birthday passed without so much as a card from him. My parents, James and Amy spent the morning cooking me breakfast. The moment I walked into the main house, alone, since Anthony insisted that he would join me after talking to the girls, I was accosted by the smell of bacon and breakfast muffins cooking. It smelled and tasted delicious.

And then there were the presents. If it wasn't for the fairies, cupcakes and flowers on the wrapping paper you would have been excused for believing that Santa had arrived early. There were well over a dozen gifts piled up on the coffee table in the lounge room. I had the most wonderful time unwrapping a pink stand mixer, beautiful toiletries and lots of sweet little baby items. Even a cute stuffed turtle toy. I hugged the little toy, after naming her Maui. I had a wonderful time with my family and was able to ignore Anthony's absence. He had ignored my messages during breakfast, asking him to join us.

Mum, Dad, James and Amy were the only people other than Anthony and I who knew about the baby at that point and so when we arrived at a nearby pub late that afternoon for my big family dinner, they thoroughly enjoyed ordering mocktails for me in secret. The rest of my family had no idea that the pretty drinks with the paper umbrellas contained no alcohol and I suspected that Anthony couldn't have cared less since he spent most of the night with his head stuck in his phone.

When the time came to order our meals, I was so embarrassed when Anthony claimed to have left his wallet at home, that I ended up ordering and paying for not just my own dinner but his as well. I knew that my parents wouldn't have hesitated to pay for our meals but I didn't want them to know that Anthony had all but ignored my birthday. When I got home from dinner, the first thing I did was throw the seven hundred dollar iPhone I'd bought for his upcoming birthday into my bag so that I could return it the following day. I was so hurt by his careless attitude towards such a big milestone that the last thing I felt like doing was spoiling him.

When he realised, as I lay in bed crying silently that night, how upset I was, he blamed the fact that his ex-wife had lived off him for years. He said that he needed a break from spoiling other people. He was sick of working hard and looking after her and the girls financially. The last thing he wanted to do was look after me as well. I didn't want to argue on my birthday and so I told him it was fine. I reminded myself how much everyone else had spoiled me before drifting off to sleep, exhausted from the day's festivities.

I tried to let go of the feeling of disappointment about the way Anthony had ignored my birthday but the next day I noticed that he was once again glued to his phone. When I returned home from returning the iPhone to the Apple Store, I noticed that he was acting even more strangely than he had been the day before. I tried to ignore the strange behaviour. It had been constantly worrying me that he'd quit his job without talking to me. I decided to try and broach the subject as I laid out the delicious Indian food I'd picked up on my way home from the shops.

"Come and grab a plate." I called out from the kitchen. I was hoping that our favourite curries would help lighten the mood as I tried to broach the contentious subject of him getting another job.

"Oh yum. Thanks, baby. What's the special occasion?" Anthony asked as he piled his plate high with a ridiculous amount of food.

"I need to talk to you about the job situation." I admitted, being careful to keep my voice neutral. "Do you think you can get something part time?"

"A part time sales role?" he laughed as he stuffed his face with butter chicken. "You know as well as I do that I can't do a job like that in part time hours."

"Maybe you could get a casual job in an electronics store or something. I asked hopefully. "You could just do a couple of shifts a week maybe?"

"Are you kidding?" Anthony asked, putting his fork on his plate before wiping his mouth. "They'd expect me to work weekends. I'm not giving up my time with my girls."

I could see that he was getting annoyed. I didn't want to make him angry but I was genuinely worried about how I was going to support us once the baby was born if he didn't get a job.

"I want to take a few months off with the baby but I can't do that if I'm supporting us both and paying for your visits with your kids." I was starting to feel hopeless, wondering if I would ever get through to him.

"Don't bring my kids into it!" He slammed his hand down on the kitchen island before standing up. "You've got plenty of money. I'm sick of you nagging me about this shit!" he screamed at me, before picking up his still half-full plate of food and emptying it in the bin.

"I'll get a job if and when I decide to do so." Anthony said before throwing the plate in the sink and storming off.

As I watched him storm out the door and up the side path, I was shocked. I sat there frozen for a minute before I remembered the plate. I walked over to the sink and my heart dropped when I saw that my beautiful Cinderella dinner plate, part of a set that I'd brought back from my first trip to Disneyland, a set that I had kept from all those years ago, had been broken clean in half.

My shock turned to anger then. I was furious. I was already paying for everything whilst trying to save for the baby because he had been unemployed for most of the time we'd been back together. He'd ignored my birthday and I was pretty sure he'd been cheating on me for months, at least since the long weekend in October when he'd so callously walked out after brushing off the news about our baby. I couldn't believe that Anthony would care so little about me despite my constant attempts to make him happy.

When he arrived back a few hours later I could see that he was still annoyed so I gave him a wide berth, claiming that I had work to finish. I glued my plate back together with my dad's help. I had taken the plate into the house, too embarrassed to admit what had happened, thankful that my father could fix just about everything, unlike Anthony who seemed intent on

     Unlovable

breaking everything. By the time he fell asleep on the lounge that night, midway through a movie, he'd barely spoken a dozen words to me all day.

I don't know what came over me but suddenly I grabbed his phone from the coffee table. Anthony had spent every minute that weekend on his phone and I needed to know if my suspicions about him cheating were right.

What I found was utterly repulsive. I had assumed that he was sleeping with his ex-wife but there, in his saved photos were pornographic pictures of the woman he'd dated for almost a year between the ex-wife and me. There were a dozen photos, dated from just before the long weekend, all the way to mid-November, just a few days earlier. He had been talking to her as recently as that day. I felt completely shattered by his betrayal.

I jumped up. The sound of me throwing his belongings into a bag woke him up. He demanded to know what the hell I was doing. But then he saw the look of rage on my face as I explained, far from calmly, what I had seen on his phone. His demeanour changed then, and he began to splutter an explanation. He tried to tell me that she had been sending him messages with those vile pictures of herself for months to try and lure him back, even though she had a new boyfriend. He claimed to have kept the pictures in case he needed them as ammunition. But ammunition against what? I demanded answers but for the first time since I'd known him, he had nothing to say.

I threw his bag outside and pushed him out the door. The last thing I cared about was where he would go so late at night. He could sleep on a park bench for all I cared. I thought back to my birthday the previous day.

My family had all spoiled me rotten. Not only had Anthony not even bothered to buy a two dollar card, he'd sat at lunch, on my thirtieth birthday, devouring the meal I'd had to buy him and messaging some woman who was sending him nudes. I was fed up. The obvious signs that he was cheating had been there for several weeks but when I realised that he really did consider me as his meal-ticket I just lost it. I guess it probably sounds strange, that I had ignored the obvious signs that he was cheating only to lose it over money.

I couldn't fathom anyone living off another person though. I had grown up watching my parents' work nights and weekends to provide for my brother and I. We had a lovely life with lovely things but I had never taken any of it for granted. I was proud of my career. My job was the one thing I'd always excelled at. And I was generous, just like my parents. No one had ever taken my generosity for granted before, until he came back into my life anyway. I had stupidly allowed him to do it before I was pregnant but realising that he didn't want to contribute to our household now that we were having a child, on top of those disgusting photos of that woman he had been cheating on me with for who-knew how long, was the last straw.

I was used to feeling like I wasn't good enough to have a man who actually loved me. A man who cared about me enough not to cheat, or a man who meant it when he told me that he valued me. I was used to boyfriends and their bad behaviour. Those other guys had never taken a cent from me though. In fact, Sam had even been generous. I still had the Tiffany necklace and Chanel sunglasses to prove it.

Kicking Anthony out gave me an instant feeling of power. In a moment of strength and clarity I thought about my mummy turtle and the way I felt that night as I watched in wonder as she laid her eggs. I knew that I could raise my baby alone. I was surrounded by my parents, brother and sister in-law and some amazing women that I felt honoured to call friends. I was sure that my cousins would start talking to me properly again when they learned that I had kicked him out. My baby wouldn't even miss that jerk because they would have everyone, including so many cousins and other little friends to play with when they arrived. The day I kicked him out I was almost twelve weeks along. I was supposed to be doing a pregnancy announcement on my social media accounts the following weekend, after I'd had my first scan. I had it all planned out with the intention of using the green turtle onesie I'd purchased the day I found out that I was pregnant. My mummy turtle had become something of a totem since finding out that I was pregnant again.

But the thought of doing the scan without him was heartbreaking too. As the day of the scan got closer, I started to regret my decision to kick him out. After all, his story about that woman wasn't entirely ridiculous and I was sure that I could convince him to at least do some cash in hand work. Even just at my uncle's car showroom. I knew they'd give him a job if I asked. That's what I told myself anyway. Going to the scan without him was too scary and so I was relieved when he agreed to go along with me.

We met outside the private hospital where I had booked the appointment excitedly the week after finding out about my little peanut, as I had started affectionately calling my baby. As soon as I saw him, I knew that he had as much of a terrible week as me. He looked like he hadn't eaten or slept in a year. Even the flowers he held out to me looked sad. He admitted that he hadn't attended the first scan for any of his other three children. Apparently, he wanted to be better for our baby. I saw the gentle side to him that I had been pulled in by so many times in the past. I ignored the familiar voice, the voice that told me to flee. I swallowed my doubts as he grabbed my hand and led me through the front doors and up to the maternity clinic.

All the doubts I had about Anthony disappeared when we saw our baby for the first time. The funny little arms and legs jumped around as our baby peanut bounced around my tummy with a case of the hiccups. I saw his eyes well up as he was overcome with emotion. I had seen the same look on his face many times before when he looked at his daughters and I knew that he too had fallen in love with our baby, just as I had done the morning that I first found out about my pregnancy.

Once the scan was finished, we headed to the hospital cafeteria for lunch. I was impressed when he ordered and then paid for our meals. He apologised for quitting his job and he apologised for the photos. He swore on his children's lives that he had not been with that woman in the pornographic pictures since a few weeks before we got back together. I needed so desperately to believe him. So, I did the dumbest thing possible. I believed him.

I know, I should have made him sweat but I wanted my little baby to have a daddy. He may not have been a perfect partner. I wasn't stupid. I knew that he wasn't shaping up to be the wonderful and loving partner that I had so desperately and gullibly believed that he was going to be. He was, however, a good dad. I had seen him with his girls enough to know that he loved his children and would always choose them.

He moved back into my granny-flat the very next day. My parents were worried sick. They had only seen a portion of the bad behaviour for themselves but they knew enough to try and convince me to cut him from my life once and for all.

"Magnolia." My dad said at dinner one night when Anthony was out with his mates doing god-knows what. "Your mum and I are really worried about you."

"Why? What about?" I asked, feeling genuinely confused. It had been a great day at work and Anthony had been in a good mood when I got home before borrowing $100 for his night out.

"Because we're watching you let this guy walk all over you." Mum chimed in, "He refuses to get a job. How are you supposed to support the baby when he constantly sits around expecting to be spoiled and treated like a bloody king?"

"He's just got a lot to deal with because of that idiot woman." I reassured them. "And he has promised to get a job after Christmas and start contributing financially."

I saw the look that my parents exchanged but chose to ignore it. Christmas was coming up. I had too much work to finish. I had to get the house ready and finish my gift shopping because, not only were we back together and back on track, we were getting his girls for a few days between Christmas and New Year's Eve. Anthony had told his ex-wife in no uncertain terms that he was going to be bringing them to my place. By some miracle she agreed. She had apparently started dating someone a couple of months earlier and had been a lot more agreeable ever since. I found it unnerving at first, expecting the threatening messages to start again. But she remained eerily silent.

I was excited at the prospect of having the girls for a few days. The eldest girl, Bronwyn, was eight. She was a quiet and reserved child. I had found it difficult to get through to her at first but eventually she seemed to come around. Then there was Michelle who was five.

Michelle was the same height as Bronwyn but personality-wise, they were polar opposites.

Michelle was outgoing and boisterous; she was the main one who'd been parroting her mother and constantly making nasty comments about my appearance when I first met her. I was a bit anxious about seeing her, but I was hoping that things would be different now that her mother had a new man to obsess over.

And then there was Lilly, the baby. I had no trouble admitting, at least to my parents, that she was my favourite. She was far too little to understand that she was supposed to hate me. Lilly was only sixteen months old when her father and I got together. She was cheeky, clever, brave and she was just about the cutest thing I had ever laid eyes on. I couldn't wait to look after her and her sisters for a few days.

And I couldn't wait to spoil them for Christmas. Amy and I had a wonderful time shopping, choosing the perfect gifts for each of the girls. I took great pleasure in wrapping them and placing them under the tree, much to Anthony's amusement. I knew that he was a massive grinch, I'd learned that the hard way back in the US all those years earlier but I assumed that having kids would have changed that.

Unfortunately, Christmas morning brought with it the same disappointment as my birthday just a few weeks earlier. There wasn't so much as a card with my name on it from him. I had taken him shopping to buy him some nice surf brand clothes. I had spent a few hundred dollars on him, and once again he couldn't even be bothered buying me a one dollar card!

I was actually relieved that afternoon when the old crazy-pants ex-wife rang to tell him that she was going away the following day. Some friend of hers had a cabin on the water down in Kiama, a short drive south of where she and the kids lived in Wollongong. The friend had just called and invited her and the girls to stay there for a week. I wasn't surprised to hear that she was taking the kids instead of letting Anthony have them like she was supposed to.

As horrible as it sounds, I wasn't just relieved, I was happy to learn that the girls were not coming to stay with us after all. I was so hurt about him not buying me anything for Christmas that the last thing I felt like doing over the holidays was to look after them all. Of course he was devastated. He had planned every day out carefully. The gifts that I had so carefully chosen, bought and then wrapped were still sitting under the tree, along with gifts that my family had brought over for the girls, thinking that they were finally going to get the chance to meet them.

As annoyed as I was with him though, I also felt sorry for him. I couldn't imagine ever having to miss out on seeing my baby on Christmas morning. It was one of the things I was most looking forward to, spoiling my own sweet little peanut. I couldn't imagine not being there to share in all the fun and excitement. There was only one solution in my mind. I told Anthony to call her back and ask if he could come down and spend the week with them.

He'd been off the phone for less than half an hour when I waved him off, in my car, to go and spend the next week with his ex-wife and children. The gifts were piled up carefully on my back seat. The new plan was that he would spend the week down the coast and then he would bring the girls up to stay with us for a few days. The original gift tags on those gifts, with both of our names written carefully in pink pen, were replaced by tags with just his name on them.

It made me sad at first but I knew he had to do it. The woman may have stopped the calls and texts but I knew that she still hated me. If she knew that the sweet little Minnie Mouse towels, plush toys and dresses were bought by me then she would have thrown them out. I wanted the girls to be allowed to enjoy their Christmas presents and not have to deal with the wrath of their mother. The gifts from my family were left under the tree though, I wasn't willing to let him put his name on those.

I spent that week catching up with my friends and family. Not having a car wasn't ideal but since most people knew about my pregnancy by then, they were all happy to come to me, or act as my taxi service. I desperately wanted to go and spend time with Bec and Hayley but I knew that there was no point while I was with Anthony, even if he was a couple of hundred kilometres away, it didn't change the fact that he was still in my life. I wasn't strong enough to deal with the way they all felt about each other and so I kept my distance. Anthony even called me every day while he was away and strangely enough the distance seemed to bring us closer together. For the first time ever, I felt like he truly appreciated me. For the first time ever, I was the one with the power. It was intoxicating.

The girls were over the moon at the sight of their dad weighed down with gifts. I believed him when he told me that he spent the week sleeping in the spare bedroom with his children. I even believed him when he told me that he had yet another serious discussion with his ex-wife on the first night. As it turned out, she had split up with her new boyfriend because she wasn't ready to give up on her and Anthony getting back together. Anthony told her that it was never going to happen, that the time had come for her to move on once and for all. He didn't tell her about our baby though. Anthony not only refused to tell his ex-wife about the fact that I was pregnant with his child, even though my tummy was starting to become more and more obvious by the day, he refused to tell his children as well. Hiding my pregnancy from them all was easy enough from a distance but trying to do so when he arrived home with the girls was going to be a different story.

From the time they arrived at my place I tried to hide my bump from them with loose tops and kaftans but it was nearly forty degrees in the shade. On the second day we went swimming at my grandparents' place. I was cooking dinner that night when I overheard Michelle tell her mother over the phone that my tummy was fat and had a baby in it.

I couldn't make out the words on the other end of the phone but I knew that she was furious, I could hear her rage as she screamed down the phone. I caught Anthony's eye as he took the phone from his daughter and walked out into the garden. I was relieved when he walked back into the house a couple of minutes later and broke the silence.

In a stern voice he told his children that telling their mother lies about me was not nice. He told them that not only was I not pregnant but I had gotten fat and that it wasn't nice to make rude comments about it. I wanted to scream out and tell them that yes, I was pregnant with their baby brother or sister. I wanted to ask him why I had to hide something so special. Our baby was not some dirty little secret but of course I kept my mouth shut. I knew that not doing so could be dangerous. I didn't want to think about what that woman would do if she knew the truth.

Chapter Twenty-Eight

had no idea at the time if the girls' mother believed whatever he told her that night. I made a point of being elsewhere when the kids spoke with her from then on. And I made a point of wearing my baggy clothes again. At almost nineteen weeks I was very obviously pregnant. I was so proud of my belly and my new 'Pammy' boobs, I had bought all sorts of lovely form fitting maternity outfits. I knew that it was only a few days though, so to keep the peace I left all my lovely new clothes in my wardrobe.

The few days of the girls' visit went by quickly enough. On the last day it was James's birthday. Amy had booked tables for our immediate family at a Greek restaurant over in the coastal suburb of Cronulla that they loved. When I tasted the food, I understood why. It was delicious and plentiful. Anthony's girls had a wonderful time playing with my nephew Joshua while the adults caught up on all the latest news and family gossip. Well, all but my own.

Despite not being able to talk about my upcoming twenty-week scan, I swallowed my disappointment and instead focussed on everyone else's excitement about holidays and job promotions. Lunch came to an end far too quickly. Anthony was determined to cram a few more memories in before his children went home and so we found ourselves headed for the beach once I had paid our share of the bill. We were parked right in front of the beach so the towels, buckets and spades had been left in the car until we needed them.

It only took a few minutes to reach the car. I had packed each of the girls a bag with their new towels, hats and snacks and then my beach bag with the sunscreen and a throw rug to sit on while they all swam. It only took a minute to grab all the bags but as we started to walk down towards the ocean pool, I remembered that my sunglasses were in the front middle console of the car. I didn't think twice when Michelle walked back to the car with me. We had gotten along beautifully for the past few days so I could never have anticipated what happened next. As soon as we were out of her father's sight, she turned towards me and then punched me as hard as she could, in the stomach.

The scream that escaped my lungs was involuntary. The pain that ripped through my body may have only lasted a few seconds but it was intense. By the time Anthony reached us, with Lilly in his arms and Bronwyn close on his heels, I was hysterical. I couldn't believe that a young child could do something so shocking and nasty. Anthony demanded to know why she would do such a thing. I guess I really shouldn't have been shocked when she burst into tears and denied what she had just done altogether.

Michelle cried hysterically, insisting that she had just been trying to feel my baby. She was doing no such thing, and he knew it but he decided that there must surely have been a misunderstanding so instead of checking to see if I was okay, he picked her up and wiped away her tears. I wanted to leave the bloody lot of them there. I wanted to get in my car and never see that child or her father again. If it was just the three of us there at that moment, I probably would have done it too. But it wasn't just us.

Bronwyn and Lilly didn't deserve to be punished for what their sister had done and so with reassurance that I was fine, just in case anyone actually cared, we headed towards the beach as planned. The next couple of hours passed in a blur. I ended up in the water when Lilly refused to go to her father, instead running up the sand and pulling my hand until I had no choice but to follow her.

The water was freezing compared with my lovely spot on the rug but it took my mind off what Michelle had done, if just for a while. By the time everyone was dried and strapped into the car it was nearly 5 pm. I knew that the girls would be a complete mess if they had to wait for dinner to be sorted out when we got home. We saw the sign for Maccas just as we were driving past the airport, so we decided on a whim to grab dinner at the drive-.

Twenty minutes later we were back in my kitchen, I was left to get the girls fed while he showered. I shouldn't have sat down but I was exhausted. I figured that we would swap when he was done with his shower, since I was still in my wet swimmers but as the minutes passed there was no sign of him. I asked the older girls to put a show on for Lilly before dragging myself off to find him. And there he was, sleeping-bloody-beauty, passed out in bed.

I couldn't believe my eyes. I marched right over and shook him, reminding him that he had three children to get ready for bed. He wasn't having a bar of it though, claiming to be too tired from his long day. I tried again but to no avail. I had always hated waking people when they were sleeping so instead of tearing the sheets off him and pushing him out of my bed like I should have, I obediently walked out and back into the kitchen to clean up the mess from dinner. The girls were, thankfully, excited about helping to lay their pyjamas out and taking turns in my pretty bathroom with the princess chandelier and the big, fluffy pink towels that I had bought especially for their visit.

I ran the shower and sent Bronwyn in first. One down, two to go I thought to myself but then Michelle reminded me that she and Lilly needed their hair washed. The last thing I wanted to be doing was, well, anything for that girl. No matter how much I tried to ignore her punching me in the stomach a few hours earlier I just couldn't. I knew she had told her mother that I was pregnant because it really was so obvious. I knew that there was so much evil coursing through that woman's veins that she wouldn't hesitate to tell her young daughter to punch a pregnant woman in the stomach. I was just so thankful that unlike the last time, her evil hadn't harmed my baby. This time her plan hadn't worked. I was relieved to feel the usual number of kicks and punches as the baby rolled around, blissfully unaware of what had happened earlier that day.

But I knew that no matter how angry and disgusted I was by Michelle's behaviour, I couldn't just leave her with dirty salty hair and so, still dressed in my swimmers, I hopped into the shower with her, washed her hair and then left her to finish washing herself. By the time the girls were all bathed and ready for bed it was after 7 pm and I was cold, uncomfortable and hungry. I hadn't ordered myself any food earlier because I was going to have leftover pasta for dinner but I realised while cleaning up the girls' mess that Anthony hadn't had a chance to eat his burger.

I popped it in the microwave for a minute to make sure it was safe for me to eat before devouring the whole thing in a few bites. I could see that the girls were engrossed in their movie, so I decided to finally go and wash my hair and get dressed. By the time I was finished in the bathroom I was surprised to see that he was no longer in my bed.

I walked out to the kitchen to find him banging containers in the fridge. When he told me that he was looking for his burger I took great pleasure in telling him that I'd eaten it. He was furious. He demanded to know why I hadn't left his dinner. The dinner that I had paid for mind you. I lost it. I knew that he was going to blame my pregnancy hormones but I didn't care, I was fed up and exhausted.

From the moment he arrived home with his children I had been running myself ragged trying to look after all of them.

The whole bloody lot of them, with the exception of little Lilly, had trashed my house. They had bossed me around and made me feel like a servant in my own home. And the thanks I got was his kid punching me in the stomach. I'd had enough. I looked up at my mummy turtle and I knew what I needed to do.

I told him to buy his own fucking dinner if he didn't like it, before turning on my heels and storming off with the bag of Maltesers I'd been saving to share with the girls that night.

When I closed my bedroom door a moment later, I felt free. I don't know what came over me but as soon as I was alone the strangest thing happened. I started to laugh. I laughed like a mad woman at the sheer ridiculousness of it all. I switched the TV on and found a movie about unrequited love. It was a movie that he hated which at that moment made it my favourite thing in the world.

While the movie played in the background I started to plan my escape. I was terrified of being alone but I knew that I had no other choice, I knew that staying with him was just too dangerous. I knew that I would miss the girls but they were no longer my concern, even little Lilly. I had loved every moment I'd spent with Anthony's youngest child in particular.

As if she knew that I needed her right then, there was a faint knock at the door. I opened it to find the sweet little two-year-old on the other side. She told me that her daddy had told her to come and see if I was okay. It was just the kind of cowardly shit that I'd come to expect from him but I didn't care.

I couldn't think of a better way to spend my last night with her. As she hopped onto my bed, asking if we could watch her favourite princess movie, it occurred to me, again, that I would probably never see her again.

I wiped my tears away as my little mate wrapped her arms around my neck. I hated the fact that my baby wasn't going to know their sisters, it wasn't the way I had planned it. as I pulled away to look at her sweet little face, framed by her jet-black curls, she reached over and kissed my belly before whispering

'I love you baby.'

Chapter Twenty-Nine

Anthony and the girls drove off the next morning after breakfast with my parents. The breakfast had been planned before the visit even started so as much as I wanted to barricade myself in my bedroom until my house was once again empty, I did what I had been doing for most of my life. I glued a smile on my face and pretended that everything was fine. But for the first time in my life, my smile wasn't there for the sake of that man. I wasn't keeping the peace in the hope that he would love me, or that he would stay.

My smile was hiding a secret. Anthony had popped his head into my bedroom the night before, shortly after Lilly fell asleep. As if everything was fine, he wanted to know if he could come to bed. I looked at him with new eyes as he stood in my doorway and then I did something that was long overdue. I told him to go and sleep in the spare room. The look on his face was priceless. I was sure he knew that the game was up.

I sat there in my bed, with the sweet raven-haired toddler sleeping peacefully next to me and thought about my relationship with her father. I had always seen him as that tall, muscular and tanned guy with the dark hair and the sexy American accent. I'd been so desperate for his love and acceptance that somehow, I'd missed what was right in front of me.

The gorgeous guy had transformed into a pudgy, bald loser. Anthony had been in Australia for so long that his sexy accent had been replaced by a weird mish-mash of Aussie and Californian. The only thing about him that hadn't changed was his ego. He was so full of himself despite the fact that he had nothing to offer.

All of those thoughts occurred to me as I sat there eating breakfast that morning. I sat in my parents' kitchen chatting, smiling and planning my escape. I saw the smug look on his face as he sat there eating and joking with everyone. He had no idea what was coming.

As I bundled the girls into my car after breakfast, I hugged each of them with all my might, even Michelle. I knew that Anthony's middle daughter wasn't a bad kid. I had witnessed her with her sisters often enough to know that she was full of love and empathy for them, just as she had been with little Joshua and any animal she came in contact with. It made me sad to think that her mother had coached her to hate me so much. I just hoped that one day she would grow up and understand how destructive that hatred could be.

As I waved them all off for the last time I faltered, wondering if there was a way to make things better but I knew I needed to be strong. I wiped the tears from my eyes and walked back down the path and into my lounge room. I looked up at my mummy turtle, knowing that I would need her strength and courage for what I was planning to do next.

Once I finished cleaning up the mess that Anthony and the girls had left in the kitchen and the spare room, I headed for my bedroom to get changed into one of my lovely, figure-hugging maternity dresses. Once I was ready, I grabbed Anthony's rucksack from the bottom of my wardrobe. As I threw the rucksack and all of his belongings onto my freshly made bed, I realised for the first time that he'd never really moved in with me. His clothes, shoes and a couple of photographs of his daughters were the only things he'd brought with him when he moved in with me, it all fit easily into the bag.

Before the disastrous week with his kids, I knew that the realisation would have devastated me but Instead I just shrugged. I carefully placed the bag down the side of my bed, smoothed my dress and headed for the door.

Anthony was driving the girls all the way back down to Wollongong. I knew that he would be gone for several hours. Dad was working that day so Mum and I had decided to take the opportunity to spend the day together. Our plan was to go out for a shopping, lunch and movie date. As it turned out, our outing was just the distraction I needed to take my mind off what I was planning to do later that day

Somehow, I managed to appear calm while we ate lunch a few hours later, at least on the outside. Mum had no idea about Michelle punching me or indeed what I was planning to do when Anthony returned that evening. I made a point of steering the conversation away from him and the girls whenever she mentioned them, instead talking about my upcoming baby shower, or the idea I'd had the night before. I was planning to ask my parents, James and Amy about going back to Maui together with the babies the following year. I loved the idea of taking my baby back to that stunning beach. Mum loved the idea of taking another family holiday to Hawaii, just as I knew she would.

The romantic comedy we watched was not the welcome distraction that I had hoped it would be though. As I sat in the dark cinema, I couldn't help but get swept up in the epic love story playing out in front of us. I couldn't help but think about everything that had happened over the years, and over the past year in particular. I thought about not just the bad things but the good things too. Like the lovely weekends away, the intimate dinners we often shared and the frequency of his declarations of love.

By the time the movie finished, I had decided that I was going to try and talk to Anthony instead of throwing him out as I had planned. After all, what kind of mother would I be if I denied my child their father?

I managed to convince myself that if I could just explain my growing frustration about him not pulling his weight financially and that surely, he would finally get another job. The money that I'd started putting away before getting pregnant was almost all gone. I had kept my mouth shut while he spent the money on his cigarettes and pot. I'd smiled along while he took credit for every gift I'd bought his daughters. I had even considered getting a second job to help re-save the money, to ensure that

I could still take a year's maternity leave but then pulled out when he complained about me working too much already.

Money wasn't the only thing that I was determined to figure out though. Sitting in bed the previous evening with just a sleeping Lilly for company once again reminded me of just how much I missed Hayley and Bec.

I had alienated my cousins, my lifelong best friends, because I hated how much they hated him. The girls had never forgiven him for the things he had done when I lived in America. The cheating, the gaslighting that made me believe everything he did was my fault. To be honest, hate was probably too mild a word. To say that Bec and Hailey despised him and his presence in my life was not at all an exaggeration.

I had believed so completely that Anthony was the only man who'd have me despite my disgusting secret, that I'd let him drive a huge wedge between us. Hayley and Bec didn't know that I was a fundamentally damaged and unlovable woman. They only knew the kind, fun and generous cousin who they seemed to think could do better. I wasn't ready to share my terrible secret with the girls but somehow, I was determined to try and reconnect and try to mend our relationship. I knew that it would be hard but I was determined to get to a place where we could all spend time together. I knew that Anthony took great pleasure in the breakdown of my relationship with my cousins but I was sure that if he would just agree to spend time with them, he would surely see what great people they were.

By the time the credits rolled I'd decided that I couldn't do it. By the time we pulled up in our driveway, next to my own car, I was sure that I could somehow still make things work. Surely, if I was just nicer, more tolerant and understanding things would finally be okay?

As I bade Mum farewell and headed down the back path that led to my granny flat, I hoped that Anthony hadn't been back long enough to notice his packed bag next to my bed. I knew that he was likely to have fallen asleep on my lounge watching TV after he got back from the long drive down south. As I turned my key in the door, I knew that my resolve to rescue myself was completely gone. Just like so many times before, I swallowed the feeling of regret because I believed that I simply wasn't strong enough to do it. I was so sure that I needed him. I would just have to figure out the rest later.

Chapter Thirty

I opened my front door and took a step inside. I was barely over the threshold when the smell hit me. I hadn't smoked weed since I was a teenager, since those nightmare years when my life was spiralling out of control. I hated the fact that he smoked it but he had always respected my wishes and kept it away from my home, or so I thought. The first thing I did when I walked into the house was run to the bathroom and vomit.

The whole house stunk. Anthony must have thought the smell would be gone by the time I arrived home. Or maybe he'd reached a point where he no longer gave a shit about pretending that he cared about me and our unborn baby. I opened the bottom cabinet to try and find some air freshener but the first thing I saw was a ceramic bong sitting on the bottom shelf.

Seeing that bong in my bathroom was the straw that broke the camel's back. I couldn't believe I'd spent the day, once again, justifying his shitty behaviour. I may not have been any good at standing up for myself but there was no way he was going to do another thing to put my little baby in harm's way.

I grabbed the bong and walked out of the bathroom as calmly as I could. As soon as he saw what I was holding he went white. I demanded to know why he would do something so disrespectful. The fucking coward actually looked kind of terrified but kept his mouth shut. I wanted to smack him with it but instead I walked to my bedroom. I calmly grabbed the rucksack from beside my bed. When I felt how light the bag was, it once again occurred to me how little he'd brought with him.

Anthony had never really moved in with me. I really was just his meal ticket while he took a break from his real family. I finally understood that he had never cared about me. It had all been some big, sick, orchestrated joke. Getting back with the stupid Aussie girl who believed that maybe, just maybe, someone could actually love her.

But it wasn't just me anymore. It was my baby. As if to encourage me, my little peanut gave a hard kick as I loaded the dirty washing I'd forgotten about earlier into his bag. I walked calmly out to the lounge room where he was watching the news like he didn't have a care in the world. I looked at the painting of my beautiful turtle on the wall behind him and took a deep breath before speaking.

"Get out." The words were automatic; it was like I was possessed. It was my first real Mumma bear moment, I guess. "I'm done". I said. I wasn't going to let him, or his ridiculous life hurt my baby the way I'd let it hurt me for so long.

Anthony always had to have the last word and that evening was no different. As we walked out the front to the driveway, he turned to face me.

"It's your own fault.' He laughed. "You're not willing to give me enough sex because you're always working. She'll do whatever I want. She'll do anything to have me so I gave her what she wanted." He muttered something else after that but I didn't hear it. I was so angry that I thought surely my head would explode.

In a way I suppose it did because before I knew what was happening, I saw the bong flying towards him. It hit him in the back of the head before falling and smashing on my driveway. He turned angrily and took a step toward me before the sound of my dad's voice stopped him in his tracks.

"Don't even think about it!." he shouted, rushing to my side. I had seen him pull up on the street outside the house a matter of seconds earlier but Anthony had not.

Chapter Thirty-One

The sight of my dad was more than that fat, bald loser could cope with. He scurried off like the rodent he was. As soon as my dad asked what was going on I lost it. I told him about the pot, about how Michelle had punched me in the stomach and about her crazy mother. By the time I got to the part about the death threats a few months earlier Mum had raced out the front to see what all the commotion was about.

"Where is he? I'm going to kill him!" Mum screamed, racing down to the street. I watched on as she frantically searched for Anthony. I had never seen my quiet, poised mother look so angry. For the first time in my life, I saw something ferocious in her. He was long gone though, luckily for him. I can only imagine what she would have done to him in that moment had she found him.

Once Dad calmed us both down, we walked into the main house and sat down to talk. As I told my parents about everything that had happened since Valentine's Day the previous year, I realised just how crazy it all sounded.

The whole thing sounded like the plot of some unbelievable movie. It was ridiculous. I had been living a nightmare. It wasn't just the toxic and dangerous situation that I had allowed myself to get mixed up in with Anthony and his deranged ex-wife. I had allowed them and so many other people to treat me like I was a worthless piece of garbage. Telling my parents finally gave me the courage to put a stop to it once and for all. I knew that I owed it to my baby to stop accepting less than what I wanted for them.

I wasn't ready to tell my parents about everything else, about the old man from all those years earlier. About the way he made me feel worthless and about the fact that I still believed the horrible things he'd said to me. That I was disgusting and a low-life. I didn't want them to worry any more than they already were at that moment and besides, I believed that they were the only people in the world who had ever truly loved me, I didn't want to risk them knowing the truth about me. I couldn't handle any more heartbreak so once again I kept it to myself.

I just wanted to think about my upcoming twenty-week scan. I had been counting the weeks until I could finally find out the sex of my baby. I knew that focussing on my scan, and then my baby shower a few weeks later, would help keep me strong as I waited to meet my baby.

I hadn't had time to think much about my baby shower over the previous week. Looking after Anthony and his children had been all-encompassing. As I thought about the amount of work I had in front of me to organise things, I tried not to think about the fact that there would be twenty-odd men attending the party with their wives and girlfriends but no longer my baby's own father. I knew that there would be an avalanche of grief and sadness to deal with about the whole big mess but first I needed to put a smile on my face and get on with things, just as I'd done so many times before.

I asked my parents if they would mind helping me get everything done for my baby shower and of course they said yes, they would love to help. I didn't want to hear what came next, that my parents wanted to take me to the police station to report the assault and the death threats. If it was just me, I would have refused but it wasn't just about me. I knew that the woman was very likely to continue her scary antics now that she knew I was having Anthony's baby. That woman was determined to destroy me and I knew that going to the police was the only hope I had of stopping her and protecting my child. I knew it was long overdue.

When we arrived at the police station an hour later, I was terrified. The thought of having to face that demented woman was almost more than I could cope with. I stopped at the door, convinced that I wasn't brave enough to confront the issue. My mum must have seen the look on my face because she hugged me then. As she pulled away a moment later, I saw the worry in her eyes. And then my dad grabbed my hand and squeezed it.

Knowing I had my parents' support gave me the courage to walk in the door and over to the desk. The constable behind the desk listened as I explained everything that had happened over the past year. I told him about the names, the nasty messages, the five-year-old who'd been coached to hate me so much that she'd punched me in the stomach and then I told him about the death threats. As he looked through the messages, I noticed for the first time how attractive he was. I wondered if he was a good partner for someone. I hoped so. His reaction to the messages certainly suggested that he was a good guy.

I could tell that he was absolutely appalled. He asked me a number of questions to try and figure out what could possibly have motivated such craziness from the woman that she could threaten to shoot me and then coach her young daughter to assault me.

"What have you said when you've come face-to-face with her?" he asked gently

"I've never actually met her." I said.

"Sorry, what do you mean?" I could see the confusion on his face. "You've never met this female?"

"Nope. She only knows what she's heard from him and the kids." I explained. "I just found out an hour or so ago that he's been cheating on me with her. They were apart for a year when he and I got together. I'm not a homewrecker." My voice cracked but I was determined not to cry.

"Oh man." He looked shocked as he spoke. "I'm so sorry. No one should have to deal with this."

"Thank you, I'm sorry for this." I apologised, his empathy made me feel silly for making a fuss.

"No. You're not the one who needs to apologise." he said sternly. "I'm going to get someone from her area command to have a very stern conversation with her. She is going to be cautioned. If she messages you again, she will be arrested."

"Oh dear." I faltered.

"Yes. Thank you." my dad said. He had walked over from the bench seat where he and Mum had sat down when we walked in. His hand on my shoulder reminded me that I didn't have to do it alone.

As we were wrapping up the attractive constable asked me to speak with one of his colleagues. I agreed, assuming that they would want to ask more questions. I just wanted to leave but when I saw the worry on my parents faces, I decided to stay and wait for the other officer. A couple of minutes later a pretty blonde woman who looked about thirty, the same age as me, walked over to the desk. The woman introduced herself as a victim liaison officer by the name of Wendy. Wendy explained, ever so gently, that there were a number of resources available to me as a victim of domestic violence. I tried to object, once again feeling silly for making such a fuss but she placed her hand over mine.

Wendy agreed with my parents and the other officer, telling me that what I had been dealing with was a clear-cut and dry case of abuse. Not only from the father of my baby but also from his ex-wife. I reached for my stomach instinctively, as if I needed to try and protect my baby from it all. I agreed to take the brochures. Wendy squeezed my arm and said the strangest thing.

"Your baby is lucky to have such a strong mum."

I squeezed her hand back. She had no idea how much I needed to hear that from a stranger. She wasn't just any stranger on the street though, she was a woman who saw the shittiest things every day. She dealt with battered women, real victims, and yet there she was telling me that she thought I was brave.

"Thank you. I don't want to take you away from helping people who really need it. Women who really need it." I said, not wanting to make a bigger deal of it.

"Please go and talk to someone about what you've been dealing with. For your sake and for that little one." she said, gesturing towards my belly.

"I will. Thank you again." And with that I grabbed the brochures and held my hands out towards my parents. The three of us walked out to the street and headed in the direction of our favourite Mexican restaurant.

I was still on a high from Wendy's comment twenty minutes later when we sat down for dinner. I knew that my high wouldn't last though. I didn't need my parents to tell me that my mental health had taken an absolute battering from the whole fucked up ordeal.

That's why I agreed when my parents insisted that Wendy was right, I needed to go and talk to somebody about what had been happening. I knew that it wasn't just recent events that I needed to finally talk to somebody about. I had been thinking more and more about that dirty old man since things started to fall apart with Anthony, months earlier, on the weekend that I first learned about my precious baby.

I knew that I needed to face what had happened to me as a fourteen-year-old girl. I needed to get to the bottom of it, once and for all, in the hope that I could finally heal and make better decisions for my future. I needed help in making plans for our future.

I couldn't imagine a time where I would ever want to date again. I knew that my mum had gotten lucky when I was just a baby. She went to that dinner party having no idea of what was about to happen. She really did find her happily ever after when she met dad so maybe there was hope for me yet. I had more important things to think about though. Once we made a plan for me to start the search for a counsellor, I not so subtly moved the conversation back to my scan and baby shower preparations.

The next few weeks ended up being so much fun. My parents both chipped in to help prepare things for my baby shower, as did James and Amy. By the Wednesday beforehand it was all hands-on deck in my kitchen and lounge room. The ladies and Joshua spent the next three days helping me. We baked buttered and iced what felt like several kilograms of cakes, cookies and sandwiches while Dad and James had a wonderful time making posters and goodie bags. The pastel green goodie bags contained the squeaky turtle toys and lays I'd purchased for the Maui themed party that Anthony had agreed to let me throw originally, much to his annoyance since he had wanted a car themed party for some strange reason. All I had left to do for the bags was to ice and decorate the cookies.

As I iced over one hundred and thirty turtle shaped cookies on the Thursday and Friday, I thought about how much I missed my cousins. I couldn't believe that they weren't there helping me prepare things. In a previous life they would have been there without question. Hayley would have been making the sandwiches and cupcakes with mum and Amy, while Bec helped me decorate the cookies.

They had both messaged before Christmas and asked if they could help with planning my baby shower. I knew that it was their way of trying to extend the olive branch and I was so excited at the thought but of course Anthony wouldn't have a bar of it. He shut the suggestion down straight away, much to my disappointment. He stopped short at telling me I couldn't invite them though so at the time I backed down and tried to at least organise everything the way I wanted it. I was looking forward to seeing them at the party.

In a way I was also relieved originally to know that my family were not going to help me plan my baby shower. I was worried that by letting any of the cherished women in my life help me with the planning and preparation, I may become vulnerable and tell them about the horrible relationship I had found myself in yet again. I didn't want to admit to anyone, including myself, just how miserable I'd let him make my life. Now that he was finally gone, I desperately wanted to fix my relationship with my cousins. It was a scary thought though because I really wasn't quite sure how to go about it.

I waited until everyone had left on the Friday night before pulling out the tub of pink fondant bows, I'd made several days earlier. I sat in front of the TV, attaching the bows to the cookies before putting them in cellophane packets and adding two into each of the goodie bags, putting the rest back into the cake box they'd been stored in. I couldn't wait to finally share with the world that I was having the little girl I'd waited so long to meet.

Chapter Thirty-Two

I hadn't told many people about Anthony and I splitting up before the day of the shower but the few people who did know, including Hayley and Bec, rallied around me and made sure that I had a wonderful day. And everybody else did too. We played games in the garden while everyone enjoyed the beautiful late February weather. We ate far too much food while everyone toasted my baby with cocktails, or in my case, mocktails. Even the children had a wonderful time sipping drinks that contained flamingo stirrers and colourful little umbrellas.

Those of us who had attended Bec and Damian's wedding reminisced about what a wonderful holiday we'd had as everyone enjoyed the Maui theme of my shower. It was so strange but wonderful to be there, in my parent's home with my whole family together again after months of awkwardness and division. I knew that there was still work to be done on mending my relationship with my cousins but for the first time since February the previous year, I felt hopeful that things were going to be okay.

By the time the party was coming to an end I realised that not a single person had missed him. I knew that my immediate family weren't massive fans of him, that fact was certainly no secret but I hadn't realised quite how much the rest of my family, as well as my friends, had also disliked him. Everyone had seen through his nice guy act except for me. The realisation didn't make me sad. Quite the opposite. It made me more determined than ever to build a new life without him.

Once everyone had left, I realised how sore my feet were. I had been standing for most of the day so when I tried to help clean up Mum insisted that Amy and I get the gifts ready to open instead. Once the kitchen was cleaned up and the rubbish taken out Mum, Dad and James joined Amy, Joshua and I in the lounge room with an assortment of leftovers to share while my nephew helped me open my gifts.

Joshua and I had a wonderful time unwrapping all of my lovely gifts and eating leftovers. To say that I had been spoiled would be a gross understatement. I was glad that I had only bought a few items of clothing for my little girl. There were beautiful little unisex onesies decorated with ducks, turtles and penguins. There were toy bunnies, teddy bears and several gift vouchers. A couple of people had blankets custom-made and even a couple of my friends and colleagues in America had sent beautiful handmade gifts.

By the time I eventually got to bed that night It was almost 10 pm. The events of the past few weeks washed over me again. I hadn't stopped since the minute I threw the bong at Anthony and turned to see my dad walking towards me. I hadn't had time to think about or process the horrible situation that I'd been living in. As I laid my head on the pillow it finally hit me like a tonne of bricks. I had been so busy and focussed on my little girl and the party in her honour that I had completely blocked out the months and years of trauma. For the first time since kicking Anthony out, I felt completely alone. I turned on the TV for company and finally fell asleep a couple of hours later wondering how the hell I was going to do it by myself.

Chapter Thirty-Three

When I woke up the next morning, I knew that I needed to get help. I'd been on such a high since finding out that I was having the little girl I had always dreamed of that I had begun to believe that my personal life was not a complete and utter disaster. The abuse from both Anthony, his ex-wife and even his child had begun to seem like nothing more than a bad dream. I really had thought that the lovely policewoman and my parents' insistence on me seeing a psychologist was overkill at the time. But that morning I knew without a doubt that I really was going to need help to overcome what had been one crazy and traumatic ordeal after the next.

I had spent so many years believing that I deserved to be treated like shit that I'd brushed off, not just Sam, Zac and Anthony's behaviour but the ex-wife's as well. I had blocked her new phone number at the advice of the police officers that I'd spoken to. I'd heard back from them the day after I went to see them. The good-looking guy rang to let me know that the woman had been cautioned. Apparently, she had tried to play the victim card to the officers who'd shown up at her door but in the end, she'd had no choice but to admit to the things she had done after they read her messages back to her.

Knowing that I never had to hear from that woman again had given me a false sense of security. But as I sat in bed that morning, I finally realised that I needed to get help. I knew that my trauma ran so much deeper than the things that had happened in the past year. I knew that it went back so much further than any of my boyfriends.

The time had come to finally face the true demon that had been haunting me for so many years. The demon who had taken my innocence and sent me on the path of self-destruction, of drugs, bad men and self-harm. I knew that I needed to get better, once and for all, so that I could be the best mother I could be for my little girl.

That's why I grabbed my phone and began searching for psychologists near Lane Cove. I managed to shortlist several different women that I liked the sound of before dragging myself out of bed and into the bathroom. I had forty minutes to shower and get ready for a day out with my mum, Amy, Hayley and Bec.

I hadn't bought any of the nursery furniture yet, thinking that I would buy everything when my maternity leave started a few weeks later. My plan had been to take Anthony with me to buy the bassinet, cot and pram. We were supposed to then order takeaway to eat while we built everything together. Mum had been nagging me for weeks, trying to convince me to get the furniture sorted out in case I went into labour early.

My brother and I had decided to arrive five weeks early and then little Joshua was born a month early too. Everyone was convinced that my little lady would make the same early appearance. The conversation had started again at my baby shower and the girls decided that I no longer had any excuse to hold off. I had agreed despite being sure that I was going to give birth no more than a day or two early but the opportunity to start rebuilding my relationship with my cousins was reason enough as far as I was concerned.

Everyone was meeting at my parents' house at 9.30 am I was sure that they were all being silly and a bit dramatic but I didn't care. I had missed Hayley and Bec so much. I was excited about spending the day shopping and lunching with them. I let the excitement of the day ahead take over and before I knew it, I was sitting at my parents' kitchen table eating croissants and drinking coffee with everyone.

We piled into Hayley's huge four-wheel drive once everyone was finished eating their breakfast and headed off on our adventure. Spending the day with my favourite women once again took my mind off everything bad that had happened. I bought so many cute pink blankets, sheets, towels and accessories that you would be excused for thinking that I was having two or three babies. When we finally got around to choosing the big-ticket items, I was beside myself when I opened a card that my dad had handed me before we headed off that morning.

I had been instructed to open the card before choosing the pram, cot and other items that I wanted. My parents had written a beautiful message about how much they loved me and couldn't wait to meet our little girl. And at the bottom was an explanation for the visa gift card. I had come clean with them at dinner, the evening that I finally found the strength to break up with Anthony, about the fact that he had almost completely cleaned out my savings account before I kicked him out.

I had thought I was going to have to use my 'emergencies only' credit card or wait until my quarterly bonus came in from work before I could afford to buy baby furniture. I was no longer going to be able to buy the beautiful and expensive items I'd had my heart set on. But my parents knew how hard I had worked to put that money away and so they had decided to surprise me and cover the cost of those items for me instead.

I tried to object at first, telling mum that I couldn't possibly let them pay for everything, that I couldn't accept such a large sum of money. I was so used to having that dirtbag take and then take some more that I had forgotten how to let people spoil me.

It was such a strange concept to me at the time. I had been showered with gifts the day before which was already overwhelming. Reading the card and seeing the sizable amount of money on the gift card that my parents had given me was just about the end of me. I bawled and I laughed. I must have looked ridiculous. Finding that everything I needed was on sale made things even more perfect. There was just enough money left at the end of our shopping trip to pay for lunch. It was the least I could do.

When we got home that afternoon we were met in the driveway by dad, James and Joshua. The sight of the two men wearing plaid shirts and tool belts, ready to build everything we'd bought that day was more than we could cope with. The girls and I laughed at the ridiculous sight before us. They looked like Bob the Builder's twin brothers. The girls and I had a wonderful time heckling them before we all headed into the house.

For the next two hours everyone helped build my little girl's nursery furniture. The thick white timber cot, matching chest of drawers and rocking chair, against the pastel pink backdrop of the room it looked like something out of a lifestyle magazine. I couldn't quite believe the transformation of my storage-space-turned-spare-room and now nursery. It was the room I had so carefully prepared for Anthony's daughters before that last, disastrous visit. Looking around at my daughter's belongings, so lovingly laid out for her, I couldn't wait for all the new memories that we would create in her room, in our home. I wiped away the single tear that rolled down my cheek.

I remembered once again, everything that was bubbling just below the surface. I remembered what I needed to do the next day. I was terrified about the prospect of telling a total stranger my story. I was scared of opening the floodgates but I knew that the threats and abuse from that crazy woman really were merely the tip of the iceberg. The thing that I had buried all those years ago, the thing that the filthy old man did, that day when he took my childhood innocence away from me. I had only ever told one person and he had taken my secret and used it against me so many times.

And I let him. I had never completely understood until than that it had started the moment I first made myself vulnerable to him. One night shortly after we first started dating, after far too many drinks, we both shared our deepest, darkest secrets. He went first and his story was terrible. It was so gory. When he was seventeen, his father's best friend went missing. The guy's wife called in a panic to tell his dad that she'd found a suicide note. For some reason Anthony's father thought it was a good idea to take his teenage son out to search for his mate.

The two of them headed to a park that the man had mentioned in his note and sure enough Anthony was the one who found his body. I was horrified when he described the way that pieces of the man's skull and brain were hanging from the tree, like Christmas ornaments from some twisted horror movie. Somehow my own secret, the shameful secret that I had buried seemed so small and insignificant compared to what he had seen.

That wasn't how he saw it though. When I told him every disgusting and shameful detail about what had happened that day, some four years earlier, he was angry, telling me over and over that what had happened to me was not okay, that it wasn't my fault and that the terrible things that man had said to me were not true. And I believed him, at least for a while.

Anthony tried to convince me at the time to tell my parents and to contact the police back at home, but I couldn't. I couldn't bear to have my parents know about what I'd done, and so not only did I refuse to tell them, I made it clear after that night that I never wanted to speak about what I had told him again.

I had moved to the other side of the world to try and run away from what had happened. I was there to try and move on, to try and forget about it, not to be constantly reminded about it. For the next couple of years, I just about managed to do exactly that. I had a job that I loved, amazing friends and I was in a loving relationship. Except that I wasn't. My job and friends were exactly what they seemed to be but discovering that Anthony had been lying and cheating almost right from the start of our relationship was truly devastating. The sweet, empathetic man I fell in love with had just been a mirage.

There were so many things that I had ignored; I justified his bad behaviour. The fights he got into in bars, his heavy drinking and so many other things. I would tell myself that he was a good guy who was acting out because of what he'd seen in the park that night. I felt like I owed it to him to justify and ignore his bad behaviour because he had entrusted me with his devastating secret, and because I had entrusted him with mine.

Finding out that he had been sleeping with other women on business trips and at parties was bad enough but when he justified it by telling me that it was all I deserved after what I'd let that old man do was just about the end of me. He tried to blame me for his actions, telling me that I was just a good for nothing whore who let old men fondle her for money.

And of course I believed him. I hadn't held a knife to my flesh once since arriving in America but his words cut me so deep that I had no choice. Knowing that I had my parents, my brother and the rest of my wonderful family and friends back at home was the only thing that saved me from doing something even more stupid at the time.

When I arrived home after that nasty breakup I was determined to find a nice guy. A nice simple Aussie guy who would love me for who I was, the kind hearted and caring woman who tried to look after everyone. But all I did was spend the next ten years running in circles, chasing shitty men who didn't care about me, only to end up pregnant and alone. I often wondered where I would have ended up if I hadn't ignored the red flags that Anthony wore like a badge of honour. Maybe I would have eventually met someone nice and had a lovely life and lots of babies who knew that they had two parents who loved them.

I even met a few nice guys when I was living in America but every time I did, especially before Anthony and I were serious, he put on the big, nice guy act and swept me off my feet … I wondered if it was all just a game to him. If it always had been. I wondered if he had been seeing his ex-wife behind my back the whole time we'd been back together. Maybe they were scheming because they thought I had money? I wouldn't have put it past either of them.

I had to snap myself out of that train of thought. I was so sick of thinking about the whole bloody mess. I had had such a wonderful weekend with my beautiful family, I wanted to cling to that. I lay in bed that night, tracing the thin scars on my arm with my fingers, thinking about all the wonderful things that lay ahead. I had never felt so determined to face my demons. It was exhilarating and bloody terrifying.

Chapter Thirty-Four

I felt so much more positive and happier about everything the following Monday morning. The shopping trip, followed by the care that was put into building the baby furniture, not to mention my dad and brother's ridiculous but hilarious outfits. It had all cheered me up so much that by the time I dialled the first psychologist's phone number, I was excited about getting my head sorted. I was ready to pop along and get myself all fixed up in a jiffy.

I wish I could say that ringing the first woman on my list was the answer to all my problems. I spoke with her on the phone, she answered on the second ring. At first, I was thrilled to be speaking with her without even having to make an appointment. But then I wasn't so thrilled. The woman seemed compassionate and gentle but it was only a matter of minutes before her manner changed. Some of the things she said made me wonder if she needed a professional more than I did.

"Why are you crying?" she said rudely. "You're not a child."

"I. Sorry." I stammered. "I'm pregnant and I've had a rough time."

"You need to start taking responsibility for your own part in your relationship breakdown." She responded without emotion. "You don't get to just blame him because you're pregnant."

I wasn't sure how to respond and so I hung up. I suddenly understood why she was available to answer her phone instead of being with a patient.

It was disheartening. I realised after that strange call that it wasn't going to be as simple as making an appointment and pouring my heart out to some stranger. Over the next three weeks I went to meet a number of other psychologists. I joked to my parents one night at dinner that it felt like I was dating. I was starting to despair at ever finding someone to help me slay my demons.

I was just about to give up altogether when I met Angela. With only weeks to go before my little princess was due to arrive, I was planning to hit pause on the whole thing. I was going to cancel the last appointment that I'd made a couple of weeks earlier, thinking that she was just going to be another bloody perfect woman who would ask me uncomfortable questions that made me cry and clam up. I hadn't felt comfortable about talking to any of the others so I assumed that she would be no different.

The appointment was booked for a couple of days after I started my maternity leave. I had forgotten to cancel the appointment between all the work I had to finish, my farewell party and the nesting that had taken over every waking minute, so I turned up to Dr Angela Jones's rooms without any expectations at all.

Actually, that's not true. I expected her to be the same cold, clinical, expressionless robot as the others.

The moment I was led by the receptionist into her room, I felt so much warmth. There wasn't a white wall or corkboard in sight. Instead, the room was painted a soft shade of blush pink. One wall was covered with all sorts of posters, including some of my favourites, from David Bowie to Pink and Nickelback. There was another wall that had a not-quite-finished mural of pink and white peonies. But it wasn't just the room. It was her.

I was barely in the door when a thin woman in blue skinny jeans and a band t-shirt wrapped her arms around me. She was about my height, and I guessed that she must be about forty-five. Her hair was the same shade of pink as the walls and as she pulled away, with her hands on my arms, looking me up and down I noticed that her left arm was covered in floral tattoos. From the moment we met I felt like I was with a long-lost friend. A friend that I could tell my deepest darkest secrets to without judgement.

And so that's exactly what I did. It was scary, letting her uncover all my broken pieces but somehow Angela managed to make me feel safe right from that first meeting. There were times that she laughed, looking mortified as I told her a crazy story, like my horror at seeing Sam weeing on my floor or some other ridiculous story about him and his friends and their stupid drunken behaviour. There were times that she held my hand and cried with me as I recounted stories of Anthony and the years of cruelty I'd endured from him in my desperation to earn his love. It took me a few sessions to find the courage to tell her anything about the old man.

One Wednesday afternoon in particular I found myself answering her questions about the ordeal and I was surprised to find that there were details that I'd never remembered before.

"Magnolia. Can you close your eyes and think back to the day in that newsagency." Angela's voice was gentle.

"I'll try." I said nervously. Dreading the thought.

"Can you tell me what you can see near the man?" She asked. "Take your time sweetheart."

"Oh wow. There was an ashtray." I could almost smell the cigarette smoke as I spoke. I curled my nose in disgust.

"Now you've told me before about the shelf full of magazines and books. What else can you see?" Her voice was so calm that I forced myself to stay there, in that terrifying room. I knew she would keep me safe.

"There's a radio. It's so old. It's not turned on. There's no music." I focused on my breathing as I spoke.

"And there's a baseball bat." It's behind the ashtray.

"Good, I don't want you to look at him. Open your eyes for me." Her voice was still gentle. I was relieved to be back in the safety of her office.

"It's so strange that I'd forgotten about those things." I said, hugging my bump. I wanted to protect her from all of it.

"It's your brain's defence mechanism. We develop ways of coping. You had a very traumatic experience that your brain has learnt to block aspects of." She said.

"I wish my brain would block the memory of him." I said. It came out sounding like a question.

"Holding onto the memory of that old man is another way your brain has been wired to protect you. I'll help you learn better ways to understand that. And to forgive yourself once and for all. Okay?"

"Thank you. I'll try." I nodded before cradling my stomach again.

"Do you want me to take you to the police?" I was confused by her question at first. I was hoping to finally deal with what had happened all those years ago. I wanted to find the words to finally tell my family. I knew it would finally give them answers about my sudden wild behaviour all those years ago. I felt like I owed my parents in particular an explanation. But why the police?

I suppose I could have just blamed my baby brain but in reality, it hadn't occurred to me that I could go to the police. A few weeks after it happened my friend and I stood outside the shop warning customers not to go in, lest they be supporting a paedophile. People turned away in droves, disgusted by our accusations but eventually someone tipped him off and he walked outside. And then he was right in front of us. He was bright red and clearly furious. My friend and I stood there terrified as he threatened to call the police and then our parents. And then he leaned in and once again whispered the words that had haunted me ever since.

"No one will believe you, and I know you both liked it, you disgusting little whores."

I had believed his words ever since. It didn't matter that before that day in the back of the newsagency I had never so much as kissed a boy. What was the point in going to the police all these years later? Angela respected my wishes to keep things between us for the time being but told me that having that man pay for what he did to me, and goodness knows how many other girls, would be a huge factor in finally being able to heal from it. It gave me something to think about and so did another interesting fact that she managed to get out of me.

Somehow when we were talking about my family during another session, I let it slip that my dad wasn't my biological father. I hadn't intended to disclose that little piece of information but something about her just compelled me to open up in ways I'd never done before. I explained how lucky my brother and I were to have such a wonderful man to look up to. And I talked about the man who had contributed to our DNA and how he had taken off on his unborn babies like a criminal in the night, never to be seen again.

It had never occurred to me that being abandoned by that guy could possibly have contributed to the way I felt about myself. It wasn't like he'd been there one day, and then gone the next. I had never even met him. James and I were only babies when our mum met Cameron, the man who raised us. We had grown up with a wonderful and loving dad. But somehow Angela knew that there was a small part of me that had never quite dealt with that abandonment.

And she was right. The more I opened up, the more Angela made me understand that I had always carried those feelings of inadequacy with me. I wondered why my brother had been so completely unaffected by it. He was so good at school and of course went on to become a doctor, just like dad. James was such a different personality to me. We were chalk and cheese despite being twins. Even before that disastrous day at the age of fourteen, I was a quiet and shy kid and had to work much harder at school than James to get even passing grades.

I had asked him once, when we were maybe twelve or thirteen, whether he would forgive our father if he ever came looking to meet us. I was surprised by his reaction.

"He's dead to me, we already have a dad." He said it with such hatred that I never dared to ask him again. I envied his strength and determination with everything he did, even the way he hated that man. Angela seemed fascinated by my brother and even asked, towards the end of one of our sessions, if I would be comfortable having him in a session.

She believed that having a frank conversation about how we were abandoned may just make me realise that James was just as scared by the experience as I was. I didn't believe for one moment that he had been affected by that man leaving us but that's not why I said no to him coming along.

I couldn't bear to think about my brother finding out about everything, not yet anyway. I knew that Angela was right. There was so much I needed to say to all of them but with only a few weeks left until my baby was due to join me, it simply wasn't the right time. I didn't want any sadness or worry overshadowing her arrival into the world. When I first decided to take the plunge and talk to someone about my past, my intention had been to do six or eight sessions before swanning off with my newly healed soul, to have my baby and live happily ever after.

Of course that's not how it works in real life. It took me those first few sessions to build up the courage to open up about the heavy secrets I'd been lugging around with me for so many years. Once I did that, we started picking it all to pieces. By the time June arrived it was all a big jumbled mess. We were going to spend the next few weeks at least starting to glue me back together but my little lady had other ideas.

Chapter Thirty-Five

The last two months of my pregnancy were such a roller coaster ride. There were so many lovely days spent with my cousins, close friends and pizza and mocktail nights with my parents. Then there were nights where I watched rom-coms with my mummy turtle and a box of chocolates for company. All wonderfully relaxing and happy nights. But then there were the raw and often devastating emotions that my sessions with Angela invoked.

Not only did Angela make me feel like I could finally talk about the old man and the abandonment issues, she also asked a lot of questions about the kind of relationships I'd had before that last disastrous experience with Anthony. I told her more about Sam and how lovely he seemed, at least at first. I talked about his drunken outbursts and the brutal way he'd discarded me before going off and marrying someone else a few months later.

And then there was Zac. I felt so stupid talking about how I'd fallen for him. I'd heard that he wasn't a very nice guy. I certainly knew that his brother wasn't but that didn't stop me from falling under his spell. He had been so charming when we met, and just like with Sam and Anthony, Zac had been on his best behaviour for a few months before the gaslighting started.

I wondered, as I explained the horrible things that he'd said, if he too had seen through my facade? I so desperately wanted to understand why the men I'd loved had been so unwilling, and indeed unable, to treat me the way I treated them.

I wasn't expecting Angela's insight into my relationships.

"Magnolia, have you ever heard of something called coercive control?"

"Coercive control? No but it sounds terrible." I replied, wondering what something that serious had to do with me.

"Coercive control is a type of abuse, usually perpetrated by a romantic partner but not always." Angela began thoughtfully. "When a person scares, bullies, humiliates, or tricks you into doing something you don't feel comfortable about. It could be something sexual like what the old man did. Threatening to tell people untrue things about you if you didn't comply."

"Well, if he hadn't done that, I might have felt brave enough to tell my parents I suppose." I shrugged, not really believing that for one moment.

"And then we have Sam essentially controlling the situation with how much you charged for your cakes. Financially controlling you is another classic form of coercion."

"Gosh, it sounds so serious when you call it that Angela." I felt embarrassed to hear the way she was describing the behaviour of those men. I had always known that none of them had treated me well but it hadn't occurred to me, with the exception of that old creep, that they were abusive as such. It wasn't like any of them had hit me.

After that particular session, at Angela's insistence, I started writing in a journal. Facing my demons in those sessions was the hardest thing I had ever attempted to do. The journal was a way to get me into the habit of writing my thoughts and feelings down every day. With my not-so-little peanut due so soon the plan was to spend time every day reflecting on my past and future and to continue through the first few weeks after giving birth, until I was ready to start seeing Angela again.

I found that writing in the journal was even fun some days. I chose a beautiful journal with sea creatures including tropical fish, whales and turtles scattered playfully throughout the pages. The pictures reminded me of the person I had become in Hawaii. On my good days I remembered how empowered I had felt on that trip. The memories drove me to try and become that woman again but this time permanently. Those were the days I found it easier to write.

Diary Entry—Sunday 4th June 2007

What a lovely surprise!

Bec, Hayley and Amy popped in this morning with beef stroganoff and some amazing feta and pumpkin muffins that were still warm. Bec baked them for me this morning. We ended up eating half of them and the girls stayed for a couple of hours. They had a great time telling stories about their kids' crazy adventures, including Bec's little girl Madison, who is the cutest, feistiest little girl I have ever met. Madison apparently won't go anywhere without an old scoop for cat biscuits that was on the floor while Bec was cleaning the cupboard one morning.

God, I missed her. Hayley too. It feels like they were never gone. I need them so much. And Mum and Amy. I'm so scared that I'm going to screw her up. The more I tell Angela about everything the more fucked up I can see it is. Somehow, I need to be strong. I want to be a good mum so desperately, just like mum and the girls all are.

And I want her to grow up with dad and James as her role models.

But enough of the heavy stuff. Save that for my session tomorrow.

I'm off to clean the floor and then I'm tempted to do nothing for the rest of the afternoon because I'm just so tired and I have my Sex in the City box set to get through before this girl gets here.

Bye for now my little baby turtles.

Magnolia xx

✧ ✧ ✧

The next day I had a morning appointment with Angela before heading to meet mum at a homemaker centre about half an hour away from home. We'd gone there to order a couple of barn-style doors for my parents' house. They had turned James's old bedroom into a grand-babies room a couple of years earlier but with the impending arrival of their second, and as it turned out, third grand-babies, since Amy and James had just announced that they were pregnant again. Mum and dad had decided to redo the room with double built in bunks and a new cot for my little girl, and eventually another cot for the newest baby. The final touch was the barn doors.

While we were there, I decided that I wanted to buy a new rug for my lounge-room and a beautiful painting of pink and white peonies that reminded me of Angela's now completed mural. As soon as I saw the painting I knew exactly where I wanted to hang it, on the wall above my little girl's cot. Angela's office had become such a safe space for me that I loved the idea of replicating that feeling in my daughter's bedroom.

As we wandered around the rug store, I noticed a strange feeling in my stomach and groin. I hadn't experienced any Braxton Hicks contractions throughout my pregnancy but from what I had read I assumed that the strange tightening sensation must surely be just that. I was not due to give birth for a couple of weeks after all so it didn't occur to me for one moment that I could have been in the early stage of labour.

The pains were so mild and disappeared completely when Mum and I sat down to eat lunch. I decided that I'd just been pushing myself too hard and assured Mum that I was fine to continue shopping. With that we headed back so that I could buy a lovely white rug with rose coloured accents. We loaded the rug, my beautiful new painting and a few groceries into the car just before 4 pm. By the time we got home I was exhausted and so, once the rug was placed carefully under my coffee table, the groceries were put away and the painting was carefully laid against the wall to be hung another time, I grabbed a blanket and snuggled up on the lounge.

I closed my eyes, hoping to have a snooze but my stomach had other ideas. I tried to ignore the grumbling sounds but they soon got the better of me. I'd never been a huge eater, even throughout my pregnancy but my little miss was not the least bit interested in helping me preserve my waistline, so I dragged myself off the lounge and over to the fridge. It didn't matter that I had just bought all manner of healthy goodies. There was nothing appealing in there, so I knew that there was only one solution, pizza.

I picked up my phone and messaged Dad. He had always been on my side when it came to the consumption of junk food so he was the one I went to, rather than Mum, when I needed a good pig out. I knew that it was a bit manipulative but at that moment I didn't care. Even my health-freak mum wasn't going to deny a pregnant woman pizza. With our order sorted I decided to put some clothes away and finish packing my hospital bag while I waited for dinner to arrive.

I lifted everything out of the bag to check what was missing. As I picked up one of the tiny little pink jumpsuits it struck me, not for the first time, how unfair it was that she was going to pay the price for my terrible taste in men. I had tried, at Angela's suggestion, to talk to him about how he was planning to be involved in our daughter's life. I shouldn't have been surprised when he played his usual mind games.

He started by saying he wanted nothing to do with the baby. Me throwing him out was unacceptable he told me. He was going to punish me by having nothing to do with her. But then he changed his mind. A couple of days after those messages I got a number of terrifying messages telling me that he was going to take the baby and raise her with that psycho woman and their kids. That was a few weeks earlier and I'd ended up freaking out and blocking his number. I remembered my original plan, the plan I had before Anthony and I got back together that last time. I couldn't believe how naive I was, to think that I wanted to do it alone. I'd been so sure of myself, so sure that I could do it by myself.

The reality of being almost nine-months pregnant without a partner was so much scarier than I ever could have imagined. But I reminded myself, as I repacked the sweet little clothes and nappies back on top of my oversize track pants and hoodie, that everything was going to be okay. I knew that we would be okay. My parents were like a pair of chickens fussing over their eggs. They were both semi-retired and absolutely bursting with excitement about having their little granddaughter a matter of metres away from their back door.

Of course, they already had Amy and James's little Joshua and another baby due in a few months, but this was different. I knew that they had spent so many years worrying about me and my bad choices. From the crazy stage in my mid to late teens to the time that I was away from them when I was living in the US. They'd watched me go from one disastrous relationship to another and then helped me through that terrible ordeal with Anthony and his psycho, whatever she was. I knew that they had found an inner peace finally, knowing that I was free of all the drama and about to become a mum.

I knew that at some point I was going to have to tell them my terrible secret. Angela and I had talked a few more times about going to the police to report what that man did to me. I wanted him to pay for what he had done, to me and God only knew how many other girls but it struck me, not for the first time, that he must surely be in his eighties. I wondered where he was and whether he was even still alive. The thought that he may have died without ever having to face what he had done was too much and so I pushed the thought aside. I wasn't ready to tell the police yet anyway.

The other thing Angela wanted me to do was tell my parents. But I didn't know how. How could I possibly tell my parents that I'd put myself in that situation? They had always tried to protect me. They knew that I had struggled on and off with my mental health for years but they had no idea why. I knew that telling them about that horrible day, so many years earlier, was going to break their hearts.

I'd read so much about sexual predators in the weeks since I'd started seeing Angela. I'd read enough to know that I wasn't what professionals would have classed as high risk. I wasn't from a poorer family; I wasn't abused as a young child and in fact I had been taught so much about stranger danger. I was just a normal, happy, teenage schoolgirl with posters on my walls and a silly crush on some guy who caught my bus before that day.

I had started to understand, thanks to the wonderful lady with the pink room and the hair to match, at least logically, that I wasn't to blame for what he did. The problem was, I'd spent so many years believing the opposite. I'd always blamed myself for being stupid enough to go into that back room. It didn't matter that I laid there silently crying as he touched me in places that nobody ever had before.

It didn't matter that I ran out of there when he was finished and it didn't matter that I never went back. I had told myself so many times that it was my fault for letting him do it. And so, I really didn't know how I would ever tell my parents. I didn't want to break their hearts but even more so, I didn't want them to think of me as a bad person. I didn't want my parents to think the things that the old man had said to me, because surely, if I'd spent so many years believing it, wouldn't they?

As I sat there with the heavy burden of it all threatening to crush me, my baby girl must've known how desperately I needed to hold her. The strangest sensation suddenly ripped through my body. I heard a loud pop and immediately I could feel that my waters had broken.

I raced into the toilet, only to discover that I was bleeding heavily. I tried not to panic as I grabbed one of the packs of maternity pads from my bathroom vanity before ringing my dad. He answered on the second ring to the sound of me freaking out.

"I'm bleeding!" I screamed. "I think she's coming."

"Okay baby. "he said, calm as ever. "We're coming now. Don't panic."

Chapter Thirty-Six

By the time my parents walked in the front door a couple of minutes later, I was bordering on hysterical, thinking for sure that I was going to lose my little girl. The little girl who was already so much a part of my life and my heart. I was thankful that dad's first instinct was to check whether she was still kicking. Realising that she seemed as happy as ever helped me to calm down. I was still thankful that we were only minutes away from the hospital where I was planning to give birth.

"She's okay, baby." Mum said. I could tell she was trying to stay calm too.

"I need my little girl." I tried to breathe. "I need her." I clutched my stomach, trying to calm down.

"Let's go and meet her then." Dad said, his excitement made me laugh through my tears as I manoeuvred myself into his car. Mum hopped in the back next to me, squeezing my hand as I buckled my seatbelt.

By the time we reached the hospital, the pains were becoming stronger and more frequent. My parents had called ahead to my obstetrician who was a close family friend and so I wasn't surprised to see her waiting as soon as we walked into the labour ward.

The next part was all a bit of a blur. For the next twelve hours I laboured. It was not easy nor was it pleasant. It was nothing like those quick and easy births I'd seen on television shows but the moment she was placed on my chest the pain was all but forgotten. in that moment the world became a better place.

She was the cutest, prettiest little baby girl I'd ever seen. With her full head of dark brown hair and her eyes so blue that they were almost purple in colour. I can't describe the feeling that washed over me but I know it wasn't unique to me. I'd heard about that love so many times before but it was the first time I believed all the hype. The moment she was placed on my chest, all the self-doubt was washed away. All the pain and trauma that I'd endured as a teenager, and as an adult. Just for a moment, it was all gone.

For the first time in my life, I felt sure. As I gazed down at my beautiful little girl, I knew that I was worthy of her. I knew that she had chosen me to be her mum, her protector, her first love. And I knew in an instant that she had been sent to save me.

My diary entry that night was only a few words in length.

Diary Entry—Monday 5th June

Grace Lottie ✿

She's perfect!

Magnolia xx

Chapter Thirty-Seven

When I gave birth to my sweet little girl, I quickly realised something. I had spent so many years chasing the dream of that one big love. Instead, I'd spent my whole adult life dating narcissistic jerks, especially Anthony. He was the tip of the iceberg. I had allowed him to live off me, cheat and play his twisted little games with his ex-wife because I truly believed that it was all I deserved. I had lost count of the number of times I'd ignored the instinct that told me to run away, to protect myself, because that old man's voice was always louder than my own inner voice.

I had silenced that inner voice, the one that always knows best, because I so desperately wanted one of those men to love me. It never occurred to me that maybe I didn't actually love any of them either. As I cuddled my little baby girl in those early days and weeks it occurred to me that the feelings I had for her were new.

The fierce need to put her needs before my own, to encourage every little thing she did and to protect her from all the bad things in the world. I knew that I would lay down my life to protect her without hesitation. I realised, without a doubt, that I had fallen in love for the first time.

Having Grace terrified me as well though. Thinking about the kind of monsters that lurked in plain sight, masquerading as regular people. Knowing that I needed to protect her gave me the courage, once and for all, to do what Angela had implored me to do in our sessions. If not for myself, then I needed to be brave for her. I needed to get that monster off the streets.

That's why, when Grace was eight weeks old, I decided that the time had come to go to the police about what that filthy old man had done to me. It was time to take a stand once and for all. It had been sixteen years since that day. I knew that he was in his sixties when he abused me and two of my friends. I decided to google him to get more current information about him. It occurred to me again that he may already be dead but I pushed the thought aside. There was no way I was going to accept that. If he was dead, then how would he ever be punished for what he'd done?

What I found a few minutes later took my breath away. There was an obituary for his wife. She had died just a few months earlier. At first, I was thrilled to have found a link to him but my excitement turned to devastation when I read that he too was dead. I can't explain the feelings that washed over me as I burst into tears. I had never been so heartbroken in my whole life.

I cried in a way that I never had before. I cried for the young girl that he had so callously destroyed all those years earlier. I had spent my whole adult life believing that I was an unlovable, worthless piece of shit because of him. I had believed the vile things he said, and I'd suffered in silence because of it for all those years. I finally had the courage, thanks to Angela but even more so because of my precious baby girl, to make him face what he'd done. How could he be dead? I didn't know what to do. I knew that my habit of spiralling, of using a blade to ease my pain whenever I felt that I wasn't in control of my life, was no longer an option now that I had Grace to take care of. So instead, I did what I should have done years ago.

I messaged my mum and asked her to come over. I didn't hear back from her straight away. I tried to keep my mind off everything as I played with Grace on the lounge room rug but the feelings of grief washed over me. I broke down, over and over again. I breathed in her delicious baby smell and kissed her sweet little head. I wasn't sure how I would find the strength to go on but I knew that I was going to have to. I was so lost in my own thoughts that it took me a few seconds to realise that Mum was standing behind me.

"What's wrong?" she asked. I could see the concern on her face. "Is Gracie okay?"

"I don't know how to tell you." my voice trailed off as I tried to compose myself.

"What? What's happened Magnolia?" My mother rarely used my name. I knew I had to say it then. I could see the worry on her face.

"I can't tell you all of it but when I was fourteen. That old man at the newsagency." I looked at my mummy turtle as I spoke, drawing strength from her and trying to find the words. "He molested me in the back room at the newsagency."

"Oh my God." she cried out, covering her mouth with her hand. "Why didn't you tell me?"

"I couldn't. I didn't know how." I said, looking at her nervously.

"I'm so sorry. Oh my goodness." The colour drained from her face as she spoke. "I would have walked in there and killed him with my bare hands. I had no idea"

And I believed her. "So many people thought he was a stand-up guy. I wasn't the only one. He said terrible things. The names he called me. I believed them all." I knew I was rambling but once I started talking, I couldn't stop.

"I just found out he's dead so he got away with it.. He did it to Katie and Ava too." I said, referring to two of my teenage friends who I hadn't seen in years. One of the girls, Ava, the one I stood outside with, warning people away from his shop, actually told me once that he was right, that what he'd done to us was fine. "I nearly went to the police once but Ava told me it was our own fault and that we knew what he was going to do. But I didn't know. I had no idea."

"What? That's ridiculous." Mum said, clearly surprised by the suggestion. "She was a pretty disturbed girl, maybe that's why?"

"I never went back there. It only happened to me once. I don't know how many times she went back ..." my voice trailed off. I didn't want to go into any of the gory details. I remembered what my friend had told me back then. That an older relative had molested her. My sadness turned to anger then. I wondered if she had ever told anyone else about what had happened to her?

"What about Katie? Have you ever spoken to her about it?" she said as she cradled Grace gently.

"I haven't spoken to her in about thirteen-years, maybe more."

I had fallen out with Katie over some money that I owed her back when I was trying to drown out the memory of him, with the drugs and alcohol, before my parents sent me off to America out of desperation. I was sure that he had done things to her as well. She had worked for him at the time and told me about how he was always touching her and the other girls and giving them free chocolate bars and magazines. I wondered aloud how many of those girls had spent their lives trying to escape the memory of that back room and I knew, before either of us said it, that I needed to try and find out.

"I'll message her." I said as I typed her name into my Facebook profile. "I'm sorry I never told you." I continued, walking to the kitchen to boil the kettle.

It was a week before Katie read and responded to my message. I was surprised but relieved to learn that when her turn came, she couldn't go through with it. She had been so terrified of him that she'd run for her life. I already knew that she continued working there for several months after her near-miss and I knew that, just like me, she hadn't told her parents or another soul about what he was doing, except for the other girls she worked with. It became their dirty little secret, just like it had been mine.

I became obsessed with learning anything I could about him after reconnecting with Katie. I found out that he had sold that newsagency several years earlier, only to buy another one in the nearby suburb of Cammeray. I shuddered as I wondered if he had a back room with a massage table in it there as well.

It may have been too late to see him suffer in jail where he belonged but I knew that I needed to tell somebody my story. I needed to expose him for the filthy paedophile that he was. And so, I started seeing Angela again. We worked through every gory detail of what that monster had done to me. And I told my dad too. I expected him to be furious, with the old man that is, and I'm sure he was but mostly he was just sad. I could never have imagined my parents' reactions before but I understood now that I was a parent myself. I understood that to them I was just a naïve kid and a bad man did bad things. It really wasn't my fault.

When I told James, Amy, Bec and Hayley they were all so sad. The girls were devastated, and I wasn't surprised that my brother was angry. He tried insisting that the man's family should pay for what their father had done to me but eventually I was able to make him understand that it wasn't their fault. They were victims in a way as well. I knew that they would find out eventually what their father had done because the next thing I did, after telling my family, was to finally go to the police.

At first, I didn't see what good it would do now that I knew he was dead but Angela insisted. She believed that other women may have come forward before, or maybe since his death to tell their own stories. Angela reminded me about the man's daughters. I knew that there was every possibility that they had been living their own nightmares because of their father. People needed to know because my story was an important part of the bigger picture. In the end I agreed because I have always been a big believer in the saying "better late than never". Telling the police was surreal and terrifying. It was so much scarier than telling them about the stalking and harassment from that woman.

For two hours I was asked over and over to go into detail about what he did. I wanted to run out of there, just like I had wanted to run out of that back room but unlike then, I stayed because I felt safe and I finally wanted to be brave. When we were nearly finished, I told them that I knew other women he'd preyed upon but of course I didn't share their details. It wasn't my place to do so. I had finally found a way to talk to the people that needed to know but I knew that we each had different layers of complexity in our lives. We each had to do what was best for us.

The best thing for me, I realised soon after telling my mum, was talking about my experience. As excruciating as it felt at the time, I realised that each time I told my story, to the police, to

Angela and with my family, each time I shared the burden with another person, it became a little bit easier to bear. That's why I decided to write about it too.

Diary Entry:

27th September 2007

It's crazy to think that I held onto this for so many years. I have despised myself. I have blamed myself. I have thought about dying SO many times because of that vile scumbag.

I wish I had been strong enough back then to do this but I will not stay quiet any longer.

I am going to write about it all. I don't know how but somehow, I am going to get my story out into the world and make sure that the Dons of this world are stopped once and for all. Maybe one day I will even have the courage to write down exactly what he did to me.

I will not be a statistic anymore and the cycle will end with me. I will hover over Grace. I will protect her from what I know is out there.

And I will not keep secrets anymore. This story literally defines me and I'm not scared of it any more.

Magnolia xx

Chapter Thirty-Eight
A year later

My story is nowhere near as unique as I would like to think. It's a twisted fairy tale, a classic story about a dumb kid who gets tricked by the big bad wolf. The kid goes on a path of self-destruction until she either dies or is rescued by her one big love. There were times over the years that the thought of my family's pain was the only thing that stopped me from doing more than cutting myself. I tried so desperately to find a prince who would kiss it all away but I now know that my terrible taste in men mixed with my desperation to feel loved was a recipe for disaster right from the start.

Until the biggest disaster of them all. Anthony. The narcissistic sociopath with the unhinged ex-wife. I had been so ready to walk away after my car crash, thinking that I couldn't possibly tolerate another minute of craziness but I'm so glad I didn't. My parents often comment on what a bad guy he was. They sometimes tell me that I should have broken it off the first time his kid parroted her mother and called me ugly and a horse. I remind them then, however, that he gave me my precious baby. My soul mate and the reason that I am finally strong enough to slay my dragons. I finally understand what it was that drew me back to him each time. She was my destiny, not him.

I have come to believe that my soul knew she would come to me. Everything bad I have tolerated from him—it all makes sense now. My sweet Grace with the big blue eyes and the soft hair that has long since changed colour, now a beautiful golden-blonde. She is my world and the love I've been so desperately searching for all these years.

Loving and protecting Grace has given me a new purpose on this earth. I hate that I couldn't give her the lovely daddy that she deserves but I try my best to fill that void for her. Everything I've done over the last year has been with her best interests in my heart and mind. She's going to grow up knowing every day how loved and cherished she is. And she's going to know that I will always be there, on the lookout for monsters. I will do anything and everything to protect her from them. I'm back into my karate lessons now too, for that very reason.

When my little girl goes to birthday parties, I'll be the mum that stays. I'll have one eye on the party host as I make small talk, and one eye on her, making sure that no one touches her. I'll be the mean mum sometimes, like when she starts getting invited to sleepovers. She may think I'm the worst mum in the world then but I don't care. I've read too many stories since I started to share mine. Stories of what some sick and twisted people do to children. I know first-hand how much a single incident can destroy a child's life.

If you're one of those parents who invites her to stay the night when she's older please understand it's not about you. It's just that I don't know you. I don't know what kind of man you're married to. The odds are that he's probably a perfectly good, decent and stand-up guy. But I'm not willing to risk it. If that makes me anything less than a good mum in your eyes then it tells me that you're one of the lucky ones. You're lucky that you don't understand what it means to live with the guilt and shame that I've lived with all these years.

But I'll not change my mind, no matter what you say or think. Grace is the love of my life. Because of her I know that I'm a good, strong and fierce woman. I'm a survivor and a fighter. She is the reason for everything I do from now on. I'm going to be the fierce mum with the tattoo on my arm that symbolises my journey to get to this place. The beautiful artwork that symbolises my babies, the two I lost and the one that I am so blessed to have with me every day.

The tattoo with the magnolia flowers, the tiny stars and the hatchling turtles that I'm going to take Grace to search for next year. I never imagined that I could be the kind of person who would get such a bold tattoo, covering most of my left forearm. Meeting Angela changed my attitude about that. I was so intrigued by her beautiful tattoos that I asked her in a session, a few months after I gave birth, what they symbolised.

I was surprised to hear that Angela had been sexually abused as a teenager as well. Her situation wasn't too different to what

I had experienced. At the age of sixteen she started cutting herself to try and ease the pain. It was all too familiar. She had done exactly the same thing as me. Each time the pain in my soul became too much, each time I was struck by emotions that I couldn't handle, I would get my knife and drive the blade into the soft skin on my left forearm until I could see the blood bubbling to the surface, just like it had done that fateful day, when I had tried to wash my shame away. Cutting my flesh was such a strange sensation. It would sting like hell, but the pain was much easier to bear than the pain that lingered in my soul. The physical pain was so much easier to cope with.

I was shocked to learn that Angela had ever been through a similar experience to me but at the same time it made sense, because she was always so attuned to my emotions throughout our sessions. She had been saved by her school counsellor who recognised the signs of a deeply disturbed and abused child.

With the help of that school counsellor, she had gone to the police and her abuser, her school principal, had been jailed for what he'd done, not only to her but to several other girls including her older sister. Angela had gone on to finish high school, and then, determined to help other people who'd been victims of abuse, she went on to become a psychologist.

Angela had dealt with her abuse but the scars on her arm served as constant reminders of what that man had done to her and so, as a graduation present to herself, she had worked with an artist friend to design her magnificent sleeve of flowers. I was so inspired by her story that I decided to do the same thing. The woman who had designed Angela's tattoo was still her good friend so she didn't hesitate to pass me her number.

Within a matter of days, I'd met with Angela's artist friend, Emma, fallen in love with the design that she had drawn just for me and had it tattooed over the scars on my arm. The tattooist noticed the scars without me even having to tell him and so he positioned the artwork in a way that they would be covered up completely. The pain of the tattoo gun was like a rebirth, the pain and the knowledge that my scars were no longer going to serve as a daily reminder of what that filthy old scumbag had done to me.

Chapter Thirty-Nine

hate that he died an innocent man. I hate that he will never face the consequences of what he did to me and God knows how many other girls. When I read his wife's obituary, I saw that he had two daughters and I've wondered so many times since reading that, whether he abused them as well. I wonder if he had grandchildren that he went on to abuse, or did he just prey on the stupid young girls who worked at his newsagent and their equally naive friends? I will never be able to answer any of those questions, any more than I am able to walk past that newsagency without the cold chill that runs down my spine at the thought of what that man was doing in there.

The people who own the business now have been there for years, I bet that they can't even begin to imagine the evil that went on before they arrived. I might have believed, under different circumstances, that he was still there haunting the place but I know he couldn't be because if there is one thing I am absolutely sure about, it's the fact that he is rotting in hell. I believe that with every ounce of conviction that I have. I'm not a perfect person and I don't know anyone who is. We all make mistakes and most of us learn from them but people who do the kinds of things he did have one destiny. I wouldn't wish it on my worst enemy, not Anthony or his wife but I hope that vile old paedophile spends all of eternity suffering for what he did here on earth.

I hope you don't think that it makes me a bad person, feeling the way I do about him. If you do, then I guess you're also happily oblivious to the kind of monsters that walk amongst us. If so, then I don't blame you. But I won't apologise for it either. I've lived a hundred lives since then. I'm a warrior because I have fought so hard to come out the other end. I'm not healed yet, my scars run deep but I'm getting there a little more each day.

Diary Entry:

5th June 2008

I can't believe Grace is one today! What a wonderful year it has been. This little girl shows me every day what it is to be cherished and adored and I feel the same way about her. She is the prettiest, most sassy and by far the smartest kid I have ever known and I can't believe she is mine.

Her Minnie Mouse party is going to be as epic as the cake Bec and I have made and I can't wait to see how she enjoys it. I got a bit carried away with the scale of it all but I don't care. I have waited my whole life for today. I'm already planning the next one!

I have learned so much about life in the past year but one thing in particular really strikes me.

I am so very loved.

I always have been as it turns out. I realise now that the only person who really thought I was unlovable was me.

It took welcoming my little girl into the world to see myself the way that she does. A perfectly flawed human who is so deserving of every ounce of the love that she and the rest of my family and friends have for me.

I am truly blessed.

Magnolia xx

The End

Unlovable includes fictionalised-but in-depth memories of
the following:

- Childhood molestation
- Portrayal of mental abuse and coercive control by a
  romantic partner
- Detailed descriptions of self harm.
- Vivid descriptions of pregnancy loss.

These themes are detailed throughout the entire story
and may cause distress for some readers.

Help is available. If you are experiencing, or have
experienced any form of abuse please call:

Australia: 1800 RESPECT: 1800 737 732
New Zealand: SHINE: 0508 744 633
United Kingdom: NDAH: 0808 2000 247
Canada: NISA HELPLINE: 888 315 6472
United States: LOVE IS RESPECT: 800 787 3224

For all other countries please visit: www.findahelpline.com

9 781923 250895